SUNSET IN PARIS

Ed Lehner

Jennifer Morse Series: Book 2

ALKIRA
PUBLISHING

Prologue

Strange humming and beeping sounds filled Jenny's ears as she slowly opened her eyes and looked around an unfamiliar room with bare off-white walls dimmed by quiet light. Even the soft light was too much for her. She squinted and tried to get her bearings. She felt something in her nose, then a soft touch on her arm, and a woman's voice said, "Oh good, you're waking up. I'll get the doctor."

"Where am I?" Jenny groaned. "Where am I? What's happening?"

She tried to move, but her body felt heavy. She noticed a tube running from her left arm to a bag hanging over her left side.

"You're in the hospital, Sweetheart. Sit tight and I'll get the doctor. He can tell you more." The woman went out the door and, a few moments later, returned with a man in a white coat.

"Hi, how're you feeling? Good to see you're awake."

"Why'm I in a hospital? What's happening?" Jenny asked through thick dry lips,

"You were brought in by ambulance an hour ago. You apparently collapsed at a bookstore downtown. From what we can determine you're a little dehydrated and are borderline anemic. And your white cell count is low. We've put you on a saline IV to get fluids into your system as well as giving you oxygen. We can remove the oxygen now. Barbara, would you?"

The nurse gently and carefully removed the cannula. "There, that's better."

"How long do I have to stay here? When can I leave? I have several more book signings I have to do. I need to go."

"Not right now. Not until we're satisfied you're sufficiently hydrated and rested. We can talk later about getting your health back to where it should be. But overall, you'll recover and be fine. I'll be back in a while and we'll talk. Meanwhile, relax and get some rest. I'll have the nurse bring you some water."

Jenny couldn't relax. She needed to complete the last leg of a ten-day East Coast book-signing tour that Marty, her agent, had set up. Lately, it seemed like she'd no sooner finished one than Marty had another set up.

Two years ago she'd gotten her book published. It had suffered a slow start, but when a TV talk-show personality had endorsed it on her show and on her book club website, it'd gone to best-seller lists, including *The New York Times*. Jenny realized instant star power, and her agent was merciless, milking the book's success to its maximum potential. Now, as Jenny lay in her hospital bed, she realized she was burned out.

Chapter 1

Exhausted, Jenny desperately wanted to be home, but the fact remained she was still two hours out from Denver with a two-hour layover and then another hour-long flight to Durango. After she'd been released from the hospital the day before, the doctor had given her some strict guidelines to get her health back on track.

She needed to get back in touch with her life and couldn't even comprehend doing any more book signings, of seeing the same expectant faces hoping for some words to save them from their lives. Same questions from the same mouths. She began to feel angry. *I'm not a goddess with all the answers to all life's problems. I wrote a book. That's all, a fictionalized book based on my early life. Everyone wants a piece of me, like I have some connection to infinite knowledge.*

She tried to sleep, but she never could sleep when flying, even in her plush business-class seat. She thought about Chris and his first book which was only a mediocre success, going to bargain books after only six months. His publisher refused his second. Maybe, in the long run, he was lucky.

She felt bad that, three years later, he was still working at the nursery and not writing. He'd been becoming more and more distant and angry toward her. She'd tried to get him into counseling and couples counseling, but he refused. She tried everything, but he just got angry and shut her out.

The plane began its descent to Denver International. She straightened in her seat and put her unopened book back into her bag.

Just as she entered the terminal, her cell phone chirped. It was Marty, her agent. "Hi, Marty."

"How was Philadelphia? Good turnouts?"

"Yeah, I guess. It all became pretty much a blur as usual until I ended up in the hospital, but I'm sure you already know about that since I was a no-show at the last three gigs."

"Yeah, I heard. Sorry about that. Got it smoothed over, and it's all good. So here's the deal, I'm lining up another European tour, London, Berlin, Copenhagen, Paris and Barcelona. It'll be about three weeks. You'll leave in a week. Pretty much all arranged—"

Jenny interrupted, "Stop! No! I can't do it, Marty, I can't. I appreciate all you do, but I'm totally burned out. Period! I need a break! I've been ordered by the doctor to get some rest and get my health back up to where it should be. Maybe in six months to a year? Just nothing before then. And Europe! With a one-week notice! Really? No. I need more lead time than one week anyway. I just can't do this anymore. Sorry."

"But Jenny, you're on top of your game. Your book is still selling like crazy. You have to keep your fans happy."

"Marty, I have sold over two million copies so far. I have more money than I know what to do with. I need a break. I want to get my life back, my health back. Get my relationship and friends back. Get my family back. I haven't seen my grandparents or my father in months. My yoga practice isn't. I miss teaching it. I haven't had a chance to run in months. I've gained weight. I'm out of shape. My health's in the tank. I haven't been to my women's group or done any counseling. I need my life back. I'm tired. So please don't push me. I need a break. I'm done." She clicked off and went to one of the B Terminal lounges for a glass of wine, check her email and social media, and wait for her flight to Durango. Her phone vibrated—Marty again. She turned it off.

The plane touched down at La Plata Regional Airport at 5:20. She picked up her bag and headed to her Jeep, hardly paying the snow-covered La Plata Mountains more than a glance. They'd lost their magic. She hadn't been into the high country in two years. She never had time, always just getting home or getting ready to leave. She didn't bother to ask her live-in partner, Chris, to take her to or pick her up from the airport anymore because it always turned into a fight. He was alway too busy and felt put upon, like it was too big a hassle for him.

She drove through her once-beloved town, hardly recognizing it anymore. It was still the same, but she'd been unable to share in its ambiance. Too busy. Always too tired.

She drove up the north valley that she'd driven so many times she knew every little nuance of the road by heart, but all she could feel was a growing knot in her stomach, dreading the next confrontation with her once-loving and supporting partner. Now she dreaded seeing him.

She pulled into the drive to the ranch house she'd bought from her friend and mentor, Will, when he and Helen got remarried three years ago. They'd decided on a newer home in town, and Will sold his house and guest house to Jenny.

Jenny loved it there, and Chris, who early on loved being there, now hated it. He felt removed from town and isolated. And it was now a thirty-minute commute rather than his ten-minute trip to work when he'd lived in town. He blamed that on Jenny as well. She couldn't understand how someone who was once so loving, supportive, and protective had turned into such a bitter angry man.

I am twenty-eight years old, and it seems I've only had two or three years of happiness.

Jenny went into the house. "Hey, Chris, I'm home. Hello? Chris?"

"Good to know," he said coldly, appearing from the bedroom. "I have to run, going out with some friends from work. See ya later." He whisked by her without a hug, without any recognition.

Jenny dropped her bags on the floor along with her heart.

Chris had gotten his book published before Jenny's. Early on, she'd urged him to get some reviews and an edit from someone other than the publisher, but he refused. The story was good but not well developed and lacked the flow of a good novel. The book started well but fizzled quickly. The book's failure had crushed him, and he completely lost interest in writing. Jenny had urged him to continue with the other stories he had in mind, but he wouldn't listen and blew her off.

Will, who was a well-published author, had helped him find a publisher. He'd offered his help with editing, but Chris refused. Jenny and Chris's relationship began to cool after her book was published and more so since she'd become a best seller. He'd become distant and cold toward her. She couldn't understand why he couldn't be happy for the success that she wanted to share with him.

Jenny stood inside the front door listening to Chris leave.

She stood there, afraid to move like she would just crumble into dust if she dared do anything other than just quietly breathe.

Cat, the cat, appeared and rubbed against her legs, purring in welcome. She reached down to pick the animal up and cuddle her. Then the tears came, Cat escaped, and Jenny got to a chair and sobbed until she couldn't anymore. She felt more alone than when she'd lived alone in the mountains for two years.

She had friends, but they all had their lives now. Will and Helen were remarried. Her closest friend, Kelly, had gotten married to Will's son, Peter, and had a six-month-old baby girl who Jenny had never seen. Even her father, Julian, had a woman friend who he was serious about. Her grandparents, Dean and Susan, were in Paris for a year. She was alone. Her health wasn't good, and she felt miserable.

It was Saturday night. Chris was going out with work buddies, and she'd just gotten home after ten days away, including time in hospital. Why couldn't he have even acknowledged her, stayed home and spent time with her? She finally got enough nerve to call Helen, hoping she'd be home. She answered.

"Hi, Helen, it's me, Jenny. Sorry to bother you. Can you talk?"

"Jenny, my God, I haven't heard from you in forever. How are you?" Helen answered brightly.

"Not so good, Helen. In fact, I'm in a really bad place right now. I don't know what to do."

"What's wrong, sweetheart? Are you sick? Where are you?"

"Oh, I'm home. And yes, I'm not well. I was in the hospital in Philadelphia. Chris is being awful and just left, and I don't know what to do. I'm sorry to bother you. Maybe I should let you go. Goodbye. Sorry." She hung up.

Her phone immediately buzzed, and she saw it was Helen. She answered.

"Jenny do not hang up on me like that again! Ever! I am coming out there right now. You stay there. Do you hear me?"

"No, no, no! I don't want you to do that. I'll be fine. Really."

"Jenny! Stop! You do not sound good. I'm coming!"

"Okay, okay. I'm sorry to bother you. I'll be here."

Twenty minutes later, Helen was at the door. After a big hug, Helen said, "Jenny, I haven't seen you since last fall, and I hate to say it, but you look terrible. You have circles under your eyes; your hair looks lifeless; you're puffy, and your complexion is sallow. And, I really don't want to say this, but you're overweight."

"I guess that sort of describes the way I feel. God, Helen, my life is so out of control. I don't know what to do." She told Helen about collapsing and ending up in the hospital. Then she went on about Chris. Her voice sounded hollow, like the way she looked and felt.

Helen said, "Jenny, I want you to come and stay with us until you get your health back. From the sounds of it, Chris won't be much help. I can't understand what he's thinking."

Jenny shook her head and, looking into space, said, "Neither do I, Helen; neither do I. But I don't want to intrude on you and Will. I'll be okay."

"You are not okay, and you will not be intruding. We have separate living quarters in the lower level of the house, and you're welcome to stay as long as you need to get yourself healthy and sort out things with Chris. I'm very serious about this, Jenny. Monday, I'm getting you an appointment with my naturopath so she can help you get your health back. Now pack what you need and let's go."

Jenny hesitated, not wanting to leave her home but

understanding what Helen was saying. She needed some R&R and she knew it. "Give me a few minutes and we can go. I want to drive my own car to have it. And I'll leave Chris a note. Oh, then there's Cat. Can I bring him?"

"Of course he can come. Will would love to see him."

Jenny went in to get some clothes and things she'd need and looked in the mirror. What she saw was her once-hard, fit, five-foot-eight body now slumped and fleshy. Her usually sharp gray eyes were dull, and her blonde hair looked washed out. *I look like shit.*

Chapter 2

Jenny dreamed she was standing in front of an empty blackboard. She was supposed to write something but didn't know what and just stood there feeling helpless. She looked out and saw thousands of people, an endless amount of people, whose faces kept changing, and they were all laughing at her.

The next morning she awoke in Helen and Will's lower bedroom and looked out the window to the spectacular view of the snow-capped La Plata Mountains. February could, historically, be the snowiest month of winter. She lay in bed for a while, thinking about how she missed her old life of having time to journal, to write, to run, to do yoga, to be with friends. She hadn't done any yoga for months. She missed teaching at Helen's yoga studio. She missed her runs with Kelly. She missed hanging out, having coffee at Ravens. She missed her therapist, Joan, and group sessions at the Women's Center. She would make it a point to call Joan today and set up an appointment. She thought of her friend Amanda in Sedona, who she hadn't seen in over two years. She couldn't understand how easily she lost her focus on what was important in her life.

She smelled a wafting scent of fresh coffee and slowly got up, put on some sweat clothes, and drifted upstairs to see Will and Helen lounging in their great room drinking coffee and reading the paper.

"Good morning, Sunshine," Will said. "Come and get a cup of coffee and sit with us. We're just starting to get moving."

Jenny did exactly that.

Will asked, "Did you sleep okay?"

"I slept like a baby. That bed is great. Thank you for having me."

"It's our pleasure. Helen tells me things aren't going too well?"

"Well, you already know, so all I can say is, no, they are definitely not. I'm guessing Helen told you everything."

"She did and I'm sorry. We'll do whatever we can for you. You know that."

"I know, Will. I know. Thanks. You've supported me, like, forever, and I keep coming back."

"It's okay. We're always more than happy to help."

"I texted my naturopath," Helen said, "and she replied back that she has an opening at 10:30 tomorrow. I'll go with you."

"Helen, you don't have to. You have things to do."

"Not really. I handed over day-to-day management of the studio to Joanne. I'm free except for my classes, and I have no classes tomorrow, so I'm free, so I'm going."

"Okay, leave about ten?"

"Ten fifteen should be fine.

The next morning, after a light breakfast, Jenny dressed in nondescript slacks, a loose sweater, and warm comfortable shoes. She and Helen drove to the naturopath's office downtown, an airy office on the second floor over a Main Street law office. They sat in a quiet, warm and inviting waiting area graced with soft colors, modern-art prints, and a water fountain bubbling away in one corner. The ambiance was serene and calming. There was no receptionist, and in a few moments, the naturopath and a client came out chatting; they gave each other a hug, and the woman left.

Helen introduced Jenny to Ann Hammond, an attractive petite woman with bobbed dark hair, wearing skinny jeans and a soft loose top. She greeted Jenny with a smile. "Happy to meet you. Come on back."

Jenny followed her into her consulting room, which felt equally as peaceful as the waiting area. Ann invited Jenny to sit and asked her what was going on. Jenny explained what had happened three days ago and showed Ann the blood panel from the Philadelphia hospital. Ann then asked her about her past medical and overall physical history. Ann's diagnosis was what the doctor had told her, she was anemic, run down, and her immune system was dangerously out of balance.

Ann got a number of bottles of supplements and muscle tested her for each one. This consisted of Jenny holding her arm straight out from her side while she held a supplement bottle in her other hand against her body. Ann would push down on her outstretched arm. If Jenny's body wanted something, her outstretched arm was extremely strong, staying where it was. If her body didn't want that particular supplement, her arm would be like jelly and fall to her side at a mere touch. She tested for four different supplements. Ann further tested her on how many times a day. She then showed Jenny how to muscle test by herself by putting the tips of her middle finger and her thumb together and pulling with the index finger of her other hand while she held a given supplement next to her body with her arm. Jenny found this all fascinating and a little strange, but she remembered how strange Amanda's healing and clearing techniques seemed to her five years ago in Sedona.

Ann reassured her, "Helen knows how to do this, and she can help you if you need. Come back and see me in two weeks, and we'll reassess your condition. Okay? Do you want to set it up now?"

"Sure. Right now I have nothing scheduled in my life."

Ann checked her appointment calendar, and they agreed on a time. "Okay, we have a time and I'll see you then. It was great to meet you. You'll be fine. And, please … get some rest."

She and Helen left and went down to the Tavern for lunch, stopping by the yoga studio on the way. Jenny looked around at the familiar space where she'd grown so much, mentally, physically, and spiritually. She hadn't meditated since she couldn't remember when. She missed teaching and the students. A lump formed in her throat.

"I'll wait outside, Helen. Take your time." She turned and left.

Helen appeared a few minutes later. "Are you okay?"

"Yeah, just realizing how much I miss teaching yoga. I miss the students. And I need to get back to my meditation practice. This book has consumed me, and my life is a mess." She laughed sarcastically. "So what's new? I was a mess when I first met you and, behold, another mess."

"You aren't a mess. You're just going through a rough patch. You need some good rest and need time to refocus."

"Yeah, and then there's Chris. I don't understand how this all happened with him. It just hurts, really hurts. I'm really glad right now that we didn't get married like I wanted.

Maybe he knew then it wasn't going to work and that's why he kept back peddling the marriage thing. Guess it'll make things easier if we do split up. The way he's been acting toward me, I'm not sure I really care what happens with him. It was so wonderful in the beginning when he was so kind and loving. Now … I don't know"—she choked back a sob—"but I love him so much. I don't want to lose him."

"I know, I know. It's hard right now, but it will get better. Promise. You need to talk with him, find out what's wrong. Maybe things aren't all that bad."

"I don't know, Helen. He's so distant. It's like he doesn't want to be around me. I don't think he even cares for me anymore. He doesn't even touch me anymore. We haven't had sex in over a year."

"Talk to him. He might be in a bad place himself and just needs to talk."

"I've tried talking to him. He just grunts and walks away. Most of the time he just leaves and goes into town. Sometimes he spends the night away. I'll try again. I'll try to catch him at the house and see. Maybe I'll catch him in a good mood."

The week went by without Jenny hearing anything from Chris. She tried calling, but her calls all went to voicemail, and he didn't return her calls. She spent her time reading, sleeping, and doing little else. The weather was cool in February with intermittent snow and not much sun. She felt listless, with no energy to do anything. She'd called for a counseling session with Joan, but she was out of town until the following Monday. She could get in on that Tuesday at 1:30.

She called her father, Julien, to let him know she was home. She didn't go into anything about her problems, opting to tell him that Chris was fine for fear of resurrecting Julien's guilt about him being in a state of alcohol and drug-induced stupor for most of her childhood. After all his counseling, he still beat himself up every time Jenny had any problems; no matter what, he blamed himself.

Julien had been paroled into her custody when he was released from prison in California over four years ago. He had a rough year or so, finally getting work, with the help of Helen, in a restaurant as a dishwasher. He worked hard and management put him in charge of running the kitchen. But he wasn't satisfied working nights. With his college degree in business management and good recommendations from the restaurant, he got a job as an office manager for a large Denver-based construction company with a branch office in Durango. He was doing well, still attending AA meetings and was now a sponsor for a young man. He had a girlfriend, Cheryl, and seemed to be happy.

On Wednesday, Helen insisted Jenny go to her yoga class. She didn't want to; she felt sloppy, had no clothes that fit and didn't want to go out of the house. Helen gave her some of her clothes that would work and almost had to drag her out the door. Class went surprisingly well for her. She ran into some people she knew and who were happy to see her. She felt pleased that she'd gone and was primed to get back into it. But after class, she was exhausted and slept most of the afternoon.

Jenny continued calling Chris several times a day, but her calls kept going to voice mail. It was winter and she knew he wasn't that busy with work. She became increasingly agitated and decided to go out to the house early Saturday morning because she was pretty sure he'd be home. She told Helen her plans.

"I'll be happy to go with you for support if you want."

"No, I think I can handle it, whatever it might be. But thanks for the offer. I may need your support when I get back."

Chapter 3

Saturday morning she was up early after a fitful night of ragged dreams, awoke in a sweat. She got dressed, grabbed a cup of coffee and drove out to the north valley to their house—her house, in truth, since she paid for it. Chris had contributed to living expenses for a while, but then things changed and he never seemed to have enough money. She didn't understand where their relationship was going, but she'd been traveling so much, she'd let it slide. She arrived and Chris's truck was there. She took a deep breath and went in.

He greeted her with, "Well, you appear. I gotta leave."

"You're always having to leave, Chris. Can you give me few minutes? We need to talk. I want to know what's wrong, why are you so angry with me. What have I done to you?"

"You're just a bother when you're here, always wanting to talk," he replied. "I don't want to talk. I told you I have to go. I like it better when you're gone. It's way easier and more peaceful."

"Chris, please don't be this way. We had something so

special. At least I thought we did."

"So tough shit. Deal with it. I have to deal with all your shit. Maybe a little support, like being home once in a while for fuck's sake."

"Chris, we've been through this so many times. I'm sorry, but it's what I needed to do. I make enough money that you can quit your job and write. I want you to start writing again. You need to. I know it's what you want."

"Yeah, right! You don't know what I want. It's always what you think I want! It's always about you and your life. I'm sick of living your life."

"I don't want you to live my life. I want you to be happy. What do you want? How can I make you happy? Please, I want us to be happy together. Chris, please, can we talk about what's making you like this? I love you. I want to be happy with you. I can't go on with you being so angry." Her voice cracked.

"Then just leave like you always do, famous Jennifer, the great writer."

Jenny felt tears coming on. "Chris, come on, that's not fair. Please. What can I do? What do you want from me?"

"Nothing. I want nothing from you. I have to piss and then I'm leaving. And, by the way, you really look like shit." He turned toward the bathroom.

His cell phone was on the counter right in front of Jenny, and as he disappeared, the screen lit up with a text message. She couldn't help but look at it.

So is the bitch still gone? Can I come out again tonight so we can get naked together and get it on? Or come to my place if she's there. Miss you. Love. Sammy

She stared at it until the screen went dark. Jenny's sadness and confusion turned into a heat of rage rising from a place so deep down she didn't know it existed. Chris reappeared.

"So who the fuck is Sammy?" she asked him. "Are you fucking her? Are you fucking her in our bed, you son of a bitch? You fucking son of a bitch. I want you out of here—NOW!"

"What the hell, you're never around. It's no big deal, just a girl from work."

"No big deal? It's a big fucking deal for me! Sounds like a big fucking deal for Sammy! No big deal? Fuck you!"

"I don't care what you think anymore. She's fun and great in bed, better in bed than you are anyway. And you've gotten fat and sloppy," he said with a chuckle, reaching for his phone.

Jenny stretched over, pulled a large butcher knife from the knife block and poked it at his throat. "Get your pig fucking ass out of here now or I swear I'll cut your heart out."

Chris saw something in her eyes that he'd never seen before. He held up both hands. "Hey, fuck you! I'm gone. Go to hell." He backed carefully out the door, ran to his truck and left quickly, spraying gravel as he tore out the driveway.

Jenny stood there, shaking. The knife fell to the floor. She clenched her fists at her sides and let out a primal scream from deep within her soul. She stood like that for a long time. Suddenly, something flashed in her mind, and she knew what to do. She grabbed her cell phone, looked up locksmiths, and found one on the north end of Durango. She called and was answered immediately.

"Frank's Lock and Key."

"Hi, I need some locks rekeyed. How soon can you be here?"

"Monday at the earliest."

"It can't wait until Monday. I need them done now."

"But I have other calls I'm heading out to."

"What's your rate? I'll double, no, triple it, if you get here right away."

"What? Really? Okay, lady. Where're you located?"

Jenny gave him the address and directions. He would be there inside an hour.

She then called the alarm company that had installed an alarm system for Will back when he'd traveled a lot. She had deactivated the service when she bought the place and now had it reactivated.

Filled with adrenaline, she went into the bedroom, stripped the comforter and sheets and hauled them and pillows out to a burn-pile area where they burned tree branches and other vegetation and debris. She then struggled getting the mattress out onto the pile, followed by the box springs. After that, she called the fire department and let them know she was doing a burn. She got a can of gas that they used for their garden tractor and poured it onto the bedding, then lit a crumpled piece of paper and tossed it on. There was a huge "whump," and it all went up in hot flames, quickly reducing the pile to ashes.

She turned and saw Frank the locksmith standing there, wide-eyed, with his toolbox. "Nice fire. Burning the bed, eh?"

"Yup. And it feels damn good too. Let me show what I want."

She had the doors to the main house rekeyed and decided to do the bunkhouse as well. Next she had him check all the window locks. She'd give her tenant the new keys and explain what was going on.

While Frank worked, she checked the alarm and set up a new entry code. She made a note to give it to her tenant. When Frank finished, she wrote him a check with a bonus.

"Ma'am, anytime you need any lock work, just please call me. Thank you."

"You are most welcome, and thank you for your quick service."

As he was leaving, she went into the bedroom, took all of Chris's drawers and dumped them out on the front lawn. Then all his hang up clothes. Then any and all items even remotely related to him: books, computer, pictures, pens, pencils, notebooks, paperclips, anything. She dumped it all out there as well.

That task completed, she called her tenant and told him the details, what to expect and what to do if Chris appeared, which he most likely would after she called and told him to pick up his stuff. She set the alarm, hung the new keys for her tenant on his door handle, and went to and Will's, thinking she needed to be there until all this blew over.

She arrived, parked, and called Chris, and, as usual, it went to voicemail. "Chris, I put all your shit out on the lawn. You should probably get it ASAP. Rain and snow are predicted for tonight. Also, the locks are changed, and the alarm has been activated, so don't even try to get in. You fucked up and I'm done. Please stay your distance and do not bother me. Hope you and Sammy have a good life; oh, yeah, until you get bored with her too. Goodbye, asshole!"

In only a few minutes, her phone chirped. She saw it was Chris and answered.

"Jenny, what the hell! You put all my stuff out. My clothes? My computer? Why? What do you expect me to do? I don't have any place to go or put all my things."

"Take it to Sammy's. She'll be happy 'the bitch' won't be in the way since you'll no longer be in 'the bitch's' house," she responded flatly.

"But she's in a small apartment with another girl. There's no room. I don't want to move in with her anyway. I want to be at the house, with you."

She laughed. "You should've thought of that before you decided to start fucking another woman. That won't work with me, Chris. Not from where I came from. I cannot and will not deal with that. Just get your shit off my property or I'm calling Goodwill to come pick it up."

"But, Jenny, be reasonable. Please. I was lonely. You were gone all the time. She and I just hooked up. It's nothing—"

She cut him off. "You were lonely? You! Were! Lonely! Ha! You, the self-proclaimed desert rat who lived in a shack by himself in Sedona. You were lonely. Bullshit!"

"Jenny, please be reasonable. I don't know where to go or what to do."

"If I was reasonable, I would've burned all your shit along with the bed. So do whatever you want. Get a storage locker. Just get your shit off my property by tomorrow or I'll make it disappear."

"You what? You burned the bed?"

"Yep. Burned it all. Don't want to ever think that you were fucking another woman in our bed. It disgusts me. And I don't want any Chris or fucking Sammy cooties. The thought of you fucking her in our bed makes me want to puke. You make me want to puke." She clicked off.

She was both crazy angry and crazy relieved. She stifled a scream and broke into uncontrollable sobs, like she was trying to wash out all of the last three years. The adrenaline wore off as suddenly as it had come, and she went into the house and down stairs and fell asleep on the bed, still fully clothed.

On Sunday afternoon she drove out to the house, and Chris's stuff was gone. All signs of him were gone. She did a fist pump for herself and smiled in satisfaction. But, still, she had to wipe tears from her eyes.

Chapter 4

Four years ago Jenny had started therapy sessions with Joan, and she'd helped her deal with her abuse as a child, and her being raped by and the suicide of her twin brother. But she was still vulnerable, especially now with the exhaustion. She'd seen too much abuse and adult irresponsibility as a youth and wouldn't put up with it ever again. She went to her appointment with Joan on Tuesday and was greeted with a long hug.

"My God, Jenny, it's so good to see you. I thought we'd lost you."

"No, you didn't lose me; it's just that my life went crazy and everything got out of hand. I sort of lost myself." She continued to tell Joan everything that had happened, from her exhaustion, ill health, and what happened with Chris.

Joan asked, "So what do you want to talk about?"

"Chris. He left me, or rather I threw him out after I found out the bastard was screwing another woman. I don't understand. He was so nuts for me in the beginning. Once his book was published and didn't do well and mine took off, well, he started to become more and more distant, finally ending up with him screwing Sammy, his new girl. I just don't understand. What's wrong with him? What's wrong with me?"

"First off, I don't think there is anything wrong with you, other than your health, which I believe, from what you've told me, you're beginning to take better care of. You'll recover, I'm sure. Now, Chris? I'm sorry for all that's happened with him. From what you just said, I would categorize him as a male that needs constant adulation and conquest, and once he achieves it, he needs to move on to the next challenge. Remember what you told me about his early career with the dot-com? And how he needed to leave after a year of apparent success? He's a Peter Pan, a boy who never wants to grow up. And I think he might be a bit of a narcissist. He saw you as vulnerable and a conquest. You then saw him as someone who might love you and support you even with your past history, and in return, you gave him what he needed. And then his book failed while yours was a success. That pushed him over the top. He simply couldn't deal with your success and his apparent failure.

"You remember we talked at length about getting into a relationship with him. You had no experience with men, even though you were twenty-five years old … no experience other than abusive cruel men. Chris appeared as a shining knight, something totally new for you. You were literally a virgin in so many ways. He had all the right things to say. And he may well have been in love with you. This is a chapter in your life that needs to chalked off to experience.

"I'm proud of you for throwing him out. You certainly put a big chink in his armor. I think the hardest blow for him was your success as a writer and his failure, and he's afraid to try to come back from failure. He'd conquered you, and then you bested him. He needed some other thing to go to that would stroke his ego, and that would be this Sammy, whoever she is. In the end, it'll always be a no-win game for him."

Joan stopped and Jenny sat for a few minutes digesting all she'd heard. "Holy shit, so I was played? That bastard!"

"Yes, in some ways, maybe, but as I said, you were inexperienced and vulnerable. As you might recall, I was leery about you getting into this but also thought it would be good for you. And he did sound like he was genuine, someone who might be good for you. We were both wrong. So are you okay with what happened? What are you thinking?"

"God, Joan, after what you just said, I feel really stupid. How could I have been so naive?"

"Because you were naive, completely naive. You went into that relationship with eyes wide open as do so many of us when we think we've found Mr. Right. So, okay, I've shared this with only a few of my clients, but I've been married three times and divorced twice. It took me three times to find the right guy, and I finally lucked out. Most men have trouble with strong women. I'm a strong woman, and you've become a strong woman now also. It takes the right sort of man who is secure in himself to understand, respect and love a strong woman."

"So you think I'm strong? I question that. I certainly don't feel strong. It hurts, Joan. Sometimes I'm not so sure of wanting to get out of bed in the morning."

"I understand. Serious relationships are hard when they fall apart. They do hurt; they can hurt a lot. Have you seen your women friends lately?"

"Just Helen. Kelly is busy being a new mom with work and all. Other than Helen, no, I haven't. I haven't had time to hardly connect with myself."

"Then it's time. I want you to come back to our group

sessions again. You could connect with some really great women there, most all are new since you were last there. Plus, you can share so much of your experience. You would be a valuable addition. We meet tomorrow night. Will you come?"

"Thanks, I will. I know I need to get myself back together. I just don't know. Right now, I'm really tired and need to go and lie down."

"One more thing before you leave. Ending a relationship as long as yours, while it may initially be a relief, can cause some heartache, second guessing, and even depression. I want you to be aware of and pay attention. It can be like a loved one dying. It takes some time to grieve. Please pay attention to your health and wellbeing, mentally, physically, and spiritually. I am going to get you a script for a mild anti-depressant. I'll make sure they're ready to pick up today."

"Joan, you know I hate drugs."

"I know, but I want you to be able to get on with your life and not be dragging around. Promise me you'll do as I ask."

"I will. Promise. I'm really tired. I need to go." She got up, gave Joan a hug, thanked her and left.

She got to her temporary residence, lay down and fell asleep. She dreamed she was in a foreign city and no one understood her, and she couldn't understand anyone there. But the people were kind and helpful, making her feel warm and cared for. She awoke mid-afternoon and groggily straggled upstairs to find Will sitting in the great room working on his laptop. "Hey, have a good rest? Want anything?"

"I think I need about a dozen shots of tequila. I really feel like crap."

"I doubt if tequila will make you feel any better. Maybe you should get out for a walk? It's a nice day, and some fresh air might do you good."

"I just don't have the energy, Will. I just want to sleep."

"Come on, I'll go with you. I need to get some air myself."

She reluctantly put on her coat and went with him into a bright sunny late-winter day. They walked for some time without speaking. Will broke the silence, "How are you feeling now?"

"Better. My head is starting to clear a little."

"I want to apologize to you."

"For what?"

"For not giving you more guidance on being more gentle with yourself after you reached author stardom. I should've advised you against letting your agent run your life and run you into the ground. I know from my own experience how easily things can get out of control."

"Not your fault, Will. I'm a big girl. I just wasn't paying attention."

"Well, I still feel I should've done something."

"Like what? You didn't know that Chris was being a jerk. You didn't know that, deep down, I enjoyed all the attention, especially early on." She paused for a few breaths. "But the few months, it all started to blur, the people at the book signings, the hotels, the cities, and, and then Chris." She choked as she swallowed a sob.

Will didn't say anything more. After walking for a while longer, he said, "Ready to head back?"

"Yeah. Thanks, Will. I love you."

"I love you too." They turned and returned to the house in silence.

Jenny decided to skip group on Tuesday night. She just didn't have the energy to go. All she wanted to do was sleep.

Chapter 5

She heard no more from Chris, which made her feel both relieved and troubled. Relieved that she didn't have to deal with him and troubled by the fact that it was evidently no problem for him to just end their relationship.

Joan had said it might not be easy, and she found that it truly wasn't. Her heart ached. She kept remembering all the fun times they had, the intimacy they had shared. She moved back and forth between anger and sadness.

After buying some new yoga clothes that would fit her, she managed to start going to yoga classes at Helen's insistence, and she got out for some short daily walks, sometimes on the trails adjacent to the house, trails that she and her best friend, Kelly, used to run on. Now it was exhausting to just walk on them. It seemed so many long years ago.

Will urged her to go and see Kelly and Peter and his granddaughter, Willow. Jenny thought back to that Thanksgiving when she met Will's son, Peter, and how she'd been attracted to him. Then on their trip together back from

Denver after she visited her grandparents, she'd told him snippets of her past, and it had made him uncomfortable. Then he and Kelly had connected, married and now had a six-month-old baby she'd never seen. Jenny felt guilty and sad about neglecting them. She drummed up the courage to call Kelly and try to make amends for her bad behavior.

Back at Will and Helen's, she took a deep breath and called Kelly, but it went to voicemail. She left a brief message and clicked off with a sigh of relief. Moments later, her phone chirped. It was Kelly.

"Hi, Kelly, I just called you."

"Yeah, I saw your message. I was busy feeding and changing Willow and had turned off my phone."

"Wow, so you're a mom. I'm so sorry for not getting in touch with you, not even acknowledging your baby. My life got out of control. That's no excuse and I'm really sorry, and I want to see you and meet Willow sometime, if you'll have me."

"Of course I want to see you, Silly Girl. Of course I do. I miss you, miss you a lot. You're my best friend, and I want to see you and catch up with all you've been doing. What are you doing now? I'm off today and Willow is settling down for a nap. Come on over."

"I have nothing going on. I'll head your way. Give me about twenty minutes."

"See ya in a few then." They clicked off.

Jenny felt nervous, then she figured out she should have a baby gift. No one was home and she panicked. She'd never had to get a baby gift before. She called Kelly back. "What can I get for a gift for Willow?"

Her voice must have sounded nervous as Kelly just laughed. "Just you will be gift enough. Get over here. Now."

Chapter 6

Kelly opened the door and gave Jenny a long hard hug. She looked the same: wild, curly dark hair and penetrating blue eyes, and she still looked so fit; it embarrassed Jenny because she knew she looked frumpy. "I have so missed you. God, I am so happy to see you."

A lump formed in Jenny's throat, and she couldn't reply except for the hug back.

"Come in and sit down. What can I get you?"

Jenny had only been in the restored and updated cottage once, right after Kelly and Peter had bought it. It was ideal for them being close to downtown and in an old but gentrified neighborhood. She saw how the house was now nicely decorated with a mix of modern and old.

"I really don't need a thing, Kelly. Thanks. When can I see Willow?"

"She just started her nap about a half hour ago. We can go in, but quietly. She was hard to get settled, and I don't want to wake her. Be very quiet. Follow me." She led Jenny into the nursery.

There she was, this little human being sleeping so peacefully. Something surged through Jenny. She couldn't remember seeing a little baby so close up. She felt such a warmth arise from deep within her that it almost took her breath away. What she wanted was to pick up baby Willow and hold her and cuddle her, to feel this little baby close to her. Finally Kelly touched her arm and motioned for them to leave. She quietly closed the door behind them.

Jenny said, "Oh my God, she is so absolutely precious. I can't believe it. She's beautiful. I want to hold her."

"You can when she wakes up."

"I can't believe you're a mother, Kelly. It's amazing. What's it like?"

"Short version, it's grueling, middle of the night feeding, little sleep, dirty diapers, and I wouldn't trade it for the world. I'm so happy, Jenny. I can't begin to tell you how happy I am. And Peter is a great dad. Does whatever he can to help out."

"How's Peter doing?"

"He's great. He loves being a lawyer. He's getting to work on some Native American tribal issues, exactly what he'd wanted to do. The people at his firm really like him and have already upped his salary. He has started mountain biking which makes me a little nervous, but he always goes with friends. He's had a couple spills, nothing serious, but some nasty road rash."

"You look great. I never saw you when you were pregnant, my fault I know. I'm sorry. I seem to have missed out on so much, being gone all the time. When I was home, I had to recover from being gone and then get ready to leave again. Then there was trying to keep Chris happy. That didn't work out so well."

"Really? What's going on with you guys?"

"We split up. I threw him out after I got back from my last trip. He was becoming more and more distant the last year. He was just being awful to me. Then I find out he's been screwing somebody named Sammy … in our bed. I kicked him out, him and all his shit. Burned the bed. He's gone and I feel miserable."

"Jenny, I am so sorry. What're you going to do?"

"Move on, I guess. What else can I do? But I can't stop thinking of all our good times up until about a year or so ago when he started being less communicative, our sex life became nonexistent, and then … Sammy, whoever the hell she is." She went on to tell Kelly about her meeting with Joan.

Kelly responded, "I'm really sorry, Jenny. Chris seemed to adore you. I can't understand him and how he changed. But Joan's assessment could make sense. I don't know what to say."

"Thanks, and there really isn't much you can say. It just is, and I need to get over it. Joan said it can take time. And—yeah, and … so, you look great. Are you working out? Yoga? What?"

"I ran up until I was six months along, did a prenatal yoga class, and have been down on the river trail running with Willow in her jogger stroller. She likes it, usually falls asleep for the whole time. Want to join me tomorrow?"

"I'd love to, but I'm so out of shape, I don't know if I could keep up, even with you pushing the stroller."

"I'm slow, and I'll take it easy with you. Please?"

"What time?"

Around 10:00. I'll meet you down at Schneider Park, or you could come by here and we could go down together."

"Do you start from here or drive down?"

"No, I start here and walk until I get to the trail."

"Great; I'll meet you here then, at 10:00."

A squawk came from the nursery. "She's awake. Come on."

They got up and went into the nursery where little Willow was gurgling, blowing bubbles, and waving her arms and legs. Jenny melted, marveling at this little person. Kelly picked her up and handed her toward Jenny. "Here, want to hold her?"

Jenny froze. "Yeah. I really want to but … but I don't know how. I don't want to hurt her."

"You're not going to hurt her. She won't break. Just hold her like I am."

Jenny reluctantly reached out, and Kelly handed her off. "Here ya go, Aunty Jenny."

Aunty Jenny. She felt tears start to form as she took the squirming little bundle of life into her arms. She carried her carefully out to the living room and sat, looking into her eyes. Willow looked up at her, gurgled, and smiled.

"Oh my God, she just smiled at me."

"She likes her new aunty."

About ten minutes later, Willow started to squirm and whine; the corners of her mouth drooped. "Okay, what do I do? She's starting to cry. I didn't do anything to her."

"She probably needs changing and is getting hungry. Here, I'll take her."

Kelly went and changed her, then sat back down, unbuttoned her blouse and began breastfeeding Willow. Jenny stared in awe of a mother and baby, joined as one.

That night Jenny dreamed that she was a mother like Kelly, and they both lived together with their children in some idyllic lush valley.

Jenny met Kelly the next morning and could barely suffer through one mile of their run. Kelly just ran along, pushing the stroller and chatting away all the while. Jenny on the other hand was struggling just to breathe and could only grunt her responses.

Back at Kelly's, Jenny crashed onto the living room floor and groaned. "God, I hurt. I hurt everywhere. I'm so out of shape. I hate myself."

Kelly laughed. "You just need to get moving. You said you're home for a while. Let's go again the day after tomorrow. I usually go out about four times a week. I'm only working a few hours a week just with some of my exclusive clients."

"I may never walk again much less run. Just let me lay here for a while, like a week."

Kelly laughed as she fed Willow. "Please stop, I'm trying to feed this baby and you're cracking me up."

Jenny loved being there with Kelly. She felt so close to her, as if the two of them were sisters.

She met Kelly for another run, but quit again after a half a mile and went back home. It was too hard, and she didn't have the energy. Helen kept coaxing her to yoga classes, but an hour class wore her out. She was now eating healthy food, not the constant flow of restaurant food, usually over a meeting when she hardly knew what he was eating. Still, she felt lethargic and had a hard time being interested in anything.

Chapter 7

Jenny met again with Joan on Monday and forced herself to go to group on Tuesday night. She recognized two women left from two years ago and saw six new faces, four younger and two older women.

Joan welcomed them and introduced them all. And then she said, "Who would like to go first?"

Jenny said, "Since I'm sort of a new person, I'll go. I was a regular here up until two years ago. Then my work caused me to travel a lot. Not only did I miss out on Joan's great counsel and my sisters in this group, but my relationship with a great guy, who turned out not to be so great, also fell apart when I found out he was screwing somebody else. We just had a breakup and, right now, I'm trying to get my head screwed back on. I was originally in counseling and group because of serious sexual abuse and bullying in my childhood. And it all still haunts me."

Everyone was quiet, digesting Jenny's speech. Marianna was the first to speak, very stoically, "I'm sorry to hear that. I was also abused the same when I was little. Welcome, sister."

Jenny didn't speak the rest of the night but listened intently to the others who delved into their issues of abuse from husbands, fathers, and other relatives. She heard about drug abuse and the gender confusion of being lesbian or trans and subsequent family rejection. After listening to the litany from some of the others, Jenny thought her problems were minuscule.

After the session was over, several of the women wanted to go out and eat a late dinner, but Jenny declined, saying she needed rest. After all the others had left, Joan asked her, "So … are you okay?"

"No, I'm not. These women are dealing with way more stuff than I am. Poor me. My guy was an asshole. So?"

"Jenny, you have to realize that your past hasn't just gone away. You have to look at yourself and how Chris's behavior has impacted you, how it impacts your past and what you're still having to work on. It doesn't all go away so easily. You've been overwhelmed these last few years, and my concern is that you've put everything aside and haven't continued to work on it. You haven't seen me in over two years, and I don't think you've been suddenly miraculously healed. You suffered before I met you, and you're suffering now. Don't try to deny it."

"Okay, dammit, Joan, okay!" she responded. "I don't need a fucking lecture! Just leave it! Okay! I am so fucking stressed right now! I don't need any more shit!"

"Okay. Sorry. Please don't get angry. I just see what's going on, and I'm concerned is all."

"I'm sorry, Joan. I'm so tired and my life sucks right now. I don't think this group is what I need. I need some rest, and I need to be somewhere away from all of this."

"You can't hide from it. It will follow you no matter where

you go. As someone once said, no matter where you go, there you are."

"I know, Joan. I know. You've taught me well. But I need rest. I just need rest."

"I understand. I do. So go home and rest. Are you taking the anti-depressants?"

"I tried but they just make me more groggy and feel worse. I hate drugs."

"I understand, but try taking a lesser dose and see what happens. Have you been writing? Journaling?"

"Okay, I'll give it a shot with a lesser dose … and, no. I haven't done any writing or journaling, not for a long time."

"Maybe it's time to start again. Have you seen Amanda, or been in contact?"

Jenny hung her head. "No. It's been over two years."

"She always had a good way of grounding you. You should call her."

"I know. I feel so bad about neglecting her friendship as well as everyone else. I'm such a bad friend. And I miss her a lot."

"You never had much practice in friendship, Jenny. It's not your fault. It's just something you need to be aware of and work on."

"Yeah, I can agree. I need to go, and so do you. Thanks, Joan. You're so great. I'm sorry. I feel like such a bitch. You've helped me so much. I love you so much."

She reached out and hugged her therapist so hard that Joan felt Jenny's tears against her neck.

The following day Jenny had an appointment with Ann, the naturopath, for her two-week checkup. Ann asked, "How are you feeling?"

"No energy. I tried running with my friend and it killed

me. A yoga class does me in. I'm always tired."

"Jenny," Ann replied seriously, "you're suffering from anemia and exhaustion. You need to eat a good healthy diet, rest, and build yourself back up again. You're young and should recover quickly, but take your time. It's only been two weeks, and it will take a while. You're not going to be up to running marathons for a while. Slow down."

"I hear what you're saying, but, well, I just want my routine back. I want to feel better."

"You will, but you need to take your time and get some rest. Period!"

Chapter 8

Jenny was tired of being a house guest and wanted to go home, but Helen didn't want her to leave, feeling she still wasn't ready to be alone. Will went off on a book-signing tour of his own, and Jenny agreed to stay until he returned home the next week.

When Jenny was working on her book, Will began on a new one—completely removed from his earlier cheap romance thrillers—which had been published and had gained the acclaim he'd been longing for all his life. He was on a similar East Coast tour to the one she'd recently returned from.

Jenny went to check on her house every few days, and all was good. Her tenant was fine and taking care of things. He worked at the ski resort during the winter and construction in summer. He was dependable and never late paying his reduced rent for his caretaker work.

She considered how vulnerable she'd begun to feel. She thought back to her years when she lived a solitary life in the mountains and in an isolated cabin a few miles north of her present house, until the cabin burned down, setting in motion a life she never would've imagined for herself.

Her phone chirped. Her caller ID registered that it was Chris. Reluctantly she answered. "Hi, Chris," she said flatly. "What?"

"Hi, Jenny. I need to talk. Are you home? I'll come out."

"No. I'm not home. And I don't want to talk."

"I'm sorry. I know I screwed up, but I really need to talk to you. Please?"

"So did your little 'Sammy' drop you like the creep you are? Now you want to come back home. No way do I want to talk to you."

"No, it's not like that at all. This is important. When'll you be home? I'll come out."

"No you won't come out. I'm not home. I don't want to see you. I don't want to be alone with you. You cheated on me, and I can never trust you again. You know my past, and you didn't honor it or me, so screw you."

"Aw, come on, Jenny. Please? I'm sorry. I was a jerk. I just want to talk. It's really important. Meet me for coffee at least? It'll be neutral ground."

Jenny hesitated. "Okay, for coffee. Tomorrow at Raven's. Ten o'clock."

"Great, Thanks. See ya then."

She clicked off.

Helen overheard Jenny's conversation. Sorry, but I couldn't help but overhear your conversation. What did he want?"

"He wants to talk."

"You're meeting him tomorrow?"

"Yeah. I don't know why. He says it's important. I can't imagine ever being with him again after the way he acted toward me."

"But you had a good relationship. Maybe you can salvage it … if you want to."

"I don't know, Helen. He was my first and only 'boyfriend.' I'm so naive about men. Maybe I'm the one who screwed it up. Maybe it's me."

"Oh, it's not you, Jenny. He's the one who cheated on you. Relationships exist on trust and support. He didn't quite make the grade on either of those. But it might be good to hear what he has to say."

"Ah, yeah, maybe. I guess I'll go see."

She slept fitfully that night with dreams of someone chasing her. Her feet felt leaden. She could hardly move. It was someone she knew, but couldn't recognize. Whoever, whatever it was kept coming closer and closer, but never close enough. She awoke panting and drenched in sweat, feeling sick to her stomach.

After stripping the bed and putting everything into the washing machine, she showered and went upstairs to find Helen having coffee and reading the paper.

"My God, Jenny, you look pale as a ghost. What's wrong? Sleep okay?"

Jenny, still feeling queasy said, "No. I had a horrible dream. I'm still shaking. It was horrible." She told Helen about it.

"Just a bad dream, sweetheart. Just breathe. Can I get you anything?"

"No thanks. I just want to sit for a minute and try to calm down. I wish Amanda was here to tell me what this was about."

"I'm not Amanda, but I would say you are reacting to your meeting with Chris today. You feel he's chasing you, and you can't get away no matter how hard you try."

"Maybe. I don't know, I'm nervous about seeing him. I'm

afraid I might let him come back, and I don't want to. I miss him. But, at the same time, I could never trust him again. And you know how I am with trust issues. It's all so messed up."

Helen couldn't help but chuckle. "Oh yes, how well I know. You'll be fine. Just be yourself. You're a much stronger woman than you were a few years ago. Trust me. You'll be fine."

Jenny got to Raven's to find Chris already sitting waiting for her. He got up and greeted her with a hug which made her stiffen and break away. She noticed he'd put on weight and looked stressed.

"Good to see you, Jenny. Can I get you something? Your favorite?"

"Thanks but I'll get it."

She returned with her cappuccino and sat across from him. "So … what do you want to talk about?"

"Well, I'm moving back to California. I was offered a job with my old tech firm where I worked before I met you down in Sedona. They want me back, and this time I set some parameters to protect myself so I don't get burned out like before. They agreed and offered me a great salary and serious bennies. I realize I suck at novel writing, as much as I thought I'd be so great at it. I was good at what I did before and am going back. And"—he hesitated—"I want you to come with me."

He threw up his hands before she could even reply. "I know, I know. I was a jerk. I screwed up. I am so, so sorry. I know I hurt you, and I'll understand if you tell me to go to hell. But I needed to ask. You're still special, and I still love you, and after my screw up, I realize just how much. I miss you. I do."

Jenny sat there stunned at what she'd just heard and how she felt after hearing what he had to say. After a few long moments with all this churning inside her head, she said, "Chris, I can't. I just can't. I don't think I could ever trust you again. What if I went with you, and then you did the same thing with another 'Sammy' that you came across? My family and friends, my support system, they're all here. I love it here. I don't want to move to San Francisco. I'm sorry Chris, but no. I can only wish you well with your new work. I'm sorry your book didn't do well. I'm sorry I wasn't able to be more attentive to you these last few years. But that was no excuse for what you did. You hurt me. Really hurt me. I loved you. I was planning on spending the rest of my life with you. But now? No, Chris. No. There's no way."

"But, Jenny, please, we can start fresh. We can move beyond this. I really want you to come with me. We could get a flat somewhere in the city. You could write. San Francisco is great. You'd love it—"

"Not going to happen, Chris. Have a good life." With that, she took her drink, got up, turned and left, not looking back, and was surprised there were no tears, even though she might never see him again. She flipped her hair and walked to her car.

Chapter 9

Will returned home and Jenny returned to her own house. She brought Cat with her, stopping briefly to buy some groceries. She also ordered a new mattress and boxspring to be delivered that afternoon.

When Jenny walked into her house, it felt empty and lifeless. She missed Chris being there. He always gave her some stability—up until the last while anyway.

She put away her groceries, sat on the couch, and stared out into the pine trees that surrounded the house, thinking about their meeting over coffee. Maybe she should go with him. She could write in San Francisco as well as anywhere. Since she'd met him and fallen in love with him, she'd felt secure and safe. Now she felt alone and frightened. Cat jumped up and curled up on her lap, purring softly.

She thought of Amanda. The more she thought of her, the more she needed to see her, to talk with her. Maybe Amanda would do some long-distance energy work on her. Maybe that would help. She knew, in the shape she was in, there was no way she could go to Sedona to see her.

She desperately wanted to feel better, to be her own self, to be happy like she'd been those few years ago after she'd come out of the mountains and had by chance met Will and how he'd helped her and cared for her when she couldn't trust anyone, especially men, fearful that they might abuse her or take advantage of her like when she was growing up in the commune in California. Then there were her grandparents, and Helen, Joan, Kelly, Amanda, and even Chris. All of them had helped her to grow and get over her abuse as a child.

But now? She was not healthy physically and was an emotional wreck. She knew she shouldn't blame herself about Chris, but she did. Maybe if she had just done something different. If she'd stayed home instead of all the traveling. If she could have somehow helped Chris to start writing again instead of letting him quit after one failure. Now he was leaving for San Francisco. Maybe she should forgive him and go with him. But she knew better. It wasn't her fault, no more her than it was for her twin brother raping her when they were fourteen years old or for him committing suicide. But it was still hard for her to reconcile everything.

She punched in Amanda's number which was answered instantly. "Jenny, it's you. What's going on? Where've you been? I haven't seen or heard from you in forever. I know something's wrong."

"Well, yeah, a few things. First let me say how ashamed I am for not being in touch with you. At least I could have called. I'm so sorry I—"

Amanda interrupted, "You don't need to apologize. What's wrong? I knew the moment I saw the caller ID."

Amanda was psychic as well as an energy healer. She'd helped Jenny release a lot of the built-up negative energy from her childhood when Jenny had met her in Sedona five years ago.

After hesitating for a moment, Jenny began to share briefly what had been happening in the last two years, her travels, her success, the toll on her health, and lastly, Chris.

"I just wish I was able to come down, but I just can't. I just don't have the energy."

Amanda remained silent for a long few moments. "I can come up to Durango to see you. I've always wanted to visit there. I could come up tomorrow."

"But there's your shop to take care of."

"I hired an assistant last year. I was getting too overwhelmed with online business, and along with my healing sessions, I had no time to run the shop, so I found a great young man who is both knowledgeable about and loves crystals and stones. He's dependable and energetic and can easily run things for a few days. It would do me good to get away anyway. I'll see you tomorrow. Give me directions."

"Wow. That'd be great. I'd love to see you and return your hospitality." She gave the directions to her house.

Chapter 10

Jenny was happy that her friend was coming to see her. She busied herself cleaning and getting the guest room together. The van arrived with her new bed. She got out extra bedding and made it up. Then she went back into town to get more groceries.

By the time she got home and had everything put away, it was late afternoon and she was exhausted. Her adrenaline had burned off, and she could barely move. She stripped down and went to her hot tub out on the back deck to soak. She then took a cold shower and, skipping dinner, fell into bed.

She dreamed that she was a princess locked in a cold stone tower in some strange land. She was standing on the roof watching the sunrise when Amanda came, riding on a white winged horse, to rescue her.

Jenny awoke with a start to the new day, realizing she was starved, not having eaten since early afternoon the previous day. Cat woke with her, stretched and came to her, purring loudly to say good morning.

She fed Cat and had a quick breakfast. Then she realized she had nothing to do but wait for Amanda's arrival. She hadn't journaled in so long that she couldn't remember when she last wrote. After rummaging around her office desk, she found her last notebook in which she'd only written on a few pages, the last entry dated over three years ago. She sat and started writing, starting from where she left off, trying to remember her life. It wasn't easy, as it all seemed like a blur. Where had she been? Who had she met? And her relationship with Chris. She tried to dissect everything, realizing that it would take her a while to catch up to present day. Around eleven o'clock she got a text from Amanda, saying that she'd gotten an early start and was already in Cortez, about an hour and a half away.

Jenny grew nervous and needed to do something to calm herself, so she kept on remembering and writing. She was lost in her journal when a knock on her door jolted her back to the present.

All Jenny could do was grab Amanda and hug her until Amanda said, "I'm happy to see you too, but please don't break me."

"I'm just so happy to see you. I'm so sorry. I'm such a terrible friend."

"Quit apologizing. You're not terrible. Good friends are friends over time and space, and we are such friends. It's great to see you." Amanda stood back and looked at her. "As a friend, I have to say you don't look so great. Sorry, but you don't. You told me a little when we talked, but, Jenny, I had no idea. You poor dear. I'm happy I came."

"I know how I look. And it's exactly how I feel. Come in. Can I carry anything in?"

"No, I have everything in this bag. Thanks. Show me your house. It looks wonderful. And it is so beautiful here in the pine trees."

Jenny showed Amanda her house, the guest room where she would stay, and guest bath. Amanda deposited her things, and they went to the living room and sat. Cat came in, jumped up by Amanda and curled up on her lap.

Jenny said, "Just put her down."

"She's fine. I like cats. She's just saying hello. So tell me what's been going on."

"It's been crazy, Amanda. It's been so crazy, I don't even know where to start, but here's the short version." She told Amanda about her last few years, ending with Chris and how she felt about it—her anger, her sadness, and her guilt that their breakup was all her fault. Finally, she shared their meeting and how he'd pleaded with her to go with him.

Amanda listened, and when Jenny was done, she sat for a long time without saying anything. Then she said, "I'm sorry about Chris. I truly am. I saw you two being so right for each other, but one thing I didn't see was for how long. I have to say that you both needed each other for that time. Jenny, you need to see what Chris has brought you, how he has impacted you and your life, and think about how different it might have been if you'd never met."

Jenny sat for a long while digesting what she'd just heard. "Interesting. I'm going to have to think about all that. It does raise some things I hadn't thought of."

"I admire you for not caving into him. I feel you did the right thing. My guess is he'll find someone else again to satisfy his need for a new adventure."

"Thanks for your support. It was hard to turn away from him. I may never see him again"—she stopped for a minute, took some deep breaths, and found a tissue to dry her eyes—"So … enough about me, how about you?"

"You know, I took your advice and went into counseling over three years ago. I'm so grateful that you urged me to do it. As you warned me, it was painful. I had to dredge up all the crap about my father's sexual abuse and my neglectful mother. It was really hard. So much of it I had put away in the back of my mind. Once I started bringing all of it to the forefront, it was a flood. After many tears and hard work, I have to say I'm happier than I've ever been.

"And I met a guy, and it's going really great. He's a few years older than me, in his early fifties, runs a landscape company."

"Don't tell me—"

"Yeah, the same guy Chris worked for. We're enjoying our time together. We spend a lot of time at his place, cooking, watching movies, eating popcorn, just being together. He's fun and nice. And no pressure for anything."

Jenny interrupted, "Yeah, I thought Chris was amazing. Ha! What a joke that was. I'm sorry. I shouldn't have said that; we had our good times, and I know it's time to move on. I want you to be happy."

"Jenny, we can't hide from trying to be happy. Being happy sometimes requires taking chances. I found that out. This thing with Scott—that's his name, Scott—we both realize that it may not last and have talked about it. He's pretty savvy, having been married and divorced. He has two boys, one in college and the other graduated and working in Phoenix.

"Sometimes two people come together for whatever reason. Sometimes it lasts forever and sometimes their time together is not meant to last forever. Maybe they're old soul mates who only need to reconnect for a brief time to satisfy their soul needs. Does this make any sense?"

"Yeah, a little. I did read that book on souls you gave me a long time ago, and I remember a chapter that touched on that."

"Also, Jenny, remember, I also talked to you about how we humans are incarnated on the planet to learn lessons we haven't yet learned from our past lives. And also, we're working on karma from our past lives. So keep that in perspective as you go through this life."

"Easier said than done. I know what you're saying from an intellectual standpoint, but it's not so easy emotionally. It's still confusing, and it hurts."

"You'll grow from this experience with Chris. And there are no rules saying you have to have a partner or a husband or children. If you find the right person, it can be wonderful, but there's no point in having someone you're not happy with or who makes you miserable. And one last thing, you're not responsible for Chris and his behavior. It was his choice, and while it makes you unhappy and sad, it's not your fault. Don't blame yourself."

"That's what everybody tells me. Maybe it's time for me to get over myself and realize it wasn't my fault." Jenny was beginning to feel lighter just being with Amanda. Her very presence seemed to bring peace and light to her and her house.

Amanda said, "I brought my massage table so I can do some energy healing for you. I'll go get it and we can do a session."

"You don't have to. You've had a long drive. You must be tired. Just sit and relax."

"I am a little tired, but doing energy work also energizes me as well. I insist."

"Okay, but then I'm taking you to town and buying you dinner."

Jenny helped get the table from Amanda's car, and they set it up in the living room. Amanda produced several candles and an incense burner from another bag along with several large crystals. She placed everything as she wanted and lit the candles and some incense. Jenny lay on the table, took several deep breaths, and closed her eyes.

Amanda didn't touch her, but Jenny felt her moving her hands over her. Her head filled with light, and she felt lighter and lighter, like she might float off the table. Warmth caressed her body. Then she felt completely free from everything, and all went quiet.

She sailed out of her house, flying higher and higher, up into the mountains. She saw her favorite place where she'd stood so many times all those years ago when she lived out of her backpack for months at a time. She remembered the freedom she felt then, freedom from people, relationships, material goods. She remembered her fear of people and how distant all that now seemed. She slowly headed back down, following a silver cord back into her body.

Gradually, she opened her eyes and tried to grasp where she was. The light was fading, like it was late afternoon. She slowly began to move her limbs. She felt different.

"Hi, sleepy head. Have a good rest?"

"What time is it? Was I asleep?"

"You were out for about an hour. I let you rest. You looked too peaceful to disturb."

"Oh my God, I think I had one of those out-of-the-body things again like the time back in Sedona when I was in the desert with Chris. There was a silver cord like the first time."

"Excellent. I removed a lot of dark matter from you. Not nearly anything like when we first met. But there was a lot of just heavy gray energy that is now gone. I hope it helps."

"I feel different, lighter." She sat up and slowly got off the table, not sure how well her legs were going to work. "I'm starved. Let's go into town for dinner. I'll call Will and Helen to see if they want to join us. I want you to meet them," she said excitedly, feeling an energy she hadn't felt in a while.

"Slow down," Amanda said, laughing. "You'll burn yourself out."

"But I feel great. Thanks for that, Amanda." She gave her a grateful, loving hug.

Jenny called and Helen said they would meet them in an hour at the Railroad Inn, one of their favorite restaurants, down by the train depot.

Chapter 11

Helen and Will were already there, seated by a window that looked out onto the now closed patio. White, year-round Christmas lights twinkled, bringing light and a sense of celebration to the early evening.

Introductions were made. A waitress appeared with menus. Another came by to fill water glasses. The waitress reappeared and took drink orders.

Amanda said, "It's so nice to meet you. Durango seems like a charming place. I already love the energy of the town and the ambiance of this restaurant."

"How long will you be staying?" Helen asked.

"I don't know, a few days for sure. I want Jenny to show me around and see the sights. We haven't seen each other in several years, and I want to catch up on her life."

"And I on hers," Jenny said.

Orders were made and conversation continued. After dinner and shared desserts, they said their goodbyes and departed. Amanda wanted to walk, so she and Jenny strolled

Main Street, looking in windows of closed stores, peeking into some of the bars, staying for a while in one to listen to the band that was playing. Then they ambled back to their car and drove back to Jenny's.

On the way, Amanda said, "Helen and Will are so nice. Is Will the man whose house you stumbled on, the one who helped you and mentored you?"

"Yeah. He's so special. I think I told you I adopted him as my father. So now I have two fathers. I want you to meet Julien while you're here. I'm so happy for him. He's doing so great. He has a good job that he likes, and a girlfriend. She's good for him and gives him something he's missed ever since my mother died when I was born. And Helen, she's been like a mother to me. She's done so much and given me so much. I truly love them both."

It was late when they returned to the house. Jenny made sure Amanda was comfortable, then they bid each other good night and retired for the night.

Jenny enjoyed a deep, peaceful, dreamless sleep, the best night's rest she'd had in a long time.

The morning came, and with newfound energy, Jenny took Amanda up into the mountains, driving up to Silverton, about fifty miles north over two 10,000-foot-plus, passes. Amanda was enthralled by the beauty and grandeur of the San Juan Mountains. The next day they went to Mesa Verde and the next, roamed around Durango.

Jenny took Amanda to meet Julien, and they had dinner at Kelly and Peter's one night. Amanda gave baby Willow a crystal which Willow grabbed and hugged. She only let go of it when she fell asleep. Jenny also arranged for Joan and Amanda to meet over lunch.

The last night before she left, Amanda asked why she

hadn't seen Jenny's grandparents.

"They're in Europe, Paris to be exact, until September. They keep wanting me to come over and spend some time with them, but I've been so busy, and now, the way I feel, I'm not sure I'm able to go."

"You are perfectly able to go. You're not sick or incapacitated. You need some rest and a change of scenery. Trust me. You need a change of scenery, and Paris would be the perfect change for you to experience."

Chapter 12

By mid-March Jenny felt better. She had more energy, had regained some strength, and shed unwanted pounds. She went running with Kelly but was still only able to do a mile or two comfortably, and she attended yoga classes regularly. Slowly, she was getting her life back, getting back into her old routine. She also journaled and worked on ideas for another book. A woman in yoga class told her Chris had left for California. She had heard nothing more from him.

As she regained her life, she became more sociable, seeing old friends and spending time going out for dinners and movies, along with hanging out at Raven's. She had a standing counseling session every two weeks with Joan but still avoided group, feeling sympathetic but too out of touch with what the other women were dealing with.

She and her father, Julien, and his girlfriend, Cheryl, got together every week or so for dinner or Sunday night pizza while watching a movie. On one such Sunday night, Jenny brought up something she'd been reluctant to, knowing how her mother's death at her and her brother's birth had sent him into depression, alcohol, and drugs. She asked Julien about her mother.

"Daddy, I'm sorry to bring this up, but I'm twenty-eight old, and I know nothing about my mother … or her family, my family. Who were they? Where was my mother from? How did you meet? I know nothing. Dean and Susan ignored my questions, saying it was something they'd just as soon forget. Nobody will tell me about her! Nobody! I want to know!"

The room went silent. Cheryl excused herself to another room. The only sound was their breathing. Julien's head dropped to his chest. Jenny could see him shaking. Finally he raised his head and looked at her with tears in his eyes.

With a quivering voice, he said, "Oh, Jenny. I loved her so much. And she died at what was supposed to be the happiest time of our lives, when you and Michael were born. We knew there were going to be two of you. She was healthy, but the delivery was hard for her. It took too long. It all went wrong. She hemorrhaged. The doctors did everything they could. But—" He choked on his words. "You know the rest that I told you when you visited me in prison. I'm still so ashamed and so sorry."

"I know, Daddy, but you need to let it go. It's been thirty years."

"Yeah, I know, I know, my counselors say the same thing. I need to let go."

"So you've talked to them about all this?"

"Of course, but it hasn't helped. Well, maybe. Yes, when I think about it, yes, it has helped, but still—"

"Maybe, then, you need to talk to me about it. About my mother, Melissa, about my other grandparents, cousins, aunts, uncles. I want to know about her, Daddy. Please?"

Another long pause, and then he began, "Well, you know I went to the University of Iowa for college, studying business management. Your mother was an economics major, and we met in an econ class that was a requisite for both of us. It was our sophomore year. We sat next to each other and became friends and study buddies. Then we realized it was more. We fell in love, madly, crazy in love. We were married the summer we graduated and moved to Denver.

"Her parents disliked me from the start; I don't know, maybe because I was from Colorado and took their daughter far away to some alien land. They were adamantly against our getting married, never even speaking to me or my parents at our wedding, just sat at their table and glared at us the whole time. Her brothers and sister seemed nice enough. They attended her funeral, but we never spoke, and I've never heard from them again.

"We both had good jobs in Denver, and Melissa was considering grad school, maybe working toward a doctorate. Our lives were good. Three years later, she got pregnant with you two. We were excited. My parents were excited. Her parents didn't seem to care one way or another. Grad school was off the table for the near future. And—" He choked again.

Jenny gave him space and waited.

"Your grandparents are Harley and Alice Burns from near New Vienna, Iowa. They're farmers. They never even wanted to see you two babies, never wanted to see their own grand-babies. And, well, you know the rest. I started drinking too much and met Dory. She introduced me to drugs. Your grandparents were pretty much raising you by that time. I wasn't fit to. I was missing work and was on notice. Then Dory wanted to go to California to a commune paradise where we would live off the land, live a life of ease. So I got you two, and we left for California, and you know how that turned out."

He paused for a long time, staring at thoughts far away, then continued, "Melissa was the middle child of five. She had two older brothers and a younger brother and sister. So you have an aunt and three uncles and probably a few cousins scattered about. I'm sorry, Jenny. It's hard not having alcohol and drugs for a crutch, but I swear I'm never going down that road again. I swear."

Jenny just sat, absorbing the information about a family she'd never known, feeling anger and relief at what she was hearing.

Julien continued, "As far as I know, Harley and Alice are still alive and farming. Melissa's one older brother, John, is an attorney, and the youngest, Mark, was working with Harley on the farm. The other two, I'm not sure of. That's all I know."

After another silence, Jenny said, "I think I'd like to go to Iowa as soon as I can get a flight. I want to see my family."

"No, Jenny. It'd be better to just let sleeping dogs lie. I'm afraid you'd just get hurt."

"The sleeping dogs have been asleep too long, Daddy. It's time to wake them up."

"Jenny, you're setting yourself up for a big disappointment. Forget it. I'm telling you, do not do this. You are setting yourself up to get hurt."

Driving north to her house later, doubt began to settle in, her bravado slipping away. *Maybe I should just forget it.* Nevertheless, when she got home she went to her computer and booked herself a flight to Cedar Rapids, Iowa.

Chapter 13

Three days later her flight landed early afternoon in Cedar Rapids. She got her rental car, found New Vienna on Google Maps, and headed out of the airport. She drove east for a few miles and then headed out of the Cedar River Valley, going north on Highway 13.

After leaving the Cedar Rapids metro area, the land began to flatten out. The views were expansive for 360 degrees, dotted by farmsteads, dying small towns with grain silos, and boarded up storefronts. It was too early in the spring for any tilling, so the land was still resting. The fields were bare, some had fall tillage, but most showed the stubble remains of corn or bean crops from the previous year.

Jenny found this landscape meditative but not calming for her jangled nerves, given the fact she was coming here unannounced and hadn't any idea where her grandparents lived. She'd looked on Google Maps and other sites to try to get a location or contact information but had struck out. She did know that New Vienna was a small town, and someone would probably know Harley and Alice Burns.

About two hours later, she arrived and drove through the little town. At the north end of town by a large stone church, she turned around and drove back to a convenience store. She went in and asked the counter person if she knew the Burns family.

A burly giant of a man with a weathered, bearded face overheard her asking the counter clerk and turned to her. "Why are you looking for them?" he asked, staring at her with his gray eyes.

"I'm Jennifer Morse, their grand-daughter," she replied steadily, despite being a little fearful of this rough-looking man. "Do you know the Burns family?"

"Yeah. I do. I'm Mark, their youngest son. So, I guess I'd be your uncle then. I thought you looked familiar, and now I know why. You look just like your mother."

Jenny stopped, staring up at this large man who was her blood relation. Her mother's brother. Her uncle. She choked on a sob.

"Do Mom and Dad know you're coming?"

"No. I wanted to call them, but I couldn't get a contact number."

"Then I don't know if it's such a good idea. They've never gotten over Melissa's getting married to your father and then her death. They've been grieving the thirty years since she died. You showing up would be like pulling a scab off a wound that's still raw. Know what I mean?"

"Yeah, 'best let sleeping dogs lie' so I've been told."

"I hate to disappoint you, but it might be for the best if you turned around and went back where you came from."

"Can I ask, how do you feel? About Melissa, I mean."

"Well, I was the baby of the family, fifteen at the time.

It shook me up pretty bad when she died. But I got over it eventually." He smiled at her. "I'm really happy to meet you. I can't believe this. How's your brother?"

"Not so good. He died about five years ago," she replied.

"I'm sorry. How'd he die if you don't mind?"

"I'd rather not get into it. Sorry."

He looked at her with kindness in his eyes. "No, that's okay. I shouldn't have pried, none of my business. It's getting late, and I gotta get back home. There's a nice motel back in Dyersville. I really don't think it'd be wise to bother Harley and Alice. They're getting on, and Dad's got a shaky ticker … had two attacks already. Probably isn't a good idea to rile him. Good to meet you though. Safe travels."

He walked by her and out the door, leaving her with a pounding heart and tears starting to form. She followed him out, got into her car, and pounded the steering wheel until it hurt her hands. Then she sat for a long few moments before starting the car and tearing out of the parking lot, heading south.

She got to Dyersville and checked into the motel, then went to her room and flopped down the bed. *What a fool I am.*

She lay there until she realized how hungry she was. She'd noticed a chain restaurant close by and walked over. She ordered a salad and a glass of wine, then several more wines. Finished and a bit tipsy, she returned to her room and went to sleep for a restless, dreamless night.

Chapter 14

The night she returned home, her cell phone chirped. It was an unfamiliar area code, but she answered it anyway.

"Jennifer Morse?" a man's voice asked.

"Yes. Who's this?

"It's your uncle Mark … from Iowa."

"Mark? What … Why are you calling?"

"Well, after I was so abrupt with you, I got home and told my wife, Mary Ellen, about meeting you. I got a royal chewing out about being rude and awful and was told that I needed to get a hold of you and apologize. Then she asked if you were the author of *Mountains in the Dawn* which she apparently read along with your grandmother, and they both loved the book. I did some checking on the internet, and when I saw your picture on the website, I knew it was you. Then I was in worse trouble. Anyway, I tracked down your information and contacted your publisher, who I had to argue with for almost an hour before they'd give me any information. I did some lying about a death in the family, and then they hooked me up with some mean woman, Marty somebody, who finally agreed.

"So then your grandmother, Alice, finds out, and she got mad at me too since she loved your book and wanted to meet her famous author granddaughter. On the downside when Dad found out, he had a fit.

"So I want to apologize for my rudeness and for not inviting you to come to the house, at least to meet Mary Ellen and our two kids. There, I said it. Now, I want to invite you to come to see us anytime you want, and you'll be welcome. Mom says she'll keep Harley in line. Will you come back?"

In spite of his rudeness to her, she had to smile at how humble he was with his wife and mother and answered, "Thanks, Mark. I really appreciate your call. It means a lot to me. Maybe I'll get back that way, but not for a while. I was pretty hurt at your dismissing me like you did. I was wanting so badly to meet you all. I really do appreciate your call, and tell Mary Ellen and your mother I said, thank you. Give me your address, and I'll send them each an autographed copy of the book."

"I'm sorry I upset you. I was scared of Mom and Dad and their reaction. I was right about Dad but wrong about Mom. I know they'd love autographed copies. So you'll will come and visit us?"

"Yes. I'd like that."

"We'd like to have you."

"Maybe in the fall then. And I need your contact information and address."

He gave what she wanted, and they said their goodbyes and clicked off. She sat for a while digesting the conversation and smiled. It was too late to call her grandparents; it would be like four in the morning in Paris. She sent a text saying she needed to talk.

She lay awake a long time thinking of her current life. She still went running with Kelly, mainly Saturdays, since Kelly was now working more hours and wasn't available that much during the week. Helen and Will, while gracious, had their own life now. Her father, Julien, was busy with work and Cheryl. Seeing her family in Iowa was a bust. She kept trying to write some short stories, but kept getting bogged down. Nothing was working for her. Jenny felt alone and was falling into a funk.

The next morning her grandmother, Susan, called in response to Jenny's last night's text. Jenny told her of her Iowa trip, Mark's call, and how she was feeling about her life. Susan didn't respond to her Iowa story, but, as usual, urged her to come to Paris. They had an extra bedroom suite at their apartment and would very much like to have her visit. Jenny said she'd consider it but let it slide.

At her appointment with Joan the next Tuesday, Jenny expressed her feelings and frustrations with life. She'd so looked forward to being at home, but things weren't the same, and she didn't know what to do. Joan wasn't much help in getting her out of her mood.

Jenny was still seeing the naturopathic doctor and was getting healthier and had more energy, but she felt listless and didn't have much interest in anything. She wanted to do some teaching at Helen's yoga studio, but all the classes had teachers until September when one teacher was leaving. Plus, she had to admit, she missed Chris's companionship.

A week later, after she'd exiled Cat to Will and Helen's, and shared some jealous goodbyes, Jenny was waking up from a comfortable overnight flight in business class. She looked out her window as the plane descended into Charles de Gaulle airport.

Chapter 15

After customs she found her grandparents anxiously awaiting her.

"Oh, Jennifer, we're so happy you're here," Susan said as she gave her granddaughter a long welcome hug.

Dean gave her a bone-crushing embrace and asked, "Are you okay? Did you get some rest on the flight?"

"Actually, after we left Dallas at seven o'clock, I had my dinner, then took a sleeping pill, curled up, and fell asleep for the whole flight. What time is it here?"

Dean answered, "It's right at twelve thirty. Let's go to the apartment. There's so much we want to show you. You'll love it here."

They grabbed her bags, got a taxi, and headed into Paris to Dean and Susan's apartment on rue Danton on the Left Bank. Along with fielding all the questions, Jenny took in the sights of the City of Lights along the way.

"Wow, this is beautiful," Jenny said as, after a ride in a tiny elevator, they entered the large, airy, modern-furnished apartment on the top floor. She dropped the bag she was carrying and walked to the large French doors and looked over the rooftops and chimneys below her. The Eiffel Tower rose into the sky in the distance. "Oh my God, this is beautiful. I can't believe this. I wish I were an artist."

Dean smiled. "This is just the beginning of what lies in store for you. Please excuse me for a bit, I have some emails I need to send. The office in Denver seems to again need my advice. They still can't run the damn place without me." He went into the other room laughing wickedly to himself.

"But, Jennifer, you are an artist," Susan said. "You're a writer. There were so many great writers who lived here, as well as great artists. You have so much to explore. Have you been writing?"

"No. I've been too preoccupied with everything."

"I know. I'm so sorry about Chris … and your trip to Iowa … doesn't surprise me. We can talk about that later, but, are you doing okay?"

"Yeah, much better. Thanks for having me here. I know already that this is what I needed to do. It was my friend Amanda who urged me to come. You remember Amanda, from Sedona?"

"Oh yes. You told us once she was a healer?"

"Yeah, a spiritual healer as well as a dear friend. I'm so lucky to have you two, my father, and all my friends, all my friends who I've neglected for too long. Did you know Kelly has a baby almost eight months old, and I just first saw her two months ago? That's how my life's been."

"And how is your father, dear?" Susan asked with still a little venom that had not completely gone away after he'd taken Jenny and Michael to that commune. Maybe Jenny had forgiven him, but Susan was still having a hard time forgiving their only son.

"Daddy's doing great. He loves his new work and has a woman friend called Cheryl. She's really good for him. I like her. He's taking care of himself and is healthy. I see him at least once a week when I've been home, which hasn't been a whole lot the last few years."

"What are you going to do now?"

"I'm taking a break, a long break. My agent had a European book-signing trip all lined up, and I had her cancel it, and told her not to book me for anything for at least a year. I'm planning on starting another project. I have some ideas for a new book. Between you and Grandpa's trust fund and all the book royalties, I have more money than I know what to do with."

"Are you investing it?"

"Yeah, with Grandpa's urging, I now have a good broker that he recommended. He's a nice guy, and I guess he's helping. I wonder many times what I would ever have done without your support, like when you sent me money and I was able to escape that commune. The women I've been in group with are less fortunate. I can never thank you two enough for what you did for me."

"We were happy that we could do it for you. You know that."

"I do, but I still can't thank you enough."

Dean reappeared. "Jenny, Susan, how do you feel like going out for a little stroll around the neighborhood and then get some dinner?"

Susan frowned. "I don't know, Dean, she should rest."

"I'm fine, really. I had a good sleep on the flight, and it's like morning at home. I'll go to bed when we get home and get a good night's sleep. I want to experience Paris. I want to freshen up, and then, let's go."

They left the apartment and started walking down rue Danton toward the Seine. Jenny was entranced with the beautiful old architecture. She wanted to duck into every shop they walked by. It all looked like some magic fairy tale place. She noticed that all the French women were stylish and beautiful and the men slim and well dressed. Dean and Susan fit right in. Wearing her usual Durango outdoor mountain attire, she felt way out of place. She made a mental note to have Susan take her shopping tomorrow.

They continued on down rue Danton, and Jenny saw two fountains and a large stone edifice enshrining a huge winged man with a sword and an evil looking creature at his feet.

"What's that?"

"That is the Fountaine Saint-Michel," Susan replied. "There are fountains and statues all over this city. Paris has such a rich history."

People sat at outdoor cafés with drinks, reading or talking, and boats filled with tourists went down the Seine. As they walked across Pont Saint-Michel toward the Ile de la Cité, Jenny looked to her right and saw the great Notre Dame cathedral. "Oh, I want to go there and see that church. Can we go?"

"Yes, of course," Susan said. "But let's wait a few days. We'll have to go early to avoid long queues. There's a lot to see here, and you'll have to pace yourself."

Jenny fell in love with everything she saw, from the slow-moving river to the great cathedral and all in between. They crossed back across the river at rue de la Cité.

Dean said, "Let's take Jenny to Shakespeare and Company."

"I've heard about it or read about it," Jenny said. "It's a famous bookstore, like from the 1920s when Hemingway and all those writers were here."

Dean nodded. "It's not the original but was reestablished by George Whitman in 1951 as the 'Le Mistral' and renamed in 1964 as 'Shakespeare and Company.' It's still run by Whitman's daughter, Sylvia. I love going there myself to browse the books."

Jenny's eyes lit up with excitement. "Oh, let's go."

They walked across the busy street along the Seine, turned left onto rue de la Bûcherie, and there it was. Jenny stood and looked at the store, and a lump formed in her throat, thinking of the history of that name, and all the famous writers that had graced this establishment.

"You two go ahead," Susan said. "I'm going into the coffee shop to get a drink. Watch your time as we need to get dinner and get Jenny back for her rest."

"I'm fine, Grandma. Don't worry."

"Jennifer, you need your rest, you can come back another day. It will still be here," Susan said like a doting mother.

"Okay, I'll keep it quick."

Jenny and Dean walked inside, and Jenny fell in love. She quickly tried to take in every nook and cranny, which were all filled with books of every genre she could imagine. No pop culture books here, but serious literature. After about thirty minutes, she found Dean and led him out the door.

"I'll be back soon," she announced to the woman at the cash register by the door.

They found Susan and headed back to Brasserie La Fontaine Saint-Michel and got a table outside where they could enjoy the late afternoon and do some people watching.

They returned to the apartment by 7:00 and then chatted for a little while. Jenny began to yawn, so excused herself to get ready for bed. She took a sleeping pill and crawled in, suddenly exhausted. She dreamed she was in a magic land, and she met a shepherd who guided her to an overlook where she could see out to forever.

Jenny awoke early. Dean and Susan were still sleeping, so she dressed, left them a note, and quietly left. Down on the street, she headed in the direction of Saint-Michel as they did yesterday. At the intersection of rue Suger, she came across a little bistro called Brasserie Le Saint André, where the smell of rich coffee assailed her nostrils. A waitress, a woman about Jenny's age, when she realized Jenny didn't speak French, spoke in perfect English—with a nice French accent—telling Jenny she could sit anywhere. Jenny chose a small table outside, and the waitress brought her a menu with French on one side and the English version on the other side.

"I will be back shortly." The French lilt to her English entranced Jenny.

Jenny sat watching the people go by, probably on their way to work. Some stopped in and got a coffee. Some customers stood at the bar drinking their coffees and espressos, reading a newspaper or talking with someone next to them. Others sat at outdoor tables reading newspapers or books.

The waitress returned, bringing Jenny's coffee, and it tasted as rich and robust with flavor as it smelled. Breakfast arrived and it was delicious. She'd never had such an omelet, light and full of taste. The croissant was light, buttery, and flakey, the butter creamy rich. She savored her food and made a mental note to have breakfast here every morning.

The waitress came back as Jenny was finishing. "Was everything all right?"

"Yes. It was totally wonderful. Thank you."

"May I sit for a moment?"

"Sure," Jenny answered.

"Thank you. I wish to practice my English, if you do not mind."

"Of course not. I'll be happy to talk with you."

"What is your name," she asked.

"Jennifer, but most people call me Jenny."

"I shall call you Jennifer. My name is Camille."

"Hi, Camille. I'm happy to meet you."

Camille asked Jenny why she was in Paris, and Jenny told her about being with her grandparents and that they were staying in an apartment on rue Danton.

"How long will you stay in Paris?"

Jenny considered this. "I really don't know. My grandparents are here through August. I may stay a week or maybe until they leave."

"Are you a student?"

Jenny laughed. "Oh no. I graduated from college about seven years ago. I'm a writer and looking for inspiration, I guess. I just needed to get away for a while."

"A writer. Have your written anything I might know?"

"I had a novel published around three years ago, *Sunrise in the Mountains*. I don't know for sure, but I think Shakespeare and Company might have a copy."

"I would love to read it. Will you sign it for me?"

"Of course, I'll be happy to. So are you a native Parisian?"

"Ah, no. I am from a small village in the Bordeaux region where we make wine. I work here for my uncle while I am a student."

"Where do you go to school?"

"The Sorbonne. I am studying international relations. But I must return to work so my uncle won't be angry with me. Will I see you again?"

"If you're here in the mornings. I'll be back. This was the

best breakfast I ever remember having."

"*Merci*. I will tell my uncle. I will see you tomorrow then."

"Hope so."

Jenny paid her bill and left, planning on another great breakfast tomorrow.

She got back to the apartment and asked Susan if they could go shopping for some more suitable clothes. The two women left and Susan took Jenny to several small shops where she outfitted herself in more suitable clothing for a woman in Paris. However, Jenny found it difficult to give up her comfortable Colorado outdoor chic and preferred it to her new clothing, which she wore infrequently, not caring about or paying any attention to some of the looks she received from both the native men … and women.

All Jenny wanted to do was go back and spend time at Shakespeare and Company. However, her grandparents wanted to show her the city. They went out early the first few mornings to get ahead of the long queues, once to Notre Dame, another to the Eiffel Tower, and another to the Louvre.

The medieval structure of Notre Dame, its history, and its grandeur entranced her. However, still not feeling in great shape, she declined climbing all the steps to the bell tower.

They had tickets to go to the top level of the Eiffel Tower. Jenny, even though she was accustomed to high mountain elevations, felt a bit queasy from the height. That was soon overcome by the views of the city some 1,083 feet below. They descended to the second level and opted for a croissant and coffee at the restaurant there. Jenny knew she might never again have coffee so rich tasting, and the croissant was beyond wonderful.

Late morning on the fifth day after she arrived, Dean came out of his office beaming and announced, "I managed to get the tickets and a place for us to stay. It was pricey, but it'll be worth it."

Susan asked, "Have you even asked Jenny if she's interested?"

Jenny asked, "Interested in what?"

"Oh, Dean has made arrangements for us to go to Monte Carlo for a Formula 1 auto race the last weekend in May."

Dean grinned. "I should've asked, but I wanted you to go with us and, well, I could get three tickets together, so I did. It'll be a great weekend whether you go to the race or not, Jenny. There'll be quite a few things to do other than the race, and Monte Carlo is a beautiful city to explore."

"Sounds interesting. I'd love to go. Will we drive?"

"No, we'll fly. It'll be faster and much easier in the long run."

"I have no idea what Formula 1 racing is, but I'm excited to go in any case. Thanks, Grandfather."

"Please, you need to start calling me Dean. Okay?"

"Okay … Dean."

"And I'm Susan. By now I think we can drop the grandfather/grandmother formality."

Jenny smiled. "All right then, Dean and Susan. But it seems weird."

They all laughed, and Dean said, "I have another email to reply to, but we should go for lunch at the Musée d'Orsay this afternoon."

After a week, Dean slowed down his tour-guide needs. Jenny had discovered the Luxembourg Gardens and found a running path around the perimeter. Her mornings were now spent going for a run, which included a lot of walking, then breakfast at her favorite bistro.

One morning after she had breakfast and showered, she walked over to Shakespeare and Company which was just opening for the day. She entered and took her time exploring all the various genres of fiction, poetry, and memoirs. She was elated to see several copies of her book in the fiction section. She purchased three obscure titles that looked interesting, and then, excited with her new books, she went back to her bistro, ordered a coffee, and read for most of the afternoon.

She also took to exploring some of the narrow little cobblestone streets in the area, looking into shops, enjoying the aromas of coffee coming from bistros, the fresh baked goods at she walked by the boulangeries, and the sweet smells from the patisseries. She wondered how the French always looked so healthy and trim when there were so many food offerings like these available everywhere you looked.

Between the now-occasional sightseeing with her grandparents, Jenny settled into reading, journaling, and drinking coffee at her favorite bistro. She and Camille became friends, sharing stories of their lives over coffee in the mornings before Camille had classes. She met Camille's uncle, Lucien, a nice man who enjoyed having her there. She liked the quiet and being in the city, while still having the time to reflect and create possible ideas for a new book.

Chapter 16

Jenny, Susan, and Dean disembarked at the Nice Cote d'Azur International Airport late Wednesday afternoon, after the short hop from Paris. The airport, located in Nice, France, was just seventeen and one-third miles from the center of Monte Carlo. They got their rental car and headed to the Port Palace Hôtel where they would stay for the next five nights.

Dean was excited as a little boy at Christmas waiting to open his presents. All he could talk about was the race and how his favorite Ferrari Factory team would do. He kept going on about how he hoped the bells in the home of Ferrari in Maranello, Italy would be ringing on Sunday, apparently a tradition when Ferrari won a grand prix race.

In her luxurious room overlooking the marina, Jenny freshened up and prepared to go for dinner, dressing in her new milk-blue dress that complemented her blonde coloring and gray eyes. She wore sensible flat sandals and carried a small purse. While being dressed more stylishly than she ever had before felt strange, it also felt like she was a grownup woman. But she really disliked carrying a purse. She went to the lobby to meet her grandparents and noticed several men giving her the once over which made her uncomfortable. She didn't like attracting attention to herself like that. But truth was, she knew she looked beautiful.

Dean had called for reservations at a restaurant on the waterfront about a fifteen-minute walk from their hotel. They arrived early and were invited to sit in the lounge. After having cocktails, they were seated in the dining room, and Dean ordered a bottle of the more modestly priced Veuve Clicquot Yellow Label champagne on recommendation from the sommelier. After they drank a toast, their waiter, a stoic young man, introducing himself as Marcel, handed out menus, and asked in broken English if there were questions. Dean asked what he would recommend, to which the waiter hesitantly responded that his favorite was the lamb chops, but the seafood was some of the best.

When Marcel returned, Dean ordered crab, Susan went for cod, and Jenny, for the lamb chops. After they made their orders, they enjoyed the view from the veranda of the Mediterranean and all the small and large yachts. The sommelier came by, and they each ordered a glass of wine to complement their food orders. Their well-presented food and wine arrived soon after. The smells were enticing, but the flavors were something to be savored.

"I could live in France forever just for the delicious food and wines," Jenny said.

Dean replied, "Amen to that."

Dinner finished, they adjourned to the lounge for an after-dinner digestif. Dean ordered Absinthe and Susan and Jenny both a Pastis. They were seated at a small table in the crowded space filled with mostly French and English-speaking people and a smattering of German. Dean and Susan finished and were ready to head back to the hotel, but Jenny, feeling heady in the cosmopolitan scene, wanted to enjoy the night a little longer and decided to stay for a while. They bid good night and left her on her own.

Now on her second Pastis, she noticed all the other tables and seats were occupied, and she began to feel uncomfortable sitting by herself with two empty seats.

A man wearing jeans, a casual jacket, sunglasses, and a New York Yankees baseball cap came up to her. "*Excusez-moi, mademoiselle, puis-je m'asseoir avec vous?*"

She shot him a not-too-friendly glance, trying to remember the few French phrases she knew from her guide book, and slowly with bad accent she replied, "*Je ne parle pas français, parlez-vous anglais?*"

He nodded and asked, "Are you English?"

"No, American." She looked at him. He was a nice-looking man, dark hair, a dark two-day growth on his face, and a bright smile, and, as she would later find out when he removed his sunglasses, intriguing dark eyes that swallowed her in.

"Please do not think me forward, but may I sit here with you? I would like to buy you another glass of what you are drinking?"

"Thank you, but no. I have had more than enough. I need to get back to my room and need a taxi, if you'll excuse me."

"Oh, please don't leave. Please stay for a little time. I would enjoy talking to you so I may speak English. Please, no problem. I am not wanting to, what you say, pick you up. I just want to talk for a while. Would that be okay, no?"

Jenny thought for a moment and said, "Yes."

"You are enjoying Monaco?"

"We just got to the hotel today, so I haven't had time to really see the city."

"You pick a busy weekend. You know Formula 1 racing?"

"Ah, no, but my grandfather does and insisted we come with him to this. I have no idea about racing?"

"Ah, yes, very fast cars on a very demanding track."

"So where's the track? My grandfather said it's in town … on streets?"

"Yes, it is on the city streets. Very famous race. It has been here since 1950. Very challenging. Very important race to win."

"On the streets? Really?"

"Oh yes. It goes right by here, but tomorrow, this will all be blocked off for the practicing. You want to come?"

"My grandfather has tickets, so I guess I'll be there, but my grandmother and I really want to go to the beach."

"Ah, but yes, you should come. See the race and the cars."

"I know nothing of this car racing, and I'm really not that interested. And who are you?"

"I am sorry, my name is Jean Luc, but please, call me Jean."

"So … you're French?"

"Yes. What is your name?"

"It's Jennifer, but everyone calls me Jenny, Jenny Morse."

"Ah, Jennifer, beautiful name. I shall always call you only Jennifer, never Jenny."

This guy was doing more than a great job of charming Jenny off her feet. "So what do you do, Jennifer Morse?"

"I'm a writer."

"Ah, a writer. What do you write?"

"Fiction."

"Fiction? What have you written? Anything I might know?"

"My first book was *Sunrise in the Mountains*. Probably something you haven't read."

"No. I have little time for reading. You must meet my father who teaches French literature at the Sorbonne. He will love to talk to you."

"Meet your father? God, my book is far from 'literature.' I don't want to be embarrassed. And I have no idea who you are, and I'm not meeting your father. I have to go."

"No, no. Please for a while. Please stay. You are a beautiful woman, and I am wanting to know you."

That just made Jenny more uncomfortable. "No. I need to leave."

"I am sorry if I offended you. We shall not talk of that anymore. Please tell me, where do you live in America? I have been to your Texas some times, and it is so big."

She paused for a moment, then decided she might indulge him a bit longer. "I live in Durango, Colorado. Not too far from Texas I guess. What were you in Texas for?"

"I work for a car manufacturer and go there for business."

"And what do you do for this car manufacturer?"

"Oh, I guess I am like a representative to make people like our cars."

"Is this some car I would know?"

"You know Ferrari?"

"Not really, but my grandfather says they race here, and he's all excited and wants the bells to ring in Maranello."

Jean Luc laughed. "So do I. You will come then? I will have a car pick you up maybe for qualifying on Saturday. Practice is very important for the drivers, but maybe not for the observers. So maybe Saturday? Where do you stay?"

"I'm at the Port Palace Hôtel, but, no, Jean Luc, or Jean, I don't think so. We have tickets. You might be, I don't know what. I don't know you at all."

"Jennifer, I would never do anything bad for you. I honor you and your beautiful nature. Truly, you must trust me. My family has a suite rented for the race. You and your grandparents will be honored guests. They must come also. You must come. I will have a car pick you up at 10:00 Saturday, and you can watch qualifying. Then Sunday for the race. Okay?"

She was hesitant, but he did invite her family as well as her, so she threw her caution away. "Okay, Jean, I'll see what my grandparents think."

"No problem, you come if you want. If not, my driver will leave, and I will be heartbroken."

She blushed from the comment and from all she'd drunk. She knew she needed to get back and to bed. "I need to get a cab. I really have to go back to the hotel now. Please excuse me."

"Please allow me to drive you home. I also must go. I must rest as I have to work tomorrow."

"Do you work at the race?"

"Yes, I do. My car is close. I shall drive you to your hotel. Cabs are scarce, and it is not safe for a beautiful woman to be on the streets by herself. Please. I promise, how do you say, 'no funny business.'"

Jenny smiled inwardly at his sincerity and with her guard down from the alcohol and his charm, said reluctantly, "Okay. I'll take a ride then."

They got up and left the bar, and Jenny couldn't help but notice his slim-waisted, broad-shouldered body and felt a twinge in her belly. Jean gave the valet his ticket, and a few minutes later she heard the growl of a car, and a small, low red car appeared. The valet got out of it with a big grin on his face. "*Belle voiture.*"

"*Merci*," Jean replied. He walked around and opened the passenger door, looked at Jenny and said, "Ready, *ma cherie?*"

Jenny had limited French, but she did know what *ma cherie* meant, and she was happy no one could see her blush. She hesitated. He seemed nice, but who knew? His family might be gangsters or something, though he had said his father was a professor at the Sorbonne. Despite her reservations, she got into the rumbling Ferrari.

Jean got in the driver's side and said, "Buckle in your seat belt, *s'il vous plait.*" Jenny did so, and he left the restaurant quickly, maneuvering the car expertly through the Monte Carlo traffic. "Jennifer, shall we take a quick ride, and I will show you some of the city?"

Maybe it was the alcohol, but she was actually enjoying riding with this confident man who she'd just met. "Okay, but not too far. Okay?"

"No. We shall not go far. I have to get rest as I have work tomorrow. Let's go." He dropped the car into a lower gear and accelerated with such force as to pin Jenny back against her seat. They flew down the coast, Jean Luc in complete control with effortless driving at speeds Jenny didn't want to know about. Though initially frightened at the speed, she soon relaxed and felt a huge rush of adrenaline as the excitement of this ride along this narrow highway with sharp curves filled her with a feeling of daring. It reminded her of the excitement she'd felt back in the San Juan Mountains at 12,000 feet when she'd looked out over the vast expanse of seemingly endless mountains. As Jean Luc skillfully shifted through the seemingly endless gears the screaming Ferrari held in its gearbox, she felt a freedom she hadn't felt in a long time.

Suddenly they were back in the city in front of her hotel.

She tingled with excitement, feeling both relief and sadness that this adventure was over, somehow, too soon, way too soon. She wanted more.

"So I will have a car here to pick you and your grandparents up at 10:00 Saturday morning? You will come?"

"I will have to talk with my grandparents. Maybe."

"Jennifer Morse, I hope I will see you again. I will not be there to greet you Saturday, but my family will and will treat you graciously. Please come."

"We'll see. Thank you, Jean Luc … Jean. Maybe we'll meet again?"

"Of yes, we shall definitely meet again. Good night *ma cherie*."

She got out, went into the hotel and to Dean and Susans' room and knocked. Dean answered and she told them of her night and relayed Jean Luc's invitation. Dean looked questioningly at her, and she could see his brain working.

"Would his name happen to be Jean Luc Bonnet?"

She frowned in thought. "I don't know. He never mentioned his last name. He told me he worked for Ferrari, maybe like in public relations or sales. He took me for a ride in his Ferrari, and we went along the coast at speeds I don't even want to think about, and it was really fun."

Dean stared at her in awe. "It has to have been him."

Jenny laughed out loud. "Dean. I have no idea. Who is Jean Luc Bonnet? I just met this guy, and all I know is that he wants us to come to his family's suite that apparently overlooks the track on Saturday for some qualifying thing. I forgot to ask him what that was. He's sending a car. That's it. 10:00 Saturday if you want to. I'd personally rather go to the beach, but if you wan—"

"Bonnet races one of the Ferrari cars. He's one of the top

drivers on the F1 circuit. I can't believe you met him. Susan, what do you think?"

"It would probably be better than sitting on bleachers somewhere. Let's go. It might be nice to meet some people.

Let's get some rest."

Chapter 17

Dean went to watch the practice sessions for the next two days while Jenny and Susan went to the beach or went shopping. Susan found a few things she liked. Jenny saw a few items, but everything was too expensive in the upscale shops they visited.

Jenny met Dean and Susan for breakfast at 8:30 on Saturday morning. After eating, they got themselves ready to meet the car—a stretch limo—which arrived promptly at 10:00. The driver opened the door, and they climbed in and sank into the plush white leather seats.

With heavily accented English, the driver said, "There is Champagne for you. Please, you may help yourselves. Please enjoy the ride."

Dean, looking a little stunned, poured each of them a flute and sat back, obviously enjoying this.

"*Merci, monsieur. Merci,*" Jenny said.

There was no reply, and the chauffeur drove slowly and gently through the city. Jenny felt quite special in the plush interior with champagne in hand. "So what is qualifying?" she asked Dean. "I don't understand."

"Each driver tries for the fastest lap that he can do, and the cars are ranked in order of fastest to the slowest. The fastest lap earns pole position or the front of the pack, so to speak. It's almost as exciting as the race itself."

Jenny grunted her acknowledgment as she sipped her champagne.

They slowed and pulled up into a narrow alley. "We arrive." The chauffeur got out and opened the door for them, then led them toward a back door and then into a foyer leading to a grand staircase. "You may choose to walk up the stairs or take the lift."

"We'll walk up, *merci*," Dean said.

"Certainly." The driver led the way up and to a large door which he opened for them. "I shall take you back to your hotel when you are ready. Tell Monsieur or Madam Bonnet and they shall contact me."

They walked into a beautiful modern apartment, no French provincial furniture or gilded framed paintings. The high ceilings were painted a soft blue; the walls were off-white. Modern paintings, from Dada through modern abstract, graced the walls. It was all stunningly beautiful.

A distinguished-looking man and a beautiful woman approached them. They were dressed elegantly, she with a blue sheer dress that she wore with style. He had on light-gray slacks, an open-collared white shirt and a cashmere navy blue coat. His dark hair was graying at the temples, and he looked like an older Jean Luc. Her hair was loose, golden and reached her shoulders. Their smiles lit up the room.

"Welcome, you must be Jennifer," the man said. "And these are your grandparents. We are so delighted you came."

He did the *faire la bise*, or cheek kissing to both women. "I wish to present my wife, Madame Danielle, and I am Robert."

Danielle exchanged cheek *la bises* as well.

Jenny greeted them with, "*Bonjour, madam* and *monsieur*. I am honored to meet you and be your guest. Yes, I am Jennifer, and these are my grandparents, Dean and Susan Morse."

"Ah, welcome. Come, come, partake of the festivities." They led them to another room with a bar and a huge table loaded with cheeses, cold meats, baguettes, croissants, and fruit, along with some things Jenny didn't recognize.

Jenny looked around at the other guests, all talking and drinking champagne and wine. She felt out of place and embarrassed, underdressed in her usual Colorado chic. She'd thought she was going to a car race, not an elegant party. However, Dean and Susan seemed to fit in seamlessly as always.

"Please go and help yourself," Danielle said. "Everyone here is very friendly and nice. Please excuse us. There are other guests arriving."

Dean got two flutes of champagne, gave one to Susan and then they went off to mingle.

I wish I had their social grace, Jenny thought.

A younger woman approached, and she saw a strong resemblance to Danielle. "Hi. Let's go over there where it's quieter," the woman said. "I am Lisette, Jean's younger sister."

"*Bonjour*, I'm Jenny. I am happy to meet you."

"Please, just use your regular English. I need the practice. I'm going to America to study this September."

"Where are you going?"

"Columbia. I want to study literature. I guess I take after my father."

"Jean Luc told me your father teaches at the Sorbonne?"

"Yes. But I don't want a French education. I want to be

away from Paris."

"Most people I know would love to come to Paris."

"Yes, but it has been my home for seventeen years, and I would like to experience somewhere different. Tell me about yourself."

"I'm a writer and live in Colorado."

"A writer? You write books? Or something else?"

"I have written one book." She told Lisette about it.

Lisette's eyes lit up with enthusiasm. "I want to read it. Is it on Amazon?"

Jenny smiled. "Yes, in both digital and print. But it's also at Shakespeare and Company."

"I will get a copy when I return to Paris then."

Jenny glanced at the other guests, then confessed, "Lisette, I feel really out of place here. I am underdressed and don't do very well at parties. Thanks for talking with me, but I don't want to keep you from the other guests."

"There are no other guests I wish to talk to. You look fine and are the only one close to my age, except for the two girls over there." She pointed to two stylishly dressed, beautiful young women. "But they are models and are stuck up. All they talk about is themselves and how wonderful they are. They're shallow and have no interest in talking to me. Come and I'll make you as beautiful as they are."

Taken aback, Jenny responded, "No, I can't bother you. I'm all right."

"No. I insist. You will hurt my feelings."

Lisette took Jenny's hand and spirited her away into her bedroom. "Come over here and sit down." She sat Jenny in front of the dressing table and proceeded to do something with her hair. Then she added some light makeup. "Now, look how beautiful you are." She stepped aside so Jenny could see in the mirror.

Jenny looked and was amazed at the magic Lisette had done. *French women must have been born with "how to look beautiful" programmed into their genes.*

Jenny and Lisette re-entered the gathering, just as a screaming whine came through the open French doors that led onto a balcony. Lisette grabbed two glasses of champagne, handed one to Jenny, grabbed her hand and said, "Come, they have started," as she led her to the balcony.

Jenny looked down. The street had been barricaded off, and a funny looking car went screaming by at an unbelievable speed for the narrow city street.

Lisette handed her earplugs. "Here, put these in your ears or the noise will make you deaf."

Jenny set her glass down and did as instructed. Just then a red car came screaming by.

"There he goes," Lisette said. "Look at him so fast. He will win today."

"Do you know that driver?"

"Yes. He is my brother, Jean Luc. He talked to you last night he said."

"He never told me his last name. So he's Jean Luc Bonnet. Oh my God, he never said. He drives one of those? Dean was right. It is him."

"Oh yes. And he drives very well. He is tied for championship points. He drives for Ferrari. You know Ferrari?"

"I'm evidently learning. He gave me a ride in one last night. I didn't know about him actually racing."

"Oh yes. Ferrari has raced cars since from the first races ever. The first race was in 1929. Ferrari is very famous, and Jean drives for them. He is very famous."

"I had no idea. He didn't say anything about driving, just

that he had to work today."

"He is shy about his success. He does not want people to like him just because of fame."

"I can understand ... and appreciate that."

"Oh, watch now, Jennifer. We can see his time and standings on the display over there." She pointed to a vertical display with names and times, but all the names were only the first three letters.

Jenny saw BON in fifth after a RIC, a VET, a VES, and a HAM. "But he's only in fifth. He's losing."

"No, no, this is the first elimination round of three and is fifteen minutes. There is time. As long as he's not eliminated, the last round is the one for pole. Do not worry."

Cars went screaming by at speeds Jenny could not believe. Then she saw him again, a red blur. She looked at the display and saw his name jump to the top. Then the first round was over and all became quiet. The bottom five wouldn't make it to the second round.

"Let's get some food, Jennifer." Lisette led her to the array of delicious-looking food. Jenny took a plate and selected some meats, cheeses and fruit along with two pieces of baguette. As she was leaving the table, the two "models" approached her, literally looking down their noses at her.

"So who are you?" the taller one asked. Her face hardly moved when she talked, like it might break if there were too much effort. She had thick lips, heavy lidded eyes, precisely cut hair, and dressed stylishly as if going to a New Year's Eve party. Her thick accent sounded Eastern European.

Jenny, already prepped by Lisette, looked her in the eyes and asked, "Who wants to know?"

"Listen, American bitch, stay away from Jean Luc. He is our friend. You stay away."

Jenny, remembering being bullied as a child, stared at the woman for a long pause, latent hostility rising from times past. "Fuck off, you skinny ass bitch," she retorted. "You don't fucking order me around. I'll do as I well damn please, and you two can go straight to hell." She gave them a fierce condescending look and waited for a reply, which did not come. The woman's mouth worked but no words formed. Jenny stared her directly in the eyes for another moment.

The other woman found her tongue, however. "Do not mess with us, American bitch, or you'll be sorry."

Jenny stared back at her. "Fuck you." She threw her glass of champagne into the woman's face. "Don't ever fuck with me." She gave her one last look of contempt, turned on her heel, and holding her head high, walked away from the two wide-eyed women. She sucked in some quick deep breaths but smiled inwardly. Several wide-eyed onlookers stood aside to let her through.

Lisette came up to her. "What did you say to them? They are still standing there looking at you with open mouths."

Jenny told her about the exchange, and Lisette laughed. "You threw champagne in her face? Good for you. They are hangers on hoping to snag Jean Luc and his money. He pays them no attention, but they keep showing up somehow. The one you talked to is Russian, and the other is from Bulgaria. Both are gold diggers. I do not understand why they even bother."

The second round began, and Jenny and Lisette put in their earplugs and went to the balcony to watch. She noticed Dean and Robert at the other end of the balcony engrossed in talking and watching the cars. At the end of this session, Jenny saw BON in fourth place and HAM at the top.

"He's not doing good, is he?" she said to Lisette.

"Do not worry, Jennifer. The next session is the important one. You will see."

The final session began with three cars blasting by. Then came the Ferrari piloted by Jean Luc, and it seemed to Jenny that he was twice as fast as the last time she saw him go by. She realized her heart was racing, and she had become completely engrossed in this racing business. She let out a whoop and raised her fist. "Kick their ass, Jean Luc."

Lisette laughed. "You are excited, Jennifer?"

"Yes. I want him to win."

She caught sight of the leaderboard just as Jean Luc's name popped up to first, and she heard a gasp from Dean and Robert all the way from where they were standing. Then they both cheered. Time was running out, and when it did, Jean Luc had just set a new track record and had won pole position, the ideal place to win this race since overtaking was so difficult on this circuit. Jenny saw red smoke floating in the air from somewhere where Ferrari fans were apparently located. The excitement ran through the suite, and champaign flutes were raised in triumph. Then the party began in earnest.

Sometime later, Robert approached Jenny who was talking with Lisette and said that she and her grandparents were invited to join them tomorrow in the pits for the race.

"What does it mean to be in the 'pits?'" Jenny asked.

Lisette replied, "We get to be down where the race really is, where everything happens. We will be up close, in a space right above the Ferrari pit area. I have been there many times, but it is always exciting and much fun. We get to see the pit stops, and we have big TVs everywhere."

Robert said, "The car will pick you up in the morning. There will be food and refreshments. Please come. I enjoy your grandparents very much."

"Have you asked them?"

"Oh yes. They are most delighted to join us but are concerned about whether you wish to see this race."

"Of course I'll come. I'm sure they're excited, especially Grandpa."

"Ah, yes. He was overjoyed at such an opportunity to participate in seeing this race. He is a true fan of Ferrari and my son. Thank you so much. I know Jean Luc will be most happy you will come tomorrow."

With that, Robert did a slight bow, turned and left.

Lisette smiled. "You are coming. I am so happy. I already like you like a big sister."

"Thank you, Lisette. That is very kind of you to say. But after this race I probably won't see you again."

"I think Jean Luc might disagree. He is very interested in you."

"What? We spent like little over an hour together. He's not interested in me."

"Oh, but he is. He told me he met the most fabulous woman. He said, 'She is so beautiful. She did not know who I am. I want to see her again after the race. But, now I must concentrate on what I am doing this weekend and I must not think of her. I will see her after the race.' That's what he told me."

"What?" Jenny asked incredulously. "I think I need to go and maybe just forget tomorrow. One thing I don't need is some lovestruck guy thinking I'm someone he wants. Been there. Done that. Don't need it. Sorry, but no thanks, Lisette. It's been fun, but goodbye." She turned to walk away.

"Jennifer, please do not go. I want you to come tomorrow. He likes you. Please do not be offended and please come tomorrow. If for nothing else, please come for me?"

Jenny stood there with her back turned to Lisette, hearing her words that were more pleading than anything else; her heart warmed. She felt something she remembered feeling many, many years ago for her brother when she was a little girl. She turned and said, "Okay, Lisette, I'll come tomorrow … for you. See you tomorrow. Thanks." Then she left.

Their car was waiting. Jenny got in, and Dean was animatedly talking of the qualifying and the race tomorrow. Susan pretended to listen intently, and Jenny had a flute of champagne.

Chapter 18

A great roar came from below as twenty-two cars started around the track in single file, revving engines and driving erratically to warm the tires to race temperature. The sound quieted for a minute or so until they all returned and lined up precisely on their grid spots, engines revving. Five red lights over the track ahead of the drivers lit up one by one. Once all were lit, they all went out, and the roar and scream of engines was so loud, Jenny felt the noise in her bones as if she might explode. The cars screamed as they frantically tried to gain position before entering into the first corner. It looked like they all might end in a pile up, but they all somehow made it through the corner without a mishap. Jenny realized her heart was beating as fast as it would if she'd just run a mile.

Lisette reached over and took Jenny's hand. "Exciting, isn't it?"

Since Jenny wore large ear-protection earmuffs, all she could do was read her lips and smile back. Yes, it was exciting to be so close to the action and activity in the pits. She'd been introduced to several people and recognized some from the party yesterday, but to her relief, the two models were missing.

Jenny looked at the leaderboard and saw BON at the top. Lisette had explained that overtaking, or passing, was very difficult on this narrow twisting circuit. Choices of tires, tire wear, and pit stops were the ultimate strategy. However, there was always the chance of an accident, a safety car, or mechanical failure that entered into the equation.

She watched for the first ten or so laps, and Jean Luc was well ahead of his nearest competition. She and Lisette went to have some food and a flute of champagne and remove their ear muffs for a few minutes. They watched the race on one of the flatscreens. Jenny enjoyed seeing coverage of more of the track than only the straight part of the circuit in front of their pit local. As she watched she saw more of the intricacies of driving a circuit like this and appreciated the skill and focus required to drive one of these machines.

A few more laps and cars began to pit for the one required tire change. Each car had to use at least two of the three available tire compounds: soft, which had the best cornering grip and was the fastest; a medium compound, or a hard compound. The soft compound, while fastest, also wore the quickest, and the hard compound, being the slowest, had the most longevity. Each team had its own tire strategy. Most of the cars started on the softer compound. Jenny couldn't see the other pit stops from her vantage point, but the Ferrari pit crew became active as Jen Luc was set to come in for new tires. Four of the crew carried out a tire and positioned themselves along with two other crew members where each wheel of the car would stop. One of the three had what looked like a power drill. Then Jean Luc came flying in to an abrupt stop, wheels positioned exactly; two other pit crew members shoved jacks under the front and rear of the car, raising it. Zing, zing, zing, zing; four tires were off; four new ones on; the jacks lowered and cleared, all happening in a blur of seconds, then Jean Luc was gone, now down to sixth place. Jenny couldn't believe the precision of the ballet that just took place.

After a number of laps, Jean Luc had regained the lead after the cars ahead of him also had to pit. The race wore on until one of the younger drivers lost it on a corner and went into a guard wall. She saw yellow flags and lights everywhere. The safety car was deployed, meaning the race had slowed, and all positions were to be held, but it meant the cars could close up gaps and all big leads were now diminished. After several laps of the cars parading past behind the safety car, the disabled car was removed, and the race resumed again. Two cars, both worthy competitors, were now on Jean Luc's tail giving renewed competition to the race. Jean Luc would have none of it and easily pulled away.

Seventy-eight laps and the checkered flag fell giving Jean Luc a solid win, his nearest competitor being a little less than a minute behind. The cars did their cool down victory lap and pulled into the paddock directly across from where Jenny stood. Lisette grabbed Jenny's hand and said, "Come on. Let's get over there."

They raced to the awards podium some fifteen feet above the track, followed by a throng of people wearing Ferrari red doing the same. But they had the advantage of being closer and got a position at the fence around the paddock as Jean Luc crawled out of his now-quiet, once-raging beast of a car. He stood on top of his car and held both hands high in the air in triumph, which was greeted by a roar from the crowd. Then he jumped down and ran to the Ferrari pit crew exchanging hugs of joy. He spied Lisette and Jenny, came over and embraced his sister, then Jenny. Even though he smelled of adrenaline and sweat, Jenny was thrilled at the embrace.

He then went and congratulated the second and third place drivers, and they disappeared into the building. Not long after, the three drivers appeared one by one on the awards platform to a cheering crowd as their names were announced. Each then had a short interview with a recently retired driver who everyone also cheered for. After the interviews, trophies were given out by the prince, the princess, and the mayor of Monte Carlo. Then the French national anthem played followed by the Italian national anthem, which all the Italians sang along to. Magnums of champagne were raised, the "Prelude to Carmen" started over the loudspeakers, and the drivers drank and sprayed each other as well as the onlookers below with the bubbly liquid. Then it was over.

"Okay," Lisette said, "let's go back to the suite where we were yesterday for the party." She grabbed Jenny's hand and led her away. Jenny had no idea where her grandparents were, but trusted that they would be at the party as well.

Back at the suite, champagne flowed and spirits were high. About an hour later, the door opened, and Jean Luc entered to cheers and congratulatory embraces from his parents and handshakes, back pats, more hugs from other guests. Jenny remained in the background with Lisette. He soon spied them and walked over. Lisette gave her brother a warm hug and kisses on both cheeks, then he moved toward Jenny, took both her hands and looked into her eyes, "I am so happy you came here today. I raced for you, Jennifer, and you brought me much luck." He gave her cheek kisses and then an embrace which took her breath away with its gentle warmth. "Did you like seeing the race?"

"Yes I did, thanks to Lisette and your family. It was so nice of you to invite my grandparents and me. Thank you."

"I apologize for not telling you who I was that night. But the paparazzi are everywhere, and I want my privacy. I was taking risk as it was by being there. But I get restless before a race and like to get out by myself to forget, if only for an hour. And by lucky chance, I meet you. Please, have some champagne and food. I need to mingle with the crowd for a while. Please don't leave until we can talk. Promise?"

Jenny blushed at his attention but wasn't sure she wanted to stay and talk.

Lisette said, "Let's go and enjoy the celebration."

Jenny spied Dean and Susan occupied by Robert and Danielle. She began to feel anxious whether from the race, the party, the champagne, or the whole day itself. She needed to leave. After making the excuse to Lisette of going to the restroom, she left quietly, got herself to an open street and found a cab. Once back at the hotel, she texted Susan to say where she was. She took a hot shower, ordered a croissant sandwich and tea from room service and curled up to write in her journal.

Her grandparents came back in the early evening. "Why did you sneak out like you did?" Susan asked. "Jean Luc, Lisette, Danielle and Robert all wondered where you went without saying goodbye or anything. I made up the excuse that you were feeling nauseous. They were disappointed, if maybe not offended."

"I'm sorry, Grandma, but I was about to have a panic attack. The whole day was too much. Then Jean Luc; I'm not sure what he wants, but whatever it is, I'm not interested."

"Oh, honey, I think he just would like to get to know you

better. He was insistent on getting your phone number from me. He felt bad that you weren't having a good time."

"Yeah. Right. I'm not interested. I'm ready to go back to Paris tomorrow."

Chapter 19

Around eleven o'clock the morning after they returned home to the Paris apartment, the building's front door buzzer rang. Dean answered, and a few moments later, he walked into the lounge room with a gigantic bouquet of flowers, brought them to an open-mouthed Jenny, and set them down on the dining room table.

"They are for Mademoiselle Jennifer Morse, and there's a card."

Jenny took the card, dreading opening it, guessing who it was from. Finally summoning some strength, she tore it open and read:

> *My dear Jennifer,*
>
> *You left the party so soon. I'm sorry, but I'm sure you had your reasons. I am in Paris for a week and would like to take you to dinner, or maybe, at the least, have coffee with you. I want to see you again and know more about*

you. Please indulge me this. I promise no funny business. I will call you.
Warm regards, Jean Luc

Jenny took a breath, inhaling the sweet smell of the flowers.

Susan came up and put her arm around her waist. "My, these are so beautiful. From Jean Luc?"

"Yes. He wants me to go to dinner with him, or maybe coffee."

"He appears to be quite interested in you," Susan said with a smile.

"I don't know why he would be. He can probably have any woman he wants. Why me? And I don't want any relationships with any man right now," Jenny said.

"You should at least have coffee with him. You don't need to have a serious relationship. Just meet him. What can it hurt?"

Jenny grunted an acknowledgment but said, "I don't need or want a man of any sort in or around my life right now. It's the last thing I want. Just let it be."

"At least call him and acknowledge his gift."

"I don't have his number. I'd just as soon forget the whole weekend. I need to go out for a while." She turned, grabbed her phone and small purse and left, realizing how much she disliked having a "purse."

The next few weeks, Jenny again spent her days roaming the cobbled streets, walking by boulangeries and smelling the warm scent of breads, often stopping for a croissant or a pain au chocolat and a coffee which she enjoyed while reading a book, or maybe while she wrote in her journal.

She noticed a man, the same man she was pretty sure she'd seen several times recently, as she walked the narrow streets. He always remained in the background, like he was stalking her.

She wasn't worried; nevertheless, she'd dug into her suitcase and found her knife with the six-inch blade she had had since she was fourteen and used for protection during the remainder of her childhood in the commune. From then on, whenever she was out by herself, she carried it, inconspicuously on a belt she rigged up all those years ago.

One week, Dean and Susan took her on a road trip out of the city to see Bordeaux, Burgundy, Champagne, and the Loire Valley. The beauty of the country, small towns and villages mesmerized Jenny. They stopped in villages for lunch at a café, and sometimes picked up things from an open market and ate in a park. Nights were spent at quaint local inns or hotels. Every place they visited was like from a fairy tale.

Back in Paris, as usual, she went to her favorite bistro on the corner, hoping Camille might be there so they could chat over a cup of coffee. She wasn't, so Jenny walked over to rue de la Bûcherie and went to Shakespeare and Company to spend time browsing books as she'd done several previous times before, never tiring of the iconic bookstore. She was looking in the contemporary Paris fiction section when one of the attendants came up to her and said, "Excuse me, but you really look like the American writer, Jennifer Morse. I've read her book. So have several others. Have you read her?"

Jenny first thought to just play along and act ignorant. This girl didn't know who she really was. But she replied, "I look like her because I am Jennifer Morse. I'm happy you enjoyed my book. Thanks." She turned back to the bookshelves she was exploring.

The attendant grinned and said, "I'll be right back."

She soon returned with a woman, who had a shock of

curly blonde hair. "Hello, I'm Sylvia, the owner, and you are Jennifer Morse," she said with a British accent. "I'm happy to meet you. How long will you be in Paris?"

Jenny, now wishing she'd kept her mouth shut, replied, "Hi, Sylvia. I'm likewise happy to meet you. I'm planning on maybe another week or so before I leave."

"Would you possibly do a reading here, at the shop? We have an opening next week and would love it if you'd spend some time with us."

Jenny paused before answering, "I … I'm not sure. I'm on vacation and have halted my touring for a while."

"I'm sorry to intrude on your vacation in our beautiful city, but really, we have sold a number of your books, and you have quite a following here. I know you would be well received. If you think you might indulge us, please call me by Wednesday so I can make arrangements. Okay?"

"Sure. I'll think it over, Sylvia, and thank you for the offer. I'll let you know one way or the other. Okay?"

"Thank you for considering, and I'll wait for your call. Here's my card so you can call me directly." With that, she smiled and left.

Jenny walked down to the Seine and stared out at the swirling waters, then looked at Notre Dame across the way. She walked by the book stalls on Quai Saint-Michel searching for something; she didn't know what. She felt a tug in her gut with an urge to write and thought about how much help Will was with her first book. Now she was on her own and was scared to death she'd never write another book.

She knew she was headed into a funk. She wanted to talk to someone, but her friends were thousands of miles away. She didn't feel comfortable expressing herself to her grandparents. She missed her sessions with Joan. She was homesick.

Her phone buzzed, showing an unknown Paris number. In spite of that, she answered, "Hello? Who are you calling?"

"Jennifer, is this you?" a male voice asked.

"Yes. Who's this?"

"It is me, Jean, Jean Luc. I have wanted to talk with you. Your grandmother gave me your number at Monaco. How are you? I missed saying goodbye at that party in Monaco. I am in Paris until Saturday and would like to take you to dinner."

There was a long pause. She could hear his nervous breathing. "Thank you for those flowers, Jean. They were very beautiful. But I don't think it would be a good idea for me to go out with you. I just got out of a long-term relationship that ended very badly and am not in the mood for men in my life right now. Thank you for asking."

"But, Jennifer, we don't have to have a relationship for me to want to take you to dinner."

Knowing she'd never get rid of him pestering her, she said, "Tell you what, I'll meet you for coffee sometime."

"How about now? Where are you?"

"Quai Saint-Michel. I can meet you at the Brasserie Le Saint André on rue Danton."

"I know the place. I will meet you there in fifteen minutes." He clicked off.

Jenny was not in any hurry for her rendezvous with Jean Luc. She continued browsing the booksellers, but almost all the books she saw were in French. There were some of print reproductions of old Paris she liked but not so much that she purchased any. Finally, she tore herself away and headed up Boulevard Saint-Michel, crossed through the plaza in front of the giant statue of Saint-Michel and up to Brasserie Le Saint André. As she walked, she spotted the same guy she'd seen several times before. He always seemed to be watching her but ducked away when he noticed she saw him. He was definitely not someone she wanted to meet, with his heavy dark beard and unkempt hair. She got to the café, found an outside table, sat and waited.

She'd barely sat down when a red motorcycle with the rider dressed in red leather screamed into a parking space about fifty feet up the street. The rider dismounted and pulled off his full-face helmet, revealing a smiling Jean Luc.

"Bonjour, ma cherie. You look beautiful. I am so happy to see you again," he said as he joined her.

"Please don't call me that. I am not 'your dear.'"

"Ah, it is just a term for addressing a beautiful woman and—"

"Please stop, Jean Luc. This is exactly why I didn't want to have dinner with you. I think I should go."

"No. Please. I will be only like a friend. I promise. But you are my lucky woman. You see how I won at Monte Carlo? You brought me that luck. I know. I wanted to invite you to come to the race in Montreal last weekend. It was a hard race without you there to bring me luck."

A waitress appeared—Jenny was thankful it wasn't Camille—and took their orders for coffees.

"Maybe you will come to the French Grand Prix in Le Castellet this next weekend? My family will be there. Lisette would like to see you."

"Jean Luc, have you lost your mind! I do not want to go to another race. I want to be with my grandparents while I'm here, and if I go anywhere, it will be back home. Forget it."

"Your grandparents can come. I will have accommodations made for you. It will be wonderful. You will fly down with my parents in my jet."

"What don't you understand about 'NO?'" She grew

angry which was conveyed by the hardness in her voice. "I'm not going to another race. I can't face your parents after I left so abruptly at Monte Carlo. I would be embarrassed for being so rude. Shakespeare and Company wants me to do a reading next week, and I'm thinking of doing it. Then I'm planning on going back home. So I do not want to participate in your wild schemes." She took a sip of her coffee, savoring the richness that the French managed to get from coffee like nowhere else she'd been.

Jean Luc looked away to somewhere distant across the street or across the city. Jenny thought he looked as if he might start to cry. He took a slow sip of his coffee, reached in his pocket for his wallet, placed some Euros on the table and said, "Then I must go. I am sorry to have bothered you with my wild schemes. I thought we maybe might be friends. I apologize for assuming more than I should. Goodbye, Jennifer Morse."

"Jean Luc, Jean, I'm sorry. I didn't want to hurt your feelings like this, but I have explained to you why I don't want anyone in my life right now. I will repeat it. I just got out of a shitty relationship with a two-timing son of a bitch that thought I was the girl of his dreams until I became successful. Then he found someone else to fuck. I will not go through that again. Please understand. I can maybe be your friend but nothing more. Still, I do not want to go to any races again. I have things I need to do, and I need to start writing again."

"Thank you, Jennifer. I am happy we can be friends. I can understand. I am too pushy. I apologize. But—"

Jenny held up her hands again. "No buts. That's it. If you want to sit back down and talk of something else, fine. But no buts. Okay?"

"Yes, okay. So please tell me about your book you have written."

Jean Luc listened attentively and quietly, his exuberance quieted as she gave him a brief synopsis of the book and its subsequent success. After she'd said all she wanted, she asked him about racing cars.

He thought for a moment, then began, "I started racing go-carts almost before I could walk. My father was an auto-racing aficionado and had always wanted to be a driver, but his life took him to academia and his failed dream fell on me. I liked driving. I was a good driver and was able to move into Formula 4 at an early age. I did well there and got a ride in GP 2 when I was sixteen."

Jenny interrupted. "So what are Formula 4 and GP 3?"

"I apologize. I should explain. Formula 4 is for transitioning from go-carts to larger open wheel racing. Then I skipped F3 to GP3 for one season and then got a ride in GP2 when I was eighteen. I was good and had gathered several sponsors. Ferrari saw me and wanted me in their junior-driver training program. I accepted, excited to be a junior driver for such a renowned team. After my second year with them, their top driver retired, and I was offered his place. Driving an F1 car is so amazing. They are precise, powerful cars. I can only say that I am very fortunate to be among the fewer than one hundred drivers in the world licensed to drive them and only twenty currently driving.

"It was a whole new world to me, wealth, fame, travel around the world, and with all that I was pursued by everyone. A young driver, I had no experience with such things. My father tried to help and come to as many of my races as he could, but he was at the Sorbonne and had his teaching, so I got an agent to manage all my affairs. But there were still the paparazzi and girls chasing me. That's why I was wearing the New York Yankees baseball cap and dark glasses the night I met you, trying to be, like incognito."

"It sounds like a fascinating life," Jenny said, "but isn't it stressful going to all those places and then driving over 200 miles per hour and competing with all those other cars? It looks terrifying to me."

"It's not so bad. I feel safer driving in a race rather than on the streets or roads. Every driver on the track has great skill level. I trust them all. Yes, I have been involved in incidents. I have crashed cars, but such things can be expected."

"Were you ever hurt?"

"Once I suffered a broken arm, but it was when I was racing go-carts at seven years old and did a stupid thing. I learned a lesson in being too aggressive. Most incidents are not so serious. But you can get seriously injured driving on the roads with all the crazy drivers who talk on cell phones or doing whatever they are doing except paying attention to driving."

She smiled. "You have a good point. I'll remember that when I'm driving from now on."

"If you might want to come to the French Grand Prix with me, I will give you a ride on the track in a car like I had the night we met, but I will have no speed limits, so you could have fun."

Jenny laughed. "I'm not going to the French Grand Prix. I'm planning to leave Paris for home in a week or so. I need to get back to my house and start writing. But all the adulation must be nice," she said, thinking about her own success and how much she disliked it. "You have all these beautiful women chasing you."

He laughed. "You mean like those two crazy women who were at the party. Lisette told me of them. I met them once at a party, and they think I am their friend. They are second-rate models that are looking for a rich man to support their lifestyle of spending much money. I am sorry they were rude, but Lisette told me how you responded. I like that you are a strong woman but am sad you are not interested in me." He laughed again.

"It's not that, Jean, you seem like a nice guy, but as I have told you, I'm truly not interested in going out with you or any man right now. I need to be alone and work."

Jean Luc nodded. "That still makes me sad, but I will understand, and I promise I will not bother you anymore. But I will be your friend. If you ever need anything, please let me know."

"Thanks for the coffee. I really must go now. I'm happy we talked. Maybe we will meet again sometime," she said with a tight smile.

"I shall await the day. I will give you a ride on a Formula 1 track."

"Ha, don't count on it. Be careful. Please." She turned and left, raising her hand in a goodbye but not looking back. She heard the motorcycle start and the sound fade away down the street.

Back at the apartment, she looked up Jean Luc on the internet. There was a lot of stories and articles about him, and when she saw his salary for the current year for driving a race car, her mouth dropped open. She stared at the figure; his earnings for the current year would be $43.5 million. What astounded her more was that he was not the highest-paid driver. After the shock of how much he earned, she skimmed some of the stories, mostly about races. There wasn't much about his private life other than a story on how he avoided all the high living that some of the other drivers in Formula 1 enjoyed.

After long consideration, she decided to do the reading at Shakespeare and Company the following Thursday. Sylvia was happy Jenny would do it and told her about how it would be a low-key intimate affair. Most readings were attended by small crowds. Sylvia told her what time to come and thanked her, said goodbye and ended the call.

Jenny felt a little unsettled about the reading and contactsd Marty, her agent, and told her. Marty was excited and immediately wanted Jenny to extend her stay, saying she would set up more signings and readings.

"No, no, no," Jenny said. "This is a one-time thing. I met the owner, and she personally invited me, and against my good judgment agreed to it. But that's it. Period. I told you I need time off."

But Marty didn't give up. "Jen, you're in Europe. I can get you into Berlin, Madrid—"

Jenny interrupted. "No, dammit! Stop! No! What is it with you people who do not understand the meaning of no!"

"But Jen—"

"I'm sorry I called. Goodbye, Marty." She clicked off. Her cell immediately buzzed. It was Marty; Jenny again blocked her number.

Chapter 20

Jenny spent the next few days with her grandparents, seeing more of Paris. She grew bored with doing nothing more than visiting shops, sitting in bistros drinking coffee, and writing in her notebook or reading a book and looked forward to getting the reading over with next week and heading back home.

Wednesday night she'd crawled into bed and was beginning to write in her notebook when she heard Dean talking to someone, on his cell phone. She overheard him saying, "That would be great. Thank you so much. It is very kind of you to invite us. We can meet you at the airport then." She heard no more as he moved away across the room.

A knock sounded on her door, and she heard Dean say, "Jenny, can I come in?"

"Sure. Anything wrong?"

He came in all excited. "I just got off the phone with Robert. They have invited us to come with them to the race in Le Castellet this weekend. Jean Luc is sending his plane to fly us down, and we leave in the morning. All arrangements have been made. We have to be at the airport at noon tomorrow."

She looked up. "No, Dean. Please count me out. I'm sorry, I appreciate their offer, but I've had enough of Jean Luc and racing. I would rather just stay here. You and Susan go and enjoy your time there."

"Jenny, all the arrangements have been made for us. The Bonnets want us to all come."

Susan came in at that point and jumped into the discussion. "Jenny, that's so ungrateful of you to not accept their hospitality. You're being rude. I just don't understand. They'll be so disappointed."

Jenny had enough and said forcefully, "No. Please listen to what I'm saying, I do not want to go. Period! You two go and have fun. Please don't make excuses for me. Okay. Tell them I appreciate their offer, but no."

Susan sighed. "Have it your way then. I simply don't understand you sometimes." They turned and left, closing the door quietly behind them.

She didn't want her grandparents angry with her, but she didn't care. While the time with them had been fun, she was starting to feel overwhelmed and smothered. She just wanted to be alone. She took a breath and continued writing in her notebook.

The next morning she heard Susan and Dean leave. It felt good to be by herself. She put in a call for a flight the following week and got an early flight out on Friday morning. She then went up to Luxembourg Gardens for a run. She loved to run the circuit up there with all the other runners who used the track. After her run, she headed down to Brasserie Le Saint André for breakfast.

Camille was working and took Jenny's order, then came

back and said, "Do you mind if I sit for a minute? Things are slow and I can talk to my American friend. How are you enjoying your time here?"

"It's been enjoyable, Camille, but I'm leaving next week."

"Oh, I'm so sorry to hear you're leaving. Are you unhappy?"

"No, I'm just ready to be back home at my own house. I've been here long enough. I need to get home and do some work on my next book. Then there's this guy I met and he seems infatuated with me. Won't leave me alone."

"Oh, a guy? Is he nice?"

"Yeah, a little too nice … a little overwhelming at times."

"Who is he? How did you meet?"

Jenny went on to tell her about Jean Luc, how they met, and how nice he was, but how she didn't want a relationship with him or anyone.

When Jenny had finished, Camille said, "*Mon dieu*, Jean Luc Bonnet? You know him? He is the most eligible man in Paris. Any woman would welcome his attention. He is very rich and famous and very kind. Did you know he has set up a national foundation for the fight to stop domestic violence against women?"

That last statement resonated deeply with Jenny with her background of childhood abuse. She took a deep breath, thinking a change of plans might be in order.

Camille left and returned with Jenny's breakfast.

"Thank you, Camille. I appreciate hearing what you told me of Jean Luc. It makes a difference in my perspective of him."

Jenny made several calls while eating her food. One was for trains for Le Castellet and another for flights. She was able to book a two o'clock flight which would get her there quicker. Then she called Susan and told her of her new plans, which, of course, made her grandmother happy.

Chapter 21

After a short hop from Paris, she arrived in Le Castellet and got a cab to take her to the Grand Prix Hôtel, aptly named since it was right next to Circuit Automobile Paul Ricard. She would be sharing a two-bedroom suite with Dean and Susan. After quickly freshening up, she found them poolside enjoying cocktails with Robert, Danielle, and Lisette.

Susan said, "I'm happy you got all those problems with your publisher worked out and could come."

Jenny glanced at her grandmother, who avoided her gaze, and said, "Ah, yeah, I'm so happy that we could resolve everything on a conference call, and I didn't have to go to New York. It's so great to see you all and be here. Sorry for the delay, but you know—"

"We are just happy you could join us. Jean will be so happy to see you," Danielle replied, "and he did so well today in practice. He thinks you bring him luck."

"Danielle, I really don't think he needs me to win. I think he does quite well on his own."

"Please sit down and join us for a cocktail. Relax after your trip. Jean will be joining us soon," Robert said.

She sat, ordered a drink, and joined in the group conversation that thankfully moved away from her. Around 5:30 Jean Luc arrived.

His eyes fell on her and lit up like street lights coming on. "Jennifer, you came after all. Maman said you could not come. But now I am very happy you are here." He came over and gave her *bisous aux joues* on both cheeks before she could get off her chair. She politely returned the *bisous*, taking somewhat longer than necessary.

He got a chair and sat next to her, and the conversation moved to practice, qualifying the next day, and the race itself. Jean Luc was upbeat and, looking at Jenny, said, "Now my luck is here. Sunday will not be a problem."

After more conversation and drinks, they all retired to their suites to get ready for dinner. Jenny already felt a little giddy with what she had to drink. She showered, which helped her to clear her head, then joined her grandparents.

Jenny wore one of her Paris dress purchase, a milky colored deep-yellow which emphasized her blonde hair and skin color, almost making her glow.

"Oh Jenny, you look radiant," Susan said, her remark echoed by Dean.

They moved down to the dining room and joined the Bonnets, who were already seated. Jean Luc rose and held a chair for her next to him. She sat down, sliding her chair closer to him than was necessary. The conversation started with Danielle complimenting Jenny on her upcoming reading at Shakespeare and Company and saying how much they enjoyed meeting her at Monaco and their disappointment that she'd left so abruptly.

"I'm sorry about that, but I had a horrible headache."

Shrugging aside the apology, Danielle continued, "Both Lisette and I have since read your novel and loved it. We want you to sign our copies."

"I promise, I will sign them for you. Thank you."

The waiters came, and Robert ordered wine and appetizers. As Jenny looked at her menu, her hand moved, like it had a mind of its own, discretely finding Jean Luc's to which she gave a quick squeeze, then pulling away immediately before he could react. She glanced over at him and found him giving her a confused smile.

During their dinner, conversation ran wildly from topic to topic until it fell onto Jenny. Robert said, "Jennifer, tell us about your book. We are wondering where the story came from."

She shuddered inwardly and searched for an answer that wouldn't divulge her own childhood abuse. "A few years ago I became involved in sexual and domestic abuse of women in Durango, where I live. I teach yoga there as well as write, and through my yoga classes, I became aware of these issues through some women I met. It seems to be an issue everywhere."

She glanced at Jean Luc who looked at her intently, then continued, "The book is based on the stories of several women I met and who shared their stories with me." She glanced at Susan who nodded, seeing that Jenny would rather not be lying about the fact that the book was truly about her.

Susan directed a question to Jean Luc, trying to change the subject. "So, Jean, how do you feel about qualifying tomorrow?"

"Like I always do; I will do my best. The car is in excellent condition, and I am looking forward to being on pole."

"He always says that," said Danielle, laughing.

Jean Luc said, "But I have Jennifer here for my good

luck. When I win, it will be because of her." He gave her a warm smile.

Dinner finished, and they ordered deserts and aperitifs. Jean Luc, skipping any alcohol, excused himself early to get rest. When the others decided to retire to the lounge, Jenny excused herself, went to her room and went to bed, happy she'd decided to come. She liked Danielle; she reminded Jenny of Helen with her elegant grace. And Robert reminded her of Will in many ways. She saw a growing friendship between them and her grandparents.

On her way up to her room, she thought she saw someone further down the hallway, but then thought it was only a shadow. Once in her room, she undressed and fell into bed for a welcome sleep, tired from the day.

Jenny and Lisette were in the pits for qualifying. Jenny liked watching all the frantic activity, which, rather than being chaotic, flowed like an orchestrated dance. Everyone knew where to be and what to do.

When she arrived Jean Luc was out on the track for the first of three rounds of qualifying. Though his times had been erratic during practice, he seemed to have settled in and was at the top of the leaderboard. His time was even better in the second round. Third round was for the coveted pole position. His first lap was good, and he was positioned to do a flying lap for time. Jenny saw his pit crew watching the monitor when they all threw their hands up in disgust. She found out he'd spun out on one of the Virage de Bendor corners. Apparently there was no damage, and he was back on the track and into the pits where a crew, with immediate purpose, went over the car and got him back out with three and a half minutes left, time for a warm-up lap and one final flying lap. Meantime, the two Mercedes and a Red Bull had bested his time. When it was all done, Jean Luc would be starting in fourth place from the second row behind both Mercedes cars and next to a Red Bull car.

Dinner was quiet that night. Jean Luc was the only one who was upbeat.

"It was an unfortunate mistake on the Virage de Bendor, so I will have to drive harder tomorrow is all. I have no problem, so no one has to be so quiet and sad. It will be a great race that I will win."

Jenny was impressed by his positive attitude, but all the same, she felt nervous for him and all she wanted was for him to be safe.

Chapter 22

Race day came, and on her way to join Lisette, Jenny ran into the two Eastern European women, the models she'd had words with at the party.

"American bitch, you will be sorry you ever messed with us," she heard one call out behind her back.

Jenny quickly turned, but they were already gone, disappearing into the crowd.

Jenny met Lisette, and they took their places in the pits with their sound-canceling earmuffs on. The formation lap was completed and cars positioned on the grid. The all-clear sign was given, and the five lights lit one by one. The cars revved in anticipation. Even Jenny's earmuffs didn't drown out the sound, and it reverberated in her chest. The lights went out, and the race began with screaming engines and squealing tires. Jean Luc had a perfect start, quickly moved into third and challenged a Mercedes. Still in a pack, all cars made it through the first turn unscathed and began to spread out.

A few seconds later, a cheer went up from the pit crew as

Jean Luc passed one of the Mercedes and moved into second place. The first lap was completed and the race settled in.

Jenny grew bored and wandered into the guest lounge, followed by Lisette. Each got a flute of champagne and sat, relieved of the ear muffs.

"Jennifer, you understand Jean Luc has a very large crush on you," Lisette said.

"I know and I've told him I'm not interested. I like your brother. He seems like a nice and gentle man. I respect him for the things he supports with his wealth. But it'd never work out between us. I live in America. He lives in France. He travels and races cars. I don't know when he'd have time for a relationship, and right now I don't want one. So it's not going to happen."

Lisette replied with a laugh. "Ah, but, Jennifer, he can be very persistent. When he wants something, he will work hard to get it. I have not seen him so happy since he met you. He was never interested in the women who chase him all the time. He never did the playboy act that so many of the young drivers do."

Jenny didn't respond to that but told Lisette about her encounter with the two models.

Lisette shook her head. "Oh, do not worry about them. They are nothing."

They finished their wine in silence with Jenny thinking about the two models, then they returned to the race, which was now on the sixteenth lap. Jean Luc was trailing the leading Mercedes by over two seconds, a lifetime in Formula 1 racing. On lap twenty-three, there was an incident involving two cars in the chicane, and a safety car was called out. A number of cars began to pit for new tires including the leading Mercedes. The hard compound tire everyone chose would carry them to the end of the race.

Jean Luc stayed out. He was now in the lead with the Mercedes pitted. But the Mercedes didn't leave the pit lane. The tire-changing crew were all standing, except for those on the left rear. Apparently they were having difficulty getting the wheel nut back on. Finally it was let loose after a thirteen-second stop as opposed to the usual two-or-so seconds it took to change the four tires.

The safety car retired, and the race resumed with Jean Luc screaming away from the nearest car on his tail. The once-leading Mercedes was now relegated to sixteenth place. From then on it was Jean Luc in the lead, and he wasn't challenged until the last two laps when the Mercedes had gotten through the pack and was within three seconds of him. But it wasn't enough. Jean Luc screamed across the finish to garner the checkered flag.

After the post-race celebrations, Jenny, her grandparents and the Bonnets retired to their hotel to relax and clean up for dinner and the post-race party.

Jean Luc joined them for dinner to cheers and toasts for his victory and hugs and *bisous* from everyone. Dinner consisted of five courses and several bottles of champagne and wine.

After several hours of food, wine, dessert, and digestifs, the group began to leave. Jon Luc walked next to Jenny as everyone left.

"Jenny, would you want to go out to the track tomorrow, and I will give you a ride like I promised?"

"What? Those cars can barely hold one person."

He laughed. "No, no. remember I told you we will ride in a two-seater like the first night we met. You will then experience the track as I do. It will be exciting. No?"

She hesitated for a moment. Dean and Susan were walking

close behind, and Dean said, "I couldn't help overhearing your offer. Jenny, you should take him up on it. Not many people get such a chance, and if you don't want to go, I'd love to."

They walked on while Jenny thought it over, and, remembering that night in Monte Carlo, decided it really would be fun. "Sure, I'd like that."

"I'll meet you here in the lobby at nine. Wear comfortable clothes. Okay?"

Chapter 23

Monday morning, Jenny met Jean Luc, and he took her to the pit garage where she was outfitted with fire-proof coveralls, gloves, and a helmet. Her nerves were on edge, and she wasn't quite sure about all this. Jean Luc also put on similar apparel.

"Jean, why all this for a car ride?"

He smiled. "Safety regulations. And now you look like a race-car driver."

"Yeah. Right. This helmet is heavy," she said, now with a new understanding about the rigorous physical training the drivers did.

He led her to the passenger seat of a low, red Ferrari two-seater. A young woman helped her to a lightly padded deep bucket seat that cradled her like a cocoon. The young woman, who introduced herself as Gabriella, then hooked her into a shoulder harness and seat belt so tight she could barely move.

"Does this have to be so tight?" Jenny asked.

"Yes. It is necessary for your ride. I'm jealous to go. It will be so much fun. Maybe someday Jean Luc will give me a ride. You must be very special."

Jenny was beginning to wonder whether this may have been a bad decision. Too late. Jean Luc was seated and belted in.

"Ready for some fun?" he asked as he started the car, which came alive with a rumble of power that was palpable. He started out with a chirp from the tires and headed out of the pit lane down the main straight. He drove fast but at a pleasant pace.

This isn't so bad, Jenny thought as she watched Jean Luc downshifting and braking for the corners. She got a feel for the track and what the drivers saw during a race.

They completed the first lap and were heading down the main straight when Jenny saw several people at the side of the track watching, one appearing to have a stopwatch. Suddenly she was flattened against her seat as Jean Luc accelerated the car to a dizzying speed. Jenny's head pressed firmly against the headrest; her chest felt heavy, and her eyes widened as she saw the first corner coming up. She knew they were going too fast, but seemingly at the last second, he downshifted and braked so hard Jenny quickly understood why she was so securely fastened in her harness. She wanted to scream, but the scream wouldn't come out.

As they drove through the first corners—a ninety-degree left hander followed quickly by a right hander—she appreciated being tightly secured in her cocoon. The track surface reverberated through the thinly padded seat. Terrific acceleration followed by more tight corners, accelerating again to insane speed, more corners, a fast, straight-and-easy right-hand corner, several tight quick ones, and the main straight again. Jenny expected that that would be it, but Jean Luc powered the screaming car even faster for another lap. She marveled at his complete control of this powerful machine. They blasted by the timekeeper in a blur, then another even faster lap, followed by him slowing to a quieter pace for another lap, then he drove into the pits and stopped.

Jenny had to make sure she was still able to breathe, thinking she hadn't taken a breath since Jean Luc had powered through the first corners. She moved her fingers and toes to make sure they still worked and noticed she was sweating. Her door opened and Gabriella unbuckled her harness, helped her out and helped her with her helmet. Jenny shook and her knees wobbled. Jean Luc spoke a few words to the crew who congratulated him on his lap times.

He came around the car. "Did you enjoy your ride?"

Jenny, standing on shaky legs, tried to speak, but all that came out was a squeak where her voice should have been.

"Jennifer, are you okay?" he asked, alarm rising in his voice.

She managed to say, "I think so. I need a moment."

"I'll get some water for you," he said, leading her inside. He gave her a bottle, and she drank greedily, now starting to feel calmer.

"Goddammit! You didn't tell me you were going to go that fast. I thought we would do a few laps so I could see the track, but no, you had to act like you were racing. You scared the shit out of me."

His eyes grew wide, and a look of panic came over him. He held his hands out, wide eyed, then a sheepish look followed, like a little boy, which she found endearing.

She knew he was only doing what he did—drive cars fast. "I'm sorry, Jean. I apologize. I just wasn't expecting that. I was scared to death. I had no idea."

"No, no, it is me who must apologize. I forget you are not familiar with such fast cars. I could have taken a few laps easier at the start and warned you I would go faster."

"It's okay, Jean. I'm sorry I snapped at you like I did. I was just so scared and excited." Her trembling ceased, and she realized how pumped up she was. She thought all her blood had probably been replaced with adrenaline. She might not sleep for a month. She felt like she could run a marathon. Then she felt a twinge, almost like sexual excitement. She wanted more.

"Do you want to drive a few laps, Jennifer?"

She looked at him incredulously. "You have to be kidding. Me? Drive that?"

"Of course. I will be with you and tell you what to do. We don't have to go fast like I did. Then you will have driven a real car," he said with a big smile.

Being already so pumped, she decided to do it. She knew Dean would be even more jealous than he already was. "Sure. If it's okay with everybody. This thing looks way more complicated than my Jeep."

"It's like any other car, only very fast. I will show you everything. Let's go."

Gabriella buckled her in again, this time in the driver's seat, but she didn't seem happy that Jenny was getting to drive. "He must be in love with you to treat you so special. Letting you drive. He has never given any woman a ride like he did. Now he is letting you drive?"

Jenny smiled up at her. "As they say, Gabriella, I'm just along for the ride."

Gabriella closed her door and Jean Luc sat beside her. "Okay, Jennifer," he said. "Have you driven a car with a clutch before?"

"No, just automatics."

"Okay. Push the clutch in when we start the car, then you

will put it in gear, then release the clutch gently as you push on the accelerator as it is very sensitive, and you can easily stall. After we get going, you won't need to use the clutch again until we stop. You will shift by pushing these paddles on the steering wheel. Brakes are very good. The steering is very quick. You won't need to worry about much else. Watch the tachometer, and do not accelerate the engine beyond the red line. We will do some easy laps, and then we can go faster. Do you have any questions?"

Jenny had a million questions but didn't know how to articulate them. She shook her head. Jean Luc showed her how to start the beast. She pushed in the clutch and started it up. She could feel the power and felt both excited and nervous. She tried to coordinate the clutch and accelerator as he had said but immediately stalled.

"It might take some tries," Jean Luc said quietly, "but you will get it."

Third time she did and headed slowly out of the pit lane onto the track.

"Okay, Jennifer. Very good. Now accelerate easily a little and get a feel for how this car handles."

Jenny did as he said. After the first few corners, she felt a stability she never knew from her Jeep. This car seemed to stick to the road surface. She could feel every nuance of the track, and the car was responsive to her slightest touch. She got a feel for the paddle shifters, the quickness of the steering, the solid braking, the stability and superb handling of the machine, and she began to feel as one with it. After negotiating the first lap, she increased her speed. Jean Luc expertly guided her into the corners, telling her when to brake, when to downshift, and when to accelerate. On the third lap, she went faster, the fourth lap faster again, and on the fifth lap, she was completely focused and drove faster than she could ever have imagined herself doing.

Jean Luc laughed. "One more, Jennifer, and push it even faster."

Jenny did, and on the back straight, she glanced at the speedometer; it read 250 kilometers per hour. Jenny didn't know how that translated into miles per hour but learned later it was around 150 miles per hour. She did as Jean Luc had done and finished with a slow lap to cool things down a bit. She'd never felt such a rush in her life; even the mountains paled in comparison. She reluctantly pulled into the pit lane and stopped. But when she unbuckled and tried to get out, her legs felt like rubber.

"Are you okay?" Jean Luc asked from the other side of the car.

"Yeah, just a little shaky. Oh my God, that was so fun. I could drive like this all day. I won't ever be able to thank you enough for letting me do this. I will never be able to drive the same." She went on blathering with excitement and from the adrenaline coursing through her veins.

Jean Luc, laughing, came over and gave her a hug, trying to calm her down. She let him hold her, feeling his hard body against hers. It felt nice. She looked up at his dark eyes and kissed him, then she kissed him harder, avoiding any tongue, but she desperately wanted to. She felt a tingle that went south of her belly, something she hadn't felt in a long time. Then her brain kicked in, and she quickly pulled back from him.

"I'm sorry. I didn't—"

"Why would you be sorry for a kiss, *ma chérie*? Maybe that kiss expresses your feelings for me? No?"

Jenny knew she'd turned beet red and fumbled to say something, still in his arms, but nothing would come.

Jean Luc broke the spell by pulling away a little. "You are a natural. Maybe Ferrari should bring you on board in their driver-training program."

"Ha, yeah right. I'm a girl and apparently this is an all-boys game."

"It truly is, but there were five women drivers that competed between 1958 and the early nineties. Sadly, they were all relegated to incomparably bad cars, so we don't really know how good a woman in a good car can compete with us 'boys.' I see your American Indy car driver Danica Patrick. She did well in spite of all the criticism from the boys about her being a woman and so much lighter than her male counterparts, which they thought gave her unfair advantage. It is sad really. It was once thought also that little girls should not drive go-karts like I did when I was little. But that is changing, and there are little girls everywhere enjoying go-kart racing. Hopefully we will see more women in F1 someday. We already have many women working in our crews. So someday—? Maybe you could be the first." He looked at her with his warm smile. "Let's get out of these coveralls and go to find some lunch."

She didn't want to admit it, but she was very attracted to him. He was nice and kind and since their talk over coffee, he hadn't been so pushy. During lunch, she asked him, "Jean, you're a rich and famous man who could have any woman he wants. So why do you think you want me, someone who is really a nobody in your circles?"

"That is precisely the reason. You are a normal woman who is not impressed by what I am. I want you to be interested in who I am as just a man. I want you to know me as a man who wants to live simply. I would like a family someday. I won't be doing this driving forever. I am thirty-two years old and already I notice my reflexes are not as they were when I was twenty. I have to push harder for focus. I sometimes get tired of the competition and pressure. My contract with Ferrari runs out in two years. I will turn thirty-four then and am planning on retiring, so only a few more years will I have this. Then I will be a nobody like when I was not this driver. All the glamour was fun for a few years, but it is old. I like being at home in Monaco or in Paris with my family." He paused, staring out beyond Jenny with a somber look. "To be truthful, I am becoming fearful. My driving is becoming less fun and is now work and pressure. This morning when we were at the track, that was fun. We got to drive fast just the two of us. No others."

"You want to retire? What will you do after? You're still young. What new adventure are you thinking?"

"I don't know, Jennifer. I don't know. I have traveled so much, I am tired of it. Maybe I will take a year and do nothing except ride bikes, read books, sit in the sun, maybe learn to meditate. I have more than enough money to live well the rest of my life. Maybe I will write a book like you. Ferrari is already pressuring me to stay with the team as a consultant and a trainer for their driver program. I might do that. Would you like to live in Maranello, Italy with me?" he finished with a mischievous look in his eyes.

She ignored the question, and they returned to the hotel in silence. Jenny's head and heart pounded with unanswered questions about her feelings around what just happened. Chris was still too fresh in her psyche. She didn't want to admit to herself what she felt for Jean Luc Bonnet. She needed to breathe.

As he pulled in to drop her off, she turned to him. "Thank you for everything, Jean. It was nice to meet you and your family. Thank you for today and for everything. You're a very nice man, and I'm sure you'll meet someone someday who you'll fall in love with."

"Ah, that will not happen."

She gave him a confused look. "Of course you will."

"No. It's too late. I have already found someone who I'm falling in love with."

She looked at him with eyes wide open. "No, Jean. Please. No. I can't." With that she gave him a peck on the cheek and quickly exited the car, walking away so fast she was almost running. She didn't want him to see the tears running down her cheeks.

That night she received a text from Helen:

Hi Jenny. It's been a while but I regret to tell you that Cat died two days ago. Will and I are both very sorry. He was such a sweetheart. He was being listless and not himself and Will took him to the vet. It was simply old age. We had no idea of his age as he was a stray, but the vet thought he was at least twenty and most likely more. We're so sorry. He had a good life. We buried him in the little pine grove behind the house.

Other news since you've been gone, Kelly and Peter are moving to Santa Fe. His law firm is opening a branch there, and they want Peter to get it up and running. They have already found a place down there and will be moving in a few weeks. Other news, we bought a little house in Mexico a bit north of Puerto Vallarta. We're tired of winters here and will

*plan on being there November through March.
We hope you'll come visit. All for now. Sorry
again about Cat. Love and hugs.*

Jenny reread the text several times in disbelief. Cat … he brought back so many memories of the first night she spent at Will's and how frightened she was of him. But how he connected with her, and how she grew to love him. He was always there. He never wanted much other than food, water, some love and pets and to snuggle up with her in bed. She cried silently for him but also for herself and how she would miss him.

Her best friend was moving away, and Will and Helen would be in Mexico half the year. Everybody was moving away. She still would have her grandparents and Julien. But that was little solace for everything else she'd just learned.

Chapter 24

Thursday night came, and after she'd a light dinner by herself at a brasserie by Place Saint-Michel, Jenny met Dean and Susan to walk over to the bookstore. She felt nervous, but as soon as she saw the store, calm come over her. Sylvia greeted her as they entered. Jenny introduced Dean and Susan, who took seats with several people already seated. Soon all the seats were full, and Sylvia introduced Jenny to the group, which brought a polite clapping.

Jenny took her seat in the front and asked if there were any questions before she began. A man in the front row raised his hand and asked her to read as she wished. Jenny had a passage marked, and she read through two chapters, then stopped and looked up from the book at the assembled group. She again received polite clapping, except for someone in the back who clapped loudly. Then she saw him; Jean Luc stood in the shadows at the back, Lisette by his side, and Danielle and Robert sat in the back row in front of them. She didn't want to see any of them, wanting to slither away and hide, but she took a breath, got her composure together, smiled and started signing books, answering a multitude of questions, and listening to praise for her book.

Things began to slow, and Sylvia stepped in, calling for an end, giving Jenny a much-needed break. Wine and cheese were available, and the crowd broke into groups talking, like everyone there were old friends. Jenny gathered her things and moved away to the side of the room, not wanting to see the Bonnet family, but Dean and Susan and the Bonnets had already found each other and were enjoying a glass of wine and conversation.

As much as she hated it, Jenny mingled with the guests, making small talk. She saw Dean motioning her over, but she ignored him, trying to avoid them, particularly Jean Luc; then she looked for Sylvia, thanked her for her graciousness and asked if there was a way out through the rear of the store. Sylvia showed her the way out to the back door.

"Be careful, though," Sylvia said, "it is very dark, but only a short way to a well-lighted, busier street. Thank you for doing the reading."

Jenny nodded. "Thank you for having me. I enjoyed it."

Using her cell phone's flashlight, Jenny started down the street, being wary of the darkened doorways. Her right hand found her knife, and she had it at the ready. She felt someone nearby before she heard him.

"Okay, American bitch," a heavily accented Eastern European voice said, "you insult my friends. Now I have you alone, and you pay."

Jenny, quick as a cat, sidestepped into a doorway as the man lunged for her. In the dim light, she saw his left hand raised, holding what she thought might be a knife, but her quickness took him off balance, and he overshot his mark.

Determined never to be a victim again, Jenny plunged the knife into his right ass cheek as hard as she could, feeling it hit flesh and sink into where it hit bone. He screamed, lost his balance, and fell into a heap on his left side. She pulled her knife out and wiped the blood on his shirt as he writhed in pain.

"American bitch. You will pay," he muttered in a venomous voice. And then he went silent.

Shit. I killed him, she thought. But she knew where she'd stabbed him wouldn't kill him. She'd dropped her cell phone in the scuffle and now quickly picked it up and shone the torch on the man. Looking more closely, she saw he had a now-empty syringe stuck into the right side of his neck. He must have fallen on it. She wanted to laugh but was too frightened.

"American bitch," he groaned.

"I really don't like being called that." She kicked him as hard as she could squarely in his face with the toe of her boot, and he said no more.

She sheathed her knife, then ran the rest of the way to the apartment. Her hands trembled so hard she could barely get the key into the lock. Once in, she slammed the door, locked it, and stood with her back against it, but she shook so hard she couldn't stand anymore. She slumped to the floor and broke into sobs.

Eventually she managed to get to her feet and go up to the apartment. She felt sick and ran to the bathroom just in time. After finishing heaving, she sat against the wall, waiting to recover, thinking, *I've carried this knife since I was fourteen and was always able to bluff my way. Now I actually used to stab a man*. The thought almost made her vomit again.

Once able to rise, she called for a cab to pick her up in thirty minutes, then she rushed to her room, quickly finished packing, took her suitcases, and raced down to the street-level door, thinking, *There are people out there who want to harm me, even kill me.*

She only had to wait several minutes for the cab. It pulled up and she cautiously walked out, looking both ways, making sure no one was lurking in the shadows. The driver got out, and she eyed him cautiously as he put her bags in the trunk. She heard police cars and emergency vehicles and saw red flashing lights.

"Charles de Gaulle, please." Her flight wasn't until early morning, but she wanted to get away from there. The police were here. They'd be checking around. There were CCTV cameras everywhere. She was probably seen running to the apartment. They'd know.

As they drove down onto Quai Saint-Michel from rue Danton, she asked the driver to pull over for a moment. "I'm leaving your beautiful city, and I must have one more look around."

"*Oui,* mademoiselle. Please take your look. I shall wait."

"*Merci.*" She walked quickly out onto the Pont Saint-Michele, looking back to make sure the cab remained there, and stopped in the middle of the bridge, looking over the rail at the dark waters of the Seine. People strolled by, so, very discreetly, she pulled the knife from her belt and dropped it into the depths. *Gone. Thankfully gone.*

Feeling much lighter, unburdened from her weapon and evidence but now defenseless, she hurried back to the cab. As they pulled away from the curb, she spied her grandparents and the Bonnets, including Jean Luc, walking toward Place Saint-Michel, probably to have dinner, probably wondering where she was. While the car drove on to the airport, she checked her phone and saw three calls and two text messages from Susan asking, "Where are you?"

She exited the cab at the airport and, feeling frightened and defenseless, carefully scanned the people coming and going. She handed the cab driver a 100 Euro note and ran to the door before he could protest the large overpayment. Once inside, she spied security guards everywhere and felt better but still wary.

Although it was late evening, the ticket counters were still open and not busy, so she went to check in for her morning flight. The attendant looked at her ticket, entered something into her computer and then said, "Mademoiselle, if you wish, I can get you a flight to Chicago leaving in one hour. Then I can get you a connecting to Albuquerque, New Mexico, which will get you there late afternoon. I'm sorry but I cannot reroute you to Denver since they are already fully booked."

Jenny considered this for a moment. *I can be away from Paris and the police. I can rent a car in Albuquerque. A three-hour drive will give me time to decompress.*

"Mademoiselle, are you okay?"

Jolted back from her thoughts, she quickly answered, "Ah, yeah. Sure. That'd be great. Thank you so much."

"It will save you spending a night on a hard bench. Plus I see you fly with American often so I can also offer you a free upgrade to first class since it is not fully booked."

Again, she looked at the attendant warily. "Oh, yeah, thank you, yes, yes, thank you."

The attendant looked at her quizzically. "Are you sure you are okay?"

"Ah, sure, yeah. Just distracted by the changes to my flight, I guess. Thank you for all your help and for the upgrade."

The attendant laughed. "Have a good flight, Mademoiselle. Here is your boarding pass and gate number."

Through security, she found her gate, where people were just beginning to board. She sent a quick text to Susan letting her know she was leaving and then boarded the plane, found her plush seat and was offered champagne before she'd hardly had a chance to sit down.

At precisely 10:00, the cabin door was shut and locked, and the engines began their whirring whine. The plane backed away from the gate and headed to the runway. The pilot announced that they were the next to take off. The giant plane rumbled down the taxiway, turned onto the runway and then a surge of pressure pushed Jenny back into her seat as the plane accelerated down the runway. After a bounce, they became airborne and the ride smoothed out. She looked out her window and saw the lights of the city, the Eiffel Tower, the Champs-Élysées, and the Seine and thought she could see Place Saint-Michel where she wondered if her grandparents were having dinner. She felt a lump in her throat and forced tears away.

An attendant came and gave her more champagne and offered selections for dinner. After eating a light dinner, Jenny asked for a pillow and blanket, turned off her overhead light, and curled up trying to sleep. Totally worn out from the excitement and trauma of the night, however, her brain was still on adrenaline overdrive from the attack, and sleep would not come.

She finally gave up and picked up the airline magazine and read an article about recreational vehicles and RV life on the road. When she'd finished the article, she put her head back and closed her eyes with her mind now fixated on what it would be like to have a small RV and go on the road for a while. She'd be away from everyone and everything, just like when she lived in the mountains for those two years with minimal contact with others. She could travel, see new places and do some writing.

After an hour layover in Chicago, she boarded the three-hour flight to Albuquerque and finally fell asleep. Much too soon, she awoke to the attendant going through the cabin getting the passengers ready for landing. They landed early afternoon. Jenny found her luggage, got her rental car and went to a nearby hotel for the rest of the day and night. She showered away all the miles and ordered out for food. Barely able to stay awake, she ate and passed out asleep by 6:30 dreaming of having her own RV and traveling the open road.

Chapter 25

After sleeping through the night until seven o'clock and feeling mostly revived, she went to the lobby for the complimentary breakfast and checked her phone. Several messages had arrived from her grandmother. It was the middle of the night in Paris, so she texted that she'd be in touch later.

She'd brought her laptop with her to breakfast and began online searches for RV dealers in the area, checking their inventory. She found a dealer that had several mini motor homes that she had read about on her flight and was interested in. She checked out of the hotel and set her GPS for the dealer's location, arriving just as they were opening.

A young salesman greeted her. "I'm Rick. Can I help you find something?"

His appearance didn't impress her: a rumpled sport coat, an open-collared shirt and a turquoise necklace that was better suited to an older woman going to the opera. He immediately grated on her, but despite that, she explained what she was looking for. He grabbed some keys and led her out to the large lot filled with travel trailers and motorhomes, some the size of buses and large trucks, others the smaller ones she wanted to look at.

She pointed to a Mercedes Sprinter. "I want to look at that one."

Rick looked skeptical. "Of course, but that's top of the line, a Mercedes-Benz Sprinter four by four. They're very pricey. I could show you some less expensive used ones."

She felt her stomach clench and her anger rising. "Listen, what don't you understand about the fact that I came here to look at that Sprinter? I've researched them, and I know what I want and what I can damn well afford. If you don't want to show it to me, I'll find someone who will." She started to turn away.

"No. No. Sorry, it's … well, it's fully self-contained and will take you most anywhere from highways and camper parks to the backcountry. It's diesel powered with plenty of power and decent fuel mileage. And it has—"

Jenny interrupted him: "I just told you I've researched them. I want to take it for a test drive."

"Of course. Let me show you—"

"Okay. Let's go then." She walked around to the driver's side.

"Ah, this is a pretty big van. Maybe I should drive and show you how."

Her nerves still on edge from her attack in Paris and jet lag, she glared at him. "Rick, are you always so condescending to women? I drive a Jeep on back-mountain roads in Colorado. I have driven a Ferrari well over 150 miles per hour at the track at Le Castellet in France. I can fucking handle this. I am moments away from telling you to go fuck yourself. Now if you have a fucking problem with me, I'll either go somewhere else or give me the goddam keys. I'm driving."

He looked at her with a wide-eyed, cowed expression. "Yeah. Sure. Sure. Sorry. By all means. You drive."

She climbed into the ergonomical well-fitting seat, looked at the dashboard, and then at the view through the windshield. She loved it already. She took a deep breath and started it, put it in gear, and slowly started out across the lot and onto the busy four-lane street. She loved the higher vantage point where she could see over other cars. She drove along carefully, getting a feel for the large, heavy van.

"I'd like to go out on the interstate for a few miles and see how it feels at higher speeds," she said as she drove onto an entrance ramp to I-40 East. "What I'd really like to do is take it into the backcountry."

Rick hesitated before stammering, "Uh, I … I, I don't know any place close by we could go to."

Jenny smirked. "I can do it soon enough. How much is this van?"

He quoted a number and followed up quickly, "But we can deal. Will you want to finance?"

"No. I'll pay cash. So give me the price if I write you a check today."

He swallowed hard. "I … I'll have to check with my boss when we get back."

She exited the interstate and turned around.

Back at the dealership, Rick said, "Let me show you the amenities in the back, where you'll be living when on the road … or off the road."

"Go talk to your boss and leave me alone. I'm not helpless and can see for myself."

He wiped his now sweaty forehead with a handkerchief, gave her a frightened look, and hustled off. She took a tour of the confined quarters, the bed, toilet, shower, refrigerator, stove, sink, storage, and the small flat screen TV. It was all she needed. It was perfect.

Ten minutes later he returned. "Okay, here's what we can do," and he quoted her a much smaller number plus a hundred dollars toward camping supplies she might need.

"Okay, let's go into your office. I'll talk to your boss. You can do better than this."

Rick stammered, "Okay, you won't need to. Here's our bottom dollar." He gave her an even lower price.

"I knew you'd have a 'bottom dollar.' I can deal with this. I need to call my bank to transfer funds and I'll write you a check or do an electronic transfer. Your call."

"Ah, let's go inside and I'll introduce you to Jessica who does the paperwork, and she'll help you with the payment method."

An hour later the transaction was complete, the check written, papers signed, title transfer signed, and a temporary cardboard license taped in the rear window. She had easily spent her $100 gift certificate on a few items she felt she'd need.

"Now I have to return my rental to Enterprise. Can you follow me and bring me back?"

Rick said nervously, "No, no need. I'll take it back and have someone pick me up. No problem. Then you can be on your way back to Durango."

Screw you, Ricky baby, she thought, *you're just excited about your commission for the $105,500 sale.*

She happily drove away from the dealership and her anxiety level began to drop, like the temperature when the sun goes down on the desert. She headed north on I-25, turned off onto Highway 550 at Bernalillo, and headed to Durango. She laughed out loud. "I'm now a Road Warrior."

The farther she got from the city, from Paris, from people,

the better she felt. She pulled off in Cuba and texted her grandmother that she was fine and on her way home and would be in touch soon.

After an uneventful trip across the New Mexico desert, she arrived home late afternoon, only stopping in Durango for food supplies. She loved the Sprinter. It was easy and fun to drive, and she was ready for the open road. She deleted eleven texts from Jean Luc.

Chapter 26

Jenny returned to an empty house. Chris was gone and now so was Cat. She unpacked a few necessities—the rest could wait—then went out to the pine grove and saw the little mound of fresh soil. Tears came and turned into a sorrowful wail. She fell to her knees and cried so hard it hurt. It all hurt: her furry little friend, Cat, and Helen and Will. Everything. Exhausted, she fell over on her side and lay there until the sun set over the hills. She dragged herself up and back to the house, then into bed, where she fell into a dreamless sleep until after eight the next morning.

She got up and got her bearings, made some coffee and calculated the time in Paris, then called her grandmother.

"Jennifer, thank heavens you finally called. Are you okay? The police have been here. They want to talk to you. Oh my, it's all so crazy. That man in the alley. Did you know him? Did you see him?"

Jenny's heart raced. *Oh shit! The police.* "Whoa. Slow down, Susan. The police? What? Why?"

Jenny's stomach churned as Susan explained what Jenny already knew.

"The police are stymied as to why he was stabbed in his posterior and not killed," Susan said. "They couldn't find any knife anywhere. And why did he have that drug? They are wondering who he might have been after and why."

When her grandmother had finished, Jenny, acting as innocent as she could, asked, "So why do the police want to talk with me?"

"Because someone saw a woman fitting your description running up rue Danton toward our apartment. That was verified by a CCTV. They interviewed everyone on the street and in the apartment building and found out that you'd suddenly disappeared."

"You know I had a flight out very early that next morning. I decided to leave early. I thought you might have invited the Bonnets back to the apartment, and I didn't want to see them or Jean Luc. When I checked in, I was told I could get a red eye to Chicago and changed my flight. That's all."

Susan said, "Well, you need to call this nice Inspector Moreau. He is quite charming and also quite handsome, I would add. He'd like you to call him to answer a few questions. Here's his number. Can you write it down?"

Jenny took down his number, hoping they couldn't pin anything on her. "All right, Grandma, I'll call him. And I'm planning to leave for an extended road trip tomorrow. I'm thinking I might head up to Oregon, and I'm going to drive the Coast Highway all the way down to LA. I need to collect my thoughts. I need to write. I'll be in touch. Thank you for everything. I'll call this Inspector Moreau. I promise."

Susan expressed her concerns about Jenny's "road trip" idea but it fell on deaf ears. They said their goodbyes and ended the call.

Jenny saw she had three more texts from Jean Luc, so she decided to see what he wanted. She saw an apology, that he had just found out that she was wanted for questioning by the police, and it was all his fault and would she please call him.

She thought for a while and decided to see what was going on. He picked up right away. "Jennifer. Are you okay? I am so sorry. I only just heard about you and the police. It's all my fault."

He sounded as panicked as her grandmother.

"Jean Luc, slow down. I'm back home in Colorado and I'm fine. I'm not sure what you're referring to."

"The models. The kidnapper. Everything. Did he attack you? Did you stab him? Cause him to have a broken nose and several missing teeth? What happened?"

"Jean Luc, the models? A kidnapper? What are you talking about?"

"Okay, I am so worried about you. I found out from some of my sources"—*He has sources?*—"that those models you had a confrontation with have close ties to an Eastern European Syndicate located in Marseille, like the Italian mafia. They had this man, Igor somebody, who was to kidnap you and hold you for ransom to get money from me. These people traffic drugs and women and are very bad. I heard this Igor was giving the police much information and the police have made arrests, including those two women that you threw champagne on. They were very bad people. I am so sorry I caused all this. Please. Can you forgive me? Did you stab him?"

Jenny had a hard time keeping from laughing. It was a serious matter, after all, but yet she loved it that she'd stabbed this Igor whoever in the ass. Now she wished it would've been that Russian bitch.

"Jean Luc, if you ever tell anyone this I will come and personally stab you in the ass, but yes, this Igor guy, whoever, or somebody attacked me, and, yes. I stabbed him in the ass. I was scared as shit, Jean Luc. Never so scared in my life. I thought I killed him. But I saw the syringe that was apparently meant for me. I remember him calling me 'American bitch.' He was an asshole, so I kicked him in the face. Now it makes sense. Oh my God. The bastard wanted to kidnap me!"

"Yes. And it was all my fault. Please forgive me."

"Jean Luc! It was not your fault. You certainly didn't plan for it to happen. And it's over. Forget it. I'm going to, now that I'm home and safe from Paris mafia. I'm heading out on a road trip, so they'll never find me, even if they are stupid enough to try."

"I do not think you have to worry now. The two women are facing charges and are in custody, so I've been told. But, Jennifer, you left without a goodbye, and I am heartbroken. Why would you avoid me?"

"I said my goodbye at Le Castellet. I didn't want to have to do it again. I was surprised you were at the reading. I just wanted to get away quietly."

"But when will I ever see you again? Are you coming back to Paris? I will be in your Austin, Texas in October to race there. Will you come?"

"I doubt it, Jean. It would be best for you to forget about me. I'm not the kind of woman you want to be with. I have too much history and most of it's not good. I always seem to cause trouble. Please, just forget me, and it will save us both from heartache." She clicked off and turned off her phone. Tears welled in her eyes. She missed Cat.

A short while later, now knowing she was not a suspect, she turned her phone back on and called this Inspector Moreau.

The phone rang and went to voicemail, so she went back to organizing for her trip. Her phone buzzed a few minutes later. It was Inspector Moreau; she took a deep breath and answered.

"Jennifer Morse?" a man with a thick French accent asked. "This is Inspector Moreau. I have only a few quick questions for you, please. And may we go to FaceTime so I may see you?"

Jenny had her hair up and was a bit sweaty and ragged looking in her t-shirt, but, nevertheless, she went to FaceTime. Her grandmother was right; the inspector was handsome with thick brown hair and hazel eyes, younger than she thought he would be.

"Ah, Mademoiselle Morse, I see you now. You are a very beautiful woman. Thank you for talking to me. I have some questions I must ask. Is this okay time?"

She blushed, caught her breath and said, "Yes, please ask away."

"First, I must tell you, you are not a suspect for anything. I must try to clarify some things. Were you attacked in the alley behind Shakespeare and Company by a man we know as Igor Valanovich?" He went on to state the date and time.

"Yes, I was attacked by a man, but I didn't see his face, and I don't know that name."

"Is this the man?" He held up a picture of a man with a swollen nose and bruised face.

Her eyes opened wide, her heart skipped a beat, and she replied, "It was so dark in that alley, I can't say. I really couldn't see that well, and I was completely in a panic. But I've seen him before, several times. There was a man who I thought was stalking me, but I paid no mind to him as he always disappeared when I glanced his way. I thought I was imagining it. But I saw him well enough at least twice to say that this is the man that was watching me, Igor whatever."

"Thank you. He was most likely waiting for the right time. Can you tell me what happened?"

Jenny told him how the event unfolded, leaving out the part of her stabbing and kicking the man.

She saw him smiling and trying to stifle a laugh. "I must ask this, did you stab Igor Valanovich in the right side of his … how can I say it, 'bum?'"

Now Jenny had to stifle a laugh. "Yes. I stabbed him in the bum."

"And where is the knife you used?"

"In the bottom of the Seine off the Pont Saint-Michele."

"You know it is illegal to carry a knife in Paris? I could charge you," he said, trying to look serious.

"No, I didn't know."

"Why did you throw the knife into the Seine?"

Reliving the event made her anger rise. "Because I was goddam scared shitless! A goddam man tried to attack me, and I was lucky to escape. I'm happy I stuck a knife in his sorry ass, and I'd do it again. I found out that that bastard was trying to kidnap me for ransom. I wish I would've killed the bastard."

Inspector Moreau's eyes grew wide and he sat up very straight. "Mademoiselle Morse, I feel I am fortunate to be thousands of miles from you. You are a woman not to be trifled with. I think Monsieur Valanovich appears to be the lucky one. Yes, he was wanting to kidnap you for ransom, but with his capture and cooperation, the Marseille police have been able to arrest a number of members of a criminal organization. We are grateful you were not hurt in the attack. How did you know about the kidnapping and ransom?"

"I talked with Jean Luc Bonnet, who was apparently supposed to pay my ransom."

"Yes, Monsieur Bonnet. He was very helpful. Your

boyfriend. No? He is a very lucky man to have such a beautiful woman.'

"He is not my boyfriend. Just friends."

"Ah, but not according to him."

"Trust me, Inspector Moreau, he's just a friend."

"Then, I am sorry you live so far away or I would ask you to dinner."

"Do all French policemen flirt with women they are questioning?"

Now he smiled. "Only with the most beautiful ones, Mademoiselle."

She smiled. "Excuse me for saying this, inspector, but you are full of bullshit."

He laughed out loud and she did too. "Thank you for talking with me, Mademoiselle Morse. It has been very much a pleasure. And please, if you ever return to our beautiful city, please let me know. My invitation to dinner will be waiting for you."

She couldn't help but grin from ear to ear. "It has been interesting. And I'll keep your invitation in mind. Goodbye, Inspector Moreau."

"Au revoir, Mademoiselle Morse."

Chapter 27

Being home felt good and Jenny realized that she wanted to stay home for a while and get grounded, that running off again, doing a road trip, maybe wasn't such a good idea. She decided to try to catch up with her life, although the attempted kidnapping left her with neither the energy nor the desire to see anyone. She thought about setting an appointment with her therapist, Joan, but already knew what she'd say, the same thing she'd told her a million times, so she scratched that idea and hunkered down, organizing her Paris notes and starting an outline for her next book. She desperately wanted to have Will give her advice again but didn't want to talk to anyone.

After a few weeks of only going out for necessities and working, one night after her dinner, her best friend, Kelly, popped into her mind, and she knew she should call her.

Kelly answered. "Jenny! Where are you? I didn't know you were back in town, but nobody's seen or heard from you. What's going on? When did you get back?"

Jenny felt a wave of guilt wash over her, knowing she

should have called her sooner. She told Kelly of needing to decompress. "Paris was overwhelming, and along with Chris's shit and my breakdown, I needed some alone time."

"What about Paris? Overwhelming? How was that? It must have been amazing."

With a sigh, Jenny said, "How long do you have? It's quite a story," and she told Kelly about her trip and all that happened.

"God, Jenny, your life is like a bad B movie. Race-car drivers, kidnapping, stabbing and who knows what else you might have done."

Jenny laughed. "That's about right. So what's up with you and Peter? How's Willow?"

"Willow's growing like crazy. She's walking all over the place and getting into everything. I didn't realize how much easier it was when she was confined to her crib or playpen. And the big news is we're moving."

"Helen gave me that news. I can't believe you're leaving. You're my best friend ever. I'm already missing you not being close."

"Yeah, it's been pretty quick. Peter's law firm is opening a branch office in Santa Fe, and they want Peter to head it. It's a great opportunity for him, and he's excited as he'll be working with a lot of the Pueblos down there. We've already bought a house a little outside the city proper. It's a beautiful Santa Fe style adobe with 360-degree views. I'm really excited."

"But what about your work? What'll you do?"

"I already put out feelers and had two offers so far. Both look good, but I'm waiting until after the move."

"So"—Jenny choked back her emotions— "When are you moving?"

"In a few weeks. This all happened so fast. We're going to rent out our house here. At this point, we don't know how long we might be there."

"But what about Will? He dotes on his little granddaughter."

"Helen probably already told you, but they've bought a place in Mexico, in some little village north of Puerto Vallarta. They're planning on going down there for winters. They're considering getting a place in Santa Fe also, maybe a condo or something for part time. Hey, I gotta go. It's already past Willow's bedtime and Peter's out. Safe travels. Talk soon."

"Bye," Jenny said in a hollow voice. Everyone she knew and cared about was moving away. All the good times being crazy with Kelly rolled through her mind like an action-adventure movie. Now she was moving four hours away. And Will and Helen, her mainstays, weren't going to be around for six months or maybe more during winters. And Helen never mentioned about them possibly moving to Santa Fe. She sat for a long time in stunned silence thinking that her life, as she once knew it, was over.

As she lay in bed, the thought wouldn't leave her, *everybody I know is leaving town*. Only Julian and her grandparents would be left. She had some friends, but no one that close. Then she thought of something she'd learned at her meditation workshop those years ago. Meditation? Something she hadn't practiced in a long time. Too long. She considered the teaching, "All one ever has is the moment they are in. There is no past; there is no future, only the present moment." Two other teachings popped into her head from that workshop: "The only certainty is uncertainty," and "Change is the only absolute," or something like that. Jenny fell into a restless sleep, dreaming of being the sole survivor of some mysterious catastrophic event.

The first thing next morning, she called Helen and was greeted by the same line she'd heard from Kelly about not knowing she was back in town.

"I'm sorry, Helen. I needed time for myself."

"You're not planning on hiding in the mountains again, I hope."

Jenny laughed. "No. Nothing so drastic. Just need time and space."

"We've been wondering, hoping you were okay. And I'm ashamed that I haven't tried to reach out to you since my text. Are you okay? How was Paris?"

Jenny took a big breath and told the same story as she'd told Kelly and received about the same response.

When Helen finished commenting on Jenny's Paris experience, she said, "We've missed you."

Taking a breath and trying to not let Helen hear her emotions, Jenny replied. "Yeah. Sucks. And you're moving to Mexico and Santa Fe?"

"What? No. I told you we bought a place in Mexico and plan on spending some time there in the winter, but Santa Fe? No. We maybe mentioned getting something there, but, no. We like it here and the kids will be fine. We'll miss them of course, but it's an easy drive."

"But what about your studio? Who's going to take care of that when you're in Mexico?"

"Amy will be the new manager. I've been grooming her to run it when I'm away. Will has always wanted to travel, and that was the cause of our divorce those years ago. He really wants to get away to warmer climes in the winter. We haven't skied in two years, and there's no reason we can't enjoy the sun and the beach."

"So Will can spend his time writing. How about you? You just going to sit around reading or doing nothing?"

"There are a lot of Americans and Canadians who come to

that area in the winter, so I plan on doing some yoga classes. There's a nice place about a hundred feet from the beach where I can have a class of maybe twenty people. Hopefully you'll come visit and spend time with us. We have two guest rooms, and you'd be welcome for as long as you want. You and Will can write. You can run on the beach and teach a yoga class if you want."

Somewhat relieved, the knot in her stomach relaxed. "You make it sound tempting. Maybe I could. With my main adventure buddy, Kelly, gone, I'm not sure what I'm going to do."

"I can understand. But it's a great opportunity for Peter. We'll miss them too, especially Willow. She's growing so fast. We're having a going-away party Friday night at our house. You'll be there. Five o'clock. Bring nothing but yourself. We're having it catered, so we won't have to fuss. I have to go. I have another call coming in, and I need to take it. See you Friday at five."

The call ended, and Jenny sat staring out into the trees and the sunlight setting over the bluffs. She thought again of Kelly and all the fun they had together, their adventures in the mountains hiking, skiing, trail running, their friendship. Then she'd had these past few years when she seemed to be constantly traveling on book tours. And when she was home, she was exhausted and spent her time resting and preparing for her next tour. Was it all worth it? She missed those years sharing time with Kelly. And Chris, maybe he was right, she hadn't been there for him.

Now dark, crickets began their nighttime chatter. The air cooled quickly, and there was nothing more to think about.

Chapter 28

August came and went. Jenny talked several times with Kelly after their move. She and Peter were settling into Santa Fe. Kelly had found a part-time position with a holistic health center and was loving it. Peter worked some long hours, but the new branch of the law firm was coming together nicely. They seemed happy.

Jean Luc was still trying to convince Jenny to come to Austin for the grand prix in early October, but she still refused.

She hadn't been out or seen anyone since Kelly and Peter's going-away party

, and she decided she needed to do something other than try to work on her book, which had ground to a halt due to her lack of inspiration and motivation. She looked out her office window, saw the camper van, and decided it was time to maybe do that road trip.

A week later, Jenny was on the road north of Monticello, Utah, entering the south end of the red rocks and desert. She was awestruck by the stark colorful landscape.

In Green River, where she stopped to top off her fuel at a truck stop, she looked through the array of trucker's supplies and found a new sheath knife with a six-inch blade to replace her old one now rusting away at the bottom of the Seine.

Electing to avoid Salt Lake City and the busy Interstate 80, she continued west on I-70 to where she found Highway 50, which bore the title of "The Loneliest Highway in the World."

As the miles passed, driving through the vast empty landscape of the Great Basin, her mind opened to reflect on the past year, her physical breakdown, Chris's betrayal, her friends, Paris, and Jean Luc and her feelings for him. Then there was the attack and how that brought back her mistrust and fear of people. She knew in her head that running away and hiding wasn't the answer, but her gut wrenched with the thought of ever relying on or trusting anyone. She thought of Helen and Will, of Kelly and Peter, her dearest friends, and felt a surge of sadness. She thought of Joan, her therapist and confidant, who had helped her with her trust issues before. She thought of Amanda and her magical ways of helping her.

Getting emotional, she pulled off to the side of the road, took some deep breaths and wiped the tears from her eyes. She wanted to call Helen or Kelly just to hear her friends' voices. She tried her cell only to discover there was no service. She took more conscious breaths and tried to find a radio station for some music but found only static. After more breaths, she shook her head to clear it of all those thoughts that wanted to flood it and continued on down the deserted road.

Ely Nevada and a KOA campground would be her first night's stop. It had been a long nine plus hours to get there. She was late getting in and exhausted. Highway 50 had, so far, lived up to its name; she'd hardly seen another vehicle.

Jenny selected the KOA since it was a commercial campground, and having never set up the camper before, she'd thought she'd feel more comfortable there. When she checked in, she selected a site as far away from the main office as she could get. It was easier than she thought to get leveled and hooked up. She sighed with relief and microwaved a frozen burrito.

She had four texts from Jean Luc wondering why she wouldn't respond, asking where she was, and what she was doing. He now seemed so far away, like some figment of her imagination. She also had a text from Susan wondering where she was and whether she was okay. Helen had joined the text worry club as well.

Her mind raced. What was she doing? Where was she going? And why? She was running away again, hiding out, not trusting anyone. Would her childhood traumas never end? She knew the attempted kidnapping in Paris reactivated all her issues of being afraid of everyone, not trusting anyone. Much later she fell into a deep and, thankfully, dreamless sleep.

She awoke early, put on her running clothes and headed out the road, where she turned into the campground which seemed to go forever out into the desert. She hadn't run since a few days before she left Paris, and it felt good to stretch her legs. An hour later she returned to her RV, showered, had a quick breakfast, and was ready to hit the road.

She considered her options and decided to take Highway 6 and head toward Tonopah, Nevada, for her next stop. She got gas and called ahead to reserve a spot at an RV park. It was less than a three-hour drive, so Jenny headed out across the Great Basin at a leisurely pace, checking out the scenery of the desolate American desert, stopping now and then to take photos.

She thought about going back to the commune where she grew up, north of Sacramento, and seeing her old friend Annie, but that thought made her stomach tighten, so she decided against it, opting to keep her original itinerary and go north to Oregon and down the coast to the Redwoods, then to Big Sur. She would take her time along the coast before heading back home. She had no demands or schedule to keep.

Tonopah was a fairly nondescript town filled with cheap motels and, since she was now in Nevada, slot machines. Her campground was okay but more like a supermarket parking lot with water and electrical and sewer hookups, devoid of any trees, plantings or visual amenities. She pulled in between a large motorhome and a fifth-wheel trailer. She ignored her neighbors and hooked up her landlines. It was ninety degrees by her cell phone weather, so she went into the van and turned on the AC, which quickly cooled down the small space.

There was a Mexican restaurant and steakhouse about a block away from the RV park, so she decided to eat out rather than have another microwaved frozen dinner. It was still daylight when she walked over, but the sun was now very low, and the desert cool was rolling in.

It was seat yourself, so she found a table for two in the corner, away from the other diners. She scanned the menu and was ready when the waiter came, ordering a margarita and three chorizo tacos.

About halfway through the meal, she ordered another margarita. Shortly, a decent cowboy band started playing. People moved onto the dance floor. After she'd finished dinner, she sat back to finish her drink and wait for the check. A nice-looking guy in need of a haircut, dressed in a plaid shirt and tight jeans, approached her.

"Care to dance?" he drawled out with a toothy grin and

wide eyes.

Jenny gave him a withering look that would have frozen the town of Tonopah.

"I take that as a 'no.'" He turned on his heel, wandered away and spoke to another man, after which they both looked at her, smiled, and walked away. Soon she saw them both on the dance floor with younger girls, smiling and talking away as they moved to the music.

He just wanted to dance. I could have been nicer. But fuck men. She thought again of Jean Luc and decided he was in a much different category.

With her bill paid, she left the restaurant, the chatter and the band. The man who'd asked her to dance and his friend stood outside the door, apparently getting some air.

As she walked by, the one who'd asked her to dance said, "Good night and have a nice evening."

Jenny felt a pang of regret hit her. She stopped and turned to him. "I'm sorry I was rude to you. I could have just said, 'No thank you' instead of glaring at you."

"Hey, no problem. You didn't want to be bothered, and I got into your space. I apologize for bothering you. You're an attractive woman and looked lonesome is all."

She smiled. "Thank you for the compliment, Cowboy. Have a good rest of the night yourself."

He laughed. "I may look the part tonight, but my name is Richard, and I'm actually a computer engineer and work in the Bay Area. Jesse and I are home visiting our families. Jesse also works in the Bay Area as an environmental engineer. We were high school friends and still hang out together. How 'bout you? You a cowgirl?"

Now completely embarrassed, happy it was dark and they couldn't see her blush, she said, "I apologize again.

Not doing too well tonight, am I? Actually I'm a writer, an author. Novels."

"Tell ya what, let me buy you a drink, and we'll let bygones be bygones."

Jenny thought for a minute. "Sure, why not, but I insist that I buy."

They walked back in and went to the bar for not one but three rounds, one from each of them. They were nice guys, a few years younger than she was. They never flirted or tried to pick her up, but when they left, Richard told Jesse that he'd get the car and Jesse should walk with her and make sure she got back to the campground safely. She was going to protest, but she was pretty drunk; it was now dark and streetlights were minimal at best, so she accepted the offer.

There were hardly any people out now, and she appreciated the male escort, especially after Paris. Back at her camper, they bade each other good night, and she went into her little house and smiled with thoughts about the night and the two nice men she'd met. She had a pleasant time and realized she might have to reassess her ideas on men.

Next morning she checked Google Maps. She could go over to the coast and north or go farther north into central Oregon and then wind down to Crescent City. She wanted to hit the coast as soon as she could, so she decided to skip Oregon and stay on Route 6 until it hooked up with Interstate 205. Then she'd follow interstates and freeways until they connected to the 101 and head north to Highway 1, the Coast Highway. She dreaded heading into city traffic, but if she timed it right, she might be able to shoot on through. On the upside, this would take her by Yosemite National Park.

Chapter 29

After a six-hour drive, she arrived at Yosemite, checked in, and drove into the park, stopping often to do short hikes and take photos of the amazing scenery. At Half Dome she spied several climbers almost to the summit, which made her queasy just watching.

Back at the campground, she noticed two women camped in a tent spot close to hers. One of them saw her looking their way, smiled and motioned her to come over. Reluctant, but seeing the woman's friendly smile, Jenny walked on over.

"Hi, I'm Angie." The woman smiled and pointed to her partner and added, "This is my wife, Sage. Where're you from?"

"Colorado. Durango, Colorado. How about you?"

"Portland, Oregon. We just got married and have a few weeks off. We're just traveling with no itinerary or destination. Just roaming. Sage is opening a bottle of wine. Sit down and have a glass, and we can exchange stories. Here's a chair." She unfolded a sling chair for Jenny.

With everyone seated and each with a large glass of wine,

Sage asked, "Traveling alone? Pretty gutsy of you. Not even a dog?"

Jenny gave her a puzzled look. "Why wouldn't I? I've been alone most of my life and get along quite well."

"Hey, no offense intended. I'm just surprised is all."

"No offense taken, but to be honest, I've had a little rough go at life recently and needed some away time from everyone and everything. Decompressing I guess."

"Anything you want to talk about … or maybe none of our business."

"It's all pretty boring stuff, except for the guy in Paris, well, two guys actually."

"Paris?" Angie exclaimed. "Nothing is ever boring about Paris. Please tell us more."

Jenny gave a brief synopsis of Jean Luc and ended with her attack the night she left and her subsequent purchase of her camper van. Even with a short synopsis, her storytelling, author, and book-signing talk modes all kicked in, and her audience of two greedily absorbed it.

"And so here I am, drinking wine and relating my life to two women I met less than a few minutes ago." She took a big sip of wine and had to smile at herself for her newfound openness.

Angie and Sage both sat staring at her. Sage was the first to comment. "Oh my God, you drove a car that fast? A fucking Ferrari? With a professional race-car driver? And he's hot after you? Oh my God."

Wide eyed, Angie said, "You stabbed your attacker in the ass? You broke his fucking nose? And we were worried about you traveling alone? Holy crap! You aren't afraid of anything. I suppose you climb mountains too?"

"No, don't do any climbing, but I lived in the mountains

by myself for two years."

Sage and Angie didn't say anything for a while, letting it all sink in, then Sage said, "You should write a book."

"Already did, *Sunrise in the Mountains.* It was sort of a best seller for a while."

"You wrote that book?" Angie's eyes grew even wider. "I loved it. You were supposed to do a book signing in Portland but it was canceled."

"Yeah, I'm sorry. I was doing too much and—" She told them about her breakdown and subsequent breakup with Chris, finding it easy and good to unload, if only to strangers. "Okay, enough about me. Tell me about you two. You just got married. Congratulations."

Angie smiled. "Thank you. We've been together for, what? Four years?"

"Actually almost five now," Sage said. "We felt it was time. Both our families still haven't accepted the fact that their daughters are lesbians and not marrying well-to-do, acceptable men, settle down and breed to have more humans to add to an already over-populated planet. Neither family attended our wedding or even sent an acknowledgment."

Angie added, "Yeah, it's hard. Nobody's speaking to us. But maybe they'll come around."

"I'm not holding my breath," Sage said, "but we love one another and both of us wanted to commit to the long haul. And we're happy. That's what counts."

Jenny thought of her own family and how messed up that dynamic was, but she had no comment, just listened.

"Sage is a naturopathic doctor," Angie said, "and I'm a divorce attorney, strictly an advocate for women, of course. I feel I do a good job protecting my clients against 'the boys.' I'm not a man hater, but there's too much testosterone out there."

The conversation continued on through the first bottle of wine, and Jenny suggested they make some dinner over at her camper which had a stove and would be easier to clean up after. They all moved over to Jenny's place and had a dinner of chicken tacos. After cleaning up, they bid good night.

After they left, Jenny sat out enjoying the early evening, thinking of these two women being married. What? Wife and wife? They seemed so happy together. Jenny wondered if she'd be happier with a woman. "No," was her answer. Even in her confused state of being, she knew she liked being with Jesse and Richard last night and enjoyed their company, just like tonight with Angie and Sage.

Dreams of strangers chasing her filled her dreams. She awoke a number of times to do some deep breathing to calm herself, but as soon as she fell back asleep, the dreams continued.

The next morning, she knew it would be afternoon in Paris, so she called Susan to let her know she was okay.

"Jenny, dear, I've been trying to reach you. Are you all right?"

"Sorry, Grandma, I had my phone off. I'm fine. I'm in California. You all okay?"

"We're all good, but we have news. Dean has been invited to be a guest lecturer at the Sorbonne teaching American Business Law … for this year and maybe the next. We're so excited. We've already rented our house in Durango. We needed a little adventure, and Dean is excited to have something to do again. The Bonnets are such great new friends, and we love having the opportunity to stay in Paris. We both love it here. Dannielle and I are now both involved with Jean Luc's foundation which has expanded to focus on specifically helping abused women in Paris as well as the rest of France. Spousal and sexual abuse is rampant here."

Jenny listened to all this and felt it like a punch in the gut.

Now her grandparents. "Wow, slow down, Susan. It sounds exciting. I'm happy for you."

"You'll have to come back now to visit. Jean Luc keeps asking about you. He's really in love with you, I hope you know."

"Yeah, he's made that quite clear, maybe not in those exact words. But I'm really not interested. I keep telling him it won't work. I don't want to be living in hotels and the rest of the time flying to them. I like my home."

"I understand, but he's really such a fine young man. He won't be racing forever."

"But his home is in France. Mine's here. He can't seem to realize that. I don't want a long distance relationship, especially with someone on another continent."

"But, Jenny, things can have a way of working themselves out."

"Yeah, like they did with Chris. I invested five years with that loser. Where's that got me? I don't want another relationship now."

"But someday?" Susan asked, sounding defeated.

"Yeah, Susan. Maybe someday."

They chatted a while longer and then ended the call.

She took her time leaving. It was a short drive to Tracy where she planned to spend the night before going around San Francisco and Oakland to head north to the Coast Highway and the ocean. So she spent more time sightseeing Yosemite, reluctantly leaving to head to interstate and freeway traffic.

She got to her campground in Tracy late, hooked up, ignored her neighbors, had a drink and popped a frozen Mexican dinner into the microwave. The rest of the night she spent trying to write. Tired from last night's restlessness, she went to bed early and, thankfully, passed out into a deep untroubled sleep.

Chapter 30

Next morning, she woke early, wolfed down a protein bar, and headed out on the freeway. As much as she wanted to avoid any city driving, she wanted to see the San Francisco Bay, so she opted to stay on I-580 which would take her by the Bay, through Berkeley, then to Bodega Bay and Wright's Beach Campground, where she planned on spending the night. It was only about a three-hour drive. She timed it right as traffic was light. She pulled off once so she could stop to see the Bay Bridge rising out of the water like some giant red sculpture.

She thought of Chris living there, but it was only a momentary thought.

A while later, she pulled into the campground a little north of Bodega Bay and found a place to back in, separated from her neighbors on both sides by short bushy trees. As soon as she parked, she ran to the beach, now far away since the tide was out. She walked along the water, listening to the low waves rolling in, enjoying the peace. The great expanse of the Pacific Ocean called to her like the Siren songs of *The*

Odyssey. The sand was solid to walk on, and it was early, so she decided on a short run to release the stress of her travels and the realization that when she returned to Durango, everyone would be gone. Pushing back tears, she changed into her running shorts, top, and shoes, and went for a much longer run than she had anticipated.

Returning to her camper, now hot and drenched with sweat, she encountered a couple walking toward her. The man was fairly tall and looked to be Mexican, and the fair-haired woman, while not beautiful, exuded a warm beauty in her smile that made Jenny immediately like her.

"Hi, neighbor," the man said. "Have a good run?" He turned to the woman. "Maybe I need to start running. Exercise would do me good."

The woman poked him. "Yeah, Mick, like you'll never even come to yoga with me." She turned to Jenny. "Excuse us. It's an ongoing thing. I'm Karen, this is Mick. Believe it or not, we're married. Why? It's a question I have yet to answer." She gave Mick a gentle poke in the ribs and smiled up into his adoring eyes.

Jenny laughed at their antics. She liked their gentle banter and the looks they gave each other, all telling how much in love they really were. "I'm Jenny, and, yeah, I had a good run. God, it's so beautiful here. I may never leave."

Karen said, "I think we're camped next to you. Are you in the dark gray Sprinter?"

"Yeah, that's me."

"Well, our motley crew is right next door. Come over and meet Hannah and Russell when you get a minute. Have a cocktail with us. We're just back from two months on the road and are unwinding a bit, so things may get out of hand. Early warning to escape while you can."

Jenny laughed. "Sure. Why not? Let me rinse off and I'll head your way. Which side are you on?"

"Over there." Mick motioned to two small tents and a van similar to hers. "Come on over. You can party with us and get wasted, so we won't be bothering you."

Jenny laughed again. "Sounds fun to me." She considered this was not at all like her, usually being much more cautious with strangers. Then she thought about how foolish she was with the two men in Tonopah. Even with that, she felt way more adventurous than usual, out of her usual comfort zone.

Jenny quickly showered, conserving water since she had no hookups and only had what was in her thirty-gallon tank. She'd bought three gallons at the grocery store for drinking, saving the camper tank for showering and cleaning.

Still debating whether to accept the invite, she sat outside looking at the ocean, considering all the places that were out there: Hawaii, Japan, China, Indonesia, Australia and on and on. A female voice awakened her from her thoughts.

"Hi, I'm Hannah. Mick and Karen said you might want to join us for a cocktail and chat. We're all just hanging out and having margaritas and wine, so come on over. You might want a wrap as it can cool down pretty quickly. So you're Jenny?"

Jenny got up and saw an attractive woman with wild hair and hauntingly cold-gray eyes like her own. She felt familiar, as if they'd met before. She pushed the thought away and said, "Yeah, I'm Jenny, Jennifer Morse to be totally formal. Thanks for the invite. I was just languishing in the beauty of the ocean. Nice to meet you." She extended her hand to be taken in by a very strong grip.

"So first time at the ocean?" Hannah asked.

"No, once before, for a few hours, at San Luis Obispo a few years ago. I lived in central California for eighteen years but never made it to the ocean. Let me grab my chair."

They both started walking. Jenny felt something strange about this woman, still thinking she knew her from somewhere. She again brushed the thought aside.

Hannah continued, "Lived here? Where're you from now?"

"Colorado. I was born in Denver, raised in California and live in Durango now."

They arrived at the camp and were greeted by Karen and Mick and a tall, good-looking man who got up to greet her. "Hi, I'm Russell. Come join us. Two choices: margaritas or chardonnay."

She thought for a moment. "I'd like a margarita, please."

Russell picked up a glass, added some ice from a cooler, picked up a pitcher and poured the crystal-clear drink, then, as a final gesture, added a lime wedge.

"Thank you." Jenny received the glass and took a deliciously refreshing drink, reminding herself to pace her drinks.

Hannah said, "Jenny was saying she's from Colorado but lived here for eighteen years. How old were you when you moved here?"

"My brother and I were just babies. My mother died at childbirth so my father relocated here." A dark cloud came over her as she remembered the commune; she wanted to avoid mentioning it. "I grew up a little north of Sacramento. I went back to Denver when I was eighteen and to college there."

With noticeable intensity, Hannah asked, "You said you had a brother? How far apart were you in age?"

"We were twins."

"I need to ask, did you maybe live in a commune?"

Jenny hesitated. "Yeah. Why?"

Hannah became agitated. "How old are you?"

Russell noticed her agitation and said, "What's going on?

You're like giving her the third degree. Slow down."

Jenny felt increasingly uncomfortable. "Maybe I should just go." She started to get up.

"No, please. No," Hannah said. "Just please, please hear me out. How old are you? I have to know. Please."

Jenny said, "I'm twenty-eight."

"Fuck! Oh fuck! Oh fuck! Excuse me." Hannah jumped out of her chair, grabbed her cell phone, and headed for the beach, punching in a number as she went.

The others all watched her, wondering what was going on. They overheard her screaming, "Goddammit, I'm fucking twenty-five years old, and I fucking want to know who my father is. Now tell me, goddammit!"

The tidal waves now rolling in hid the rest of the conversation. A few minutes later, she returned, looking like she'd seen a ghost. With a trembling voice, she asked, "Jenny, is your father by any chance Julien Morse?"

Jenny sat up straight, eyes widened. She paled. "Yes, Julien's my father. What's this about?"

The other three just sat there, barely breathing, with their eyes wide and glancing back and forth between the two women.

Hannah took a deep breath. "He's mine too. We're sisters."

There were three audible gasps, and three sets of eyes moved from Hannah to Jenny, seeing her stunned-deer-in-the-headlights expression. Jenny dropped her drink and slumped over in her chair. Mick was closest and was there to catch her and lay her gently on the sand. Karen grabbed a towel and got some ice from the cooler.

Jenny's eyes opened slowly, seeing four faces she seemed to vaguely recognize. "What happened? You were all there, and Hannah was talking about something and everything went black."

Hannah held ice on her forehead. "I'm so sorry. What I said was too abrupt. I'm sorry."

"What were you saying? Something about Julien? Oh my God! Father? Sisters? Sisters? You and me? That can't … How is that possible? I need to get up."

Hands got her up and back into her chair. Mick handed her a glass of water and ice. She quaffed down a healthy slug. "So tell me what the hell this is about."

Hannah moved a chair and sat facing her. "Here's the story. My mother, Meg, lived in that commune and had a brief affair with Julien resulting in her getting pregnant with me. She knew you and your brother, even took care of you for a while. But things were getting out of hand at the commune with drugs and sex parties, so she bailed. She begged Julien to bring you two and leave with her, but he refused to leave and refused to let her take the two of you with her. She left and went to live with my grandparents and finished her bachelor's degree along with giving birth and caring for me. She went on to earn her master of fine arts in painting.

"She then moved into an artist's co-op in San Francisco where she met her partner, Frank, the greatest guy ever, well except for maybe Russell," she said with a wink. "Mom hit it big on the art scene and has done very well with her art. She is represented in galleries throughout the West, especially cities like LA and Frisco. She and Frank live in Sausalito. Russell and I have a place there too. So how's Julien? What can you tell me about him?"

With her head about to burst with all this information, Jenny said, "Excuse me. I need some space for a minute to process this." She got up and walked toward the ocean. She heard Russell say, "No, Hanna, let her go."

Jenny walked along the incoming tide, letting the sound settle her nerves. *A sister? Her mother cared for us? I need to go back.*

She returned to the camp and sat down again. Mick offered her a drink which she refused. "I'm sorry. I needed to process this for a minute. You were asking about Julian. He's living in Durango. He has a great job with a large general contractor that is out of Denver and has a branch office in Durango where he was recently appointed general manager. He has a great girlfriend. I keep hoping they'll eventually get married."

"What else? What was he like as a father?"

Jenny made a point to look at everyone hanging on every word and said, "Maybe some other time."

Russell nodded. "Karen, Mick, let's go make some food. Leave these two to talk." The three of them left for the front of the van where food prep was to take place.

Jenny and Hannah sat for a few minutes, not knowing what to say. Jenny broke the silence. "A sister. Family. And we meet here at a campground on the Pacific Ocean. I … I don't know what to say. It's so completely weird and so wonderful. Hannah. Hannah. Hannah. My God, I need to know everything about you."

"And I need to know everything about you, but maybe now's not the time or place. What are your plans? Are you heading back home?"

"I had planned on going to the Redwoods and spending some time there. I'm a writer and need time to reflect and write."

Hannah thought for a moment. "So would you mind a passenger? Someone you don't know but would like to? Someone who needs time to do some writing herself?"

"You're a writer too? Really? How weird is that?"

"It's a different type of writing. I'm a singer/songwriter and have a bunch of ideas running around in my head. Oh yeah, Russell and Mick are my bandmates who make everything happen. Without them, well—"

"Oh God, I'm so wound up giddy with all this … Of course. It'd be great. We could be sisters. We could learn everything about each other. It'd be so much fun to have you."

Jenny paused and looked at Hannah, then went over and embraced her. Hannah returned the embrace. Suddenly Jenny began to cry softly on Hannah's shoulder. Hannah held her tighter and also cried. They stood for a long while before parting and wiping their eyes on their sleeves.

"I'm sorry," Jenny said. "It's just, just too much to take in."

"I know. My mother told me about you two kids. I know she loved you both and felt some responsibility for you both, but she'd never tell me about Julien. As much as I begged, never, until tonight when I told her about you. She's completely out of her mind knowing we met. She wanted us to come back tonight so she could meet you. But, hey, us sisters are going to the Redwoods. God, I already love you."

Jenny took a moment before she could answer, her voice quivering, "I already love you too."

They heard a shout, "It's food. Come now before I throw it out."

Jenny and Hannah each poured a margarita and headed over to find everything prepared for tacos. Delicious spicy smells permeated the ocean air. Everyone dove in.

While eating, Hannah told everyone of their plans, calling it a sister's writing retreat. Russell seemed a little miffed, but Hannah told him to grow up. It would only be for a week or so.

"But we have our Friday gig now that we're back."

"You and Mick can handle it. You two are great together. I've heard you jamming."

"But everyone comes to hear you, not us."

"Then they'll have to get over it. Tell them the truth, that I'm on a writer's retreat. I need some time to write some more tunes to keep them entertained. If they have a problem, too bad. I seriously need some time."

With all cleaned up, the three pulled out their instruments: guitars for Hannah and Russell and bass for Mick. Jenny and Karen sat back, hunger satiated, fresh drinks in hand while the band tuned and began playing.

"They're really good," Jenny whispered to Karen.

"Yeah. They've played festivals and venues from the Midwest to here and back. People are drawn to Hannah's music. Of course the guys help. We have a lot of fun on the road, but it can become a little tedious sometimes. It's always good to get back home."

They sat and listened, and a few other campers came over for the free impromptu session, clapping and cheering after each song. By nine o'clock, Jenny was starting to yawn. The ocean air, her run, all the emotions of the day were wearing on her, and she needed to hit her bed.

During a break, she wished all a thank you and good night over the pleas for her to stay for a while longer, but she shook her head. "I'm falling asleep. The music is great, but I need my bed."

She lay in bed with the windows open for the cool sea air. The music rolled in, lulling her to sleep, then she heard who she thought were Hannah and Russell arguing.

"How can you just leave? Two weeks? What are you thinking? We have our weekly gig. We have to practice. We have another tour coming up in three months. How can you just pack up and leave with your wacky so-called sister?"

"Wacky sister? Fuck you. You and Mick can handle two weeks. You both have plenty of your own material. And practice? Practice what? We haven't had a new tune in over two years. I don't need to practice this old shit we've been doing for years. You want a new CD? What're we gonna do? Oldies revisited? I need time to write, and I never have a chance when I'm around you. There's always something you want to try new, but you never give me the chance. All your anal shit is being the same as when we met. I thought you were over all that, but no. You're as fucking nitpicky anal as ever. I'm going."

Jenny heard Karen say, "Guys. Guys. Slow down."

Then Mick added, "Yeah, Russell. It'll be fun with just us guys. A new 'boy band' in the making. Both of you. No need to be doing this."

Russell said, "But going off with this woman she thinks is her long lost sister? Give me a break. All this commune shit with your mother and this Julien whoever, it's all crazy."

Hannah spoke up with a shaky voice, "How fucking dare you! My mother lived there. She did what she needed to do and did the best she could. You lived off her and Frank's hospitality for two years. Now you, what? Think she's beneath you? Ha! Fuck you. I'm done."

Jenny heard what sounded like a chair falling over against something followed by a rustling, then Russell saying, "But Hannah, you just can't leave."

"Oh can't I? Just watch me. See me. This is me leaving."

A few minutes later, Jenny, now wide awake with her heart racing, heard a tapping on her door. She opened it to Hannah, standing there with her guitar, backpack, and a sleeping bag.

"Can I come in?" she asked, her voice quivering.

"Of course, please."

"Did you overhear all that? God, he makes me so mad sometimes I could just slap him. He gets into his old controlling self-righteousness; thinks he needs to control the whole show. I'm sorry. Can I crash on your floor or something? I can't be in the tent with him right now." Tears ran down her face.

Jenny grabbed some tissues. "The bed is big enough for both of us. You'll sleep there with me. No floor. We're sisters and can pretend we're young girls. It'll be fine. Are you sure you're okay?"

"I think I am now. Thanks. Now I'm really tired."

As they lay there and Jenny heard Hannah's breath deepen into sleep, she felt a great warmth in her heart. For the first time, she realized that this was what love really felt like.

Chapter 31

In the morning the two women spoke only a few words to each other, as if they were afraid of last night and their discovery. There was too much to say, and neither knew where to start.

As they drove into Fort Bragg, Hannah broke the silence, wistfulness in her voice. "Russell and I stayed here when we first met. It was so beautiful then. It was an amazing time. We were so much in love."

Jenny asked how they'd met, and Hannah told her of her hitchhiking across the West and how Russell had picked her up in Western Iowa and how much of a nerd he was, shy and so reserved, controlled and cautious. She chuckled at the memory and went on about how she coaxed him into a sweat lodge at the Rosebud Reservation. She thought for a moment. "I believe that sweat might have been the catalyst for his awakening to life. It seemed that his emotional anchor seemed unhinged afterward."

"What's a sweat lodge?" Jenny asked.

"Think of a really long hot sauna in pitch black, crammed in with a bunch of other people in a circle sitting on a dirt floor where everybody prays."

Jenny furrowed her eyebrows. "Sounds like a whole lot of fun."

Hannah laughed. "It is truly a beautiful experience. Maybe you and I should make a trip up to the Res."

"Or, maybe not. So … what happened after the sweat lodge?"

"Well, we ended up traveling together, becoming friends, discovering each other and enjoying all the sights we saw along the way. He was a beginner, or maybe intermediate-level guitar player, and we started playing music and did a few open mics along the way until … until I started falling in love with him.

"Then my own shit started getting in the way, and I got scared and bailed. I went to a retreat center where I'd been before and got my head screwed back on and the courage to tell him about when I was in a really bad time in my life; when I almost died due to a drug overdose, got busted, and spent two years on probation. My so-called boyfriend at the time got busted for distribution and is still in the slammer as far as I know. Then there were the sex videos"—she looked away and wiped her eyes with her sleeve— "I can't go into that right now. Russell met me there at the retreat center, and he decided to do a four-week retreat by which time my commitment would be finished. I think he got a lot from his experience with the incredible Tibetan teacher who is the mainstay of the center. We left there, and the rest is pretty much history."

"Wow, that's quite a story. Hey, here's our campground. It's early, but let's check in and then go explore."

"Yeah, I only packed for two days, so I need a few things, like more underwear."

They asked the camp host when checking in and were told there weren't any stores in town for what they needed. Best shot would be Santa Rosa or Eureka.

After spending the next day shopping for Hanna, driving through some beautiful landscapes, and sharing more of their lives, they camped and settled in for the night.

The next morning they explored the Redwoods National Park in awe of the giant trees. Jenny couldn't get enough photos of the giants and Hannah posing. They checked out The Big Tree, 306 feet tall with a sixty-eight-foot circumference and a twenty-two-foot diameter, some 1,500 years old. By noon they were back at the campground, having lunch, then they settled into some writing. The next few days followed the same pattern.

Jenny loved being with Hannah. It was like they'd known each other forever. She was comfortable to be with, smart, and had wisdom beyond her years. They shared their stories. Jenny's mostly were all recent; she avoided getting too far back into her past.

The night before they were to head down to Sausalito, they made a nice dinner with cocktails during prep time and had wine with their food. By the time dinner was finished, they were both pretty tipsy and giggling at some stupid thing Jenny had said when Hannah looked at her and said with all seriousness, "Why are you avoiding anything about when you were growing up? All I ever hear about is Durango. What really went on after my mother left?"

Jenny paused, peering out into the giant trees in the fading light. "Okay, but it's not very pretty. It can be encapsulated into a youth surrounded by drugs and alcohol, neglect, and sexual abuse. I was sexually abused by my father's, ah, our father's mistress. Then I was raped when I was fourteen.

That's when I started carrying a hunting knife, the same one I stabbed good ol' Igor in the ass with. My grandparents hired a private investigator who eventually found Michael and me. They sent us each a nice sum of money for our eighteenth birthday. I escaped to Denver with mine. Michael, I don't know what he did with his.

"My grandparents supported me through college which I'm surprised I ever made it through because I'd gotten to the point where I didn't trust anyone and had become completely anti-social. After graduation, I hitchhiked to Durango and spent the next two years hiding in the mountains or in a small deserted cabin in winter.

"Then the cabin burned down, and I met Will when I needed a place to camp for a night. We got hit by an early snowstorm and the ensuing circumstances led him to become my savior, mentor, and father figure. I love him more than I can ever say.

"He helped me in so many ways, plus mentoring me through my first book which turned out to be a success. I dumped my cheating boyfriend, went to Paris, met a race-car driver, almost got kidnapped, stabbed the bastard, and now here I am with my sister, Hannah." She finished by turning to look at Hannah.

Hannah was about to speak, but stopped for a moment to consider, then asked, "So where's Michael in all this? He's your twin, right?"

Jenny answered with harsh bitterness, "He turned into a misogynistic, violent creep, got arrested for attacking several women and committed suicide in jail. I was almost one of his victims. The shock of it put me in the hospital with a nervous breakdown. I've since found out, through hypnosis, that he was the one who raped me when I was fourteen. He was completely sick and twisted. I try not to hate him, and I guess have pretty much forgiven him. The circumstances he grew up with shaped him. I was lucky I escaped into my own world early on."

There was a long pause until Hannah said, "I'm sorry. God, I can't imagine. I'm so sorry. Are you okay?"

"Yeah. After all my therapy and with some really great friends, I'm doing better. I guess I'm still feeling the effects of my ex being a two-timing cheat. The kidnapping thing didn't help. But then you and I met and found out who we are to each other. I'm happy right now, very happy."

"So a race-car driver? What's that about?"

Jenny related the story of Jean Luc and his wanting a relationship with her and her refusal of his overtures.

Hannah said hesitantly, "He sounds like a decent guy. And you just don't like him?"

"Yeah, I like him, really like him a lot. He's really sweet, charming, considerate, wealthy beyond belief, and really good looking. But I just got rid of Chris. He turned out to be such an ass. I don't know if I can ever trust another man, especially with my past trust issues. It all seems too much at the wrong time. Know what I mean?"

"I see your point, but sometimes, things present themselves and you need to pay attention. The universe gives us things when we least expect but when it thinks we are ready for it or need a new challenge to face, whether good or bad. It's like when Russell picked me up when I was hitchhiking. God, he was such a nerd. Completely out of his element. I couldn't even begin to tell you what his element even was. He was so completely clueless about life.

"But I knew he was safe. After my own stupid idea of hitchhiking around the country and getting picked up by truckers who wanted a quicky for giving me a ride. Then there were the drugged-up or drunk cowboys. Russell was very safe, afraid of his own shadow.

"I think somehow, he saved me from my own drama, and I think I saved him from his. He's really a sweet guy, and I know I went off on him harder than I should've. I turned off my phone when we left and haven't looked at it since. I wanted some space, and we need to talk face to face, not through texting. That night when I discovered who you were wasn't the right time for him to start his control thing with me."

Jenny poured each of them the remaining wine. "I'm sure he's fine. And thank you for the advice about paying attention to what's given you. I'll think on it."

Chapter 32

The Spanish colonial house was beautiful. Jenny felt nervous and a bit giddy as they walked to the front door. Hannah opened it without knocking. "Hey. Anybody home?"

"In here, Hannah, in the kitchen. You're early," came a female voice.

A moment later an older version of Hannah appeared, wiping her hands on a towel. She saw Jenny, stopped in her tracks, and stared. "Oh my God, oh my God, you're Jennifer. Oh my God, let me look at you. You're so beautiful."

Hannah's mother, Meg, stood there for another few moments, looking at her, then came and threw her arms around Jenny in a seemingly never-ending hug. "I never thought I'd ever see you again, and here you are. Serendipity is an interesting and wonderful thing. I can't believe it. Come in. Come in. How's Michael? Do you see Julian?"

"Whoa, slow down, Mom. We have time. We just got here. Where's Frank?"

"He's out on a job and will be back around six. I just came

in a while ago and started prepping for dinner. Come in and let's sit. Can I get you anything, Jenny? Iced tea? Water? I just cannot believe this is happening. You kids were so beautiful. I cared so much for you and begged Julian to leave with me. It broke my heart to leave you there. I'm sorry. I'm just so excited. Can I get you anything? Iced tea? Water?"

Jenny swallowed and took a breath. "Water would be fine."

Hannah said, "Mom makes great iced tea. I'll get them. You two can talk."

Meg's eyes shone with delight. "So, Jenny, tell me about yourself; what are you doing now? Where are you living? Where's Julian? Do you see him ever?"

Jenny answered her questions, dreading the one she knew would eventually come, the "What about Michael?" question.

When Jenny finished her narration, Meg said, "Julian was going downhill with drugs and alcohol when I left. He never got over your mother dying. I worried for you kids and thought about returning several times to see if you were okay, but life always got in the way. When did you leave the commune?"

"Right when I turned eighteen. I got the hell out. It was awful living there with the constant drunken orgies, and the kids were horrible bullies. Thank God I had my books and could hide away most of the time. Then there was Annie. She was sort of my protector and did her best at being my home-school teacher. She did a good job as I was able to pass my GED and get into college."

"I remember Annie and a few of the others. So where's Michael? What's he doing?"

"He's dead. Committed suicide."

Meg's eyes widened and she sucked in a breath. "I don't understand. He's dead? Suicide. What do you mean?"

Jenny again told the sordid story of him raping her, his

choices, and his abuse of women, now realizing just how much anger she still had toward him even with her efforts at forgiveness.

Hannah returned with a tray with three tall glasses of iced tea and relieved them with the distraction from the news about Michael. Meg directed her attention to Hannah. "Is Russell managing okay with you being gone?"

Hannah set the tray down and handed Jenny and her mother each a tall glass of tea. "I wouldn't know. We had a fight the night before Jenny and I left, and I've had my phone off. Maybe I should check." She got her phone. "Wow, it still has some charge left. Let me look. Yeah, he sent several texts." She paused to read them. "Oh my God, listen to this, 'Hannah, I'm sorry. You were right. I'm being an idiot again and I apologize. I'm going up to Ashland to the retreat center to meet with Rinpoche and get some grounding. I'll be up there for at least two weeks. Enjoy your time with Jenny. That is such a wonderful surprise for you. See you soon. Love you always.'

"Just when I'm so pissed at him, he does something like this. Now I can't wait to see him."

They heard the back door open, and in walked a tall man with a chiseled face and a square jaw, a sleeveless t-shirt drawn across a broad chest with muscular tattooed arms hanging out. His narrow waist held up blue jeans. Jenny's eyes widened, and she felt her heart beating faster.

"Hannah, you're back. Come here and give me a big hug."

Hannah jumped up and rushed into his arms. "Hey, Frank. Great to be back."

His gaze fell on Jenny. "And you are Jenny. Man, I can see a resemblance between you two, same high cheekbones, same eyes, and both beautiful women. Come here and let me give you a hug."

Jenny blushed both at his remark and her racing heart. She hesitated, then got up and was crushed into a hug against a hard male body, like she remembered having from Jean Luc. That didn't help her racing heart at all.

Meg said, "Okay, I have everything ready for dinner. It's cocktail time. We usually do margaritas and go to the hot tub for a soak. Will you join us?"

"Of course," Jenny replied. "I've missed my tub and my soak time. And I'll try a margarita, but not strong, please."

Frank laughed. "You got it, three not strong and one regular for me." He left for the kitchen.

"Let's get our things out of the van, Jenny. You'll be staying here in the guest bedroom. Our place is too small, and I know Mom wants us both here."

On the way in with what they needed, Hannah counseled Jenny, "We usually soak naked. If that makes you uncomfortable, I'll say something to Mom and Frank."

Jenny considered this interesting factor. She'd always soaked naked by herself and with Chris, early on. It would be okay with Hannah maybe, but with Frank and Meg? "I don't know. I think I need to pass."

"Oh, come on. It'll be fine. Nobody's gonna stare or try to embarrass you." Hannah laughed. "I remember the first night when Russell was here, I forgot to forewarn him. You should have seen his expression when he discovered everyone was naked. I couldn't stop laughing. It was precious."

Jenny was trying to quell her desire to see Frank naked. *Why am I so obsessed with Frank?*

"I really don't think I can be naked in front of Meg and Frank. There's too much baggage from when I was a girl. I just can't do it. Please don't let me stop you all."

"Okay, I can understand that, but please come and hang out … after we're in. I suppose we are a little bohemian in some regards. But we're harmless."

Frank had made a pitcher of margaritas, either weak or strong, only he knew. Once he, Meg and Hannah were situated, Jenny felt okay to join them near the tub. She had her drink and sat close enough to participate in the conversation which centered around Jenny and Hannah, their discovery of being half sisters, and their trip together.

Meg asked, "What are your plans? What happens next?"

Hannah spoke first. "I'd like it if Jenny would maybe spend a few weeks here. I need to catch up on a few things, like talking to Russell when he gets back. Then I'd like to go with Jenny to Durango to meet my father, if all that would be okay with you, Jenny."

"Sure. I have no schedule to be anywhere. I'd like that."

Later after dinner, they sat out by the fire pit, enjoying the sunset and dessert.

Meg sniffed and wiped her sleeve across her eyes. "I'm so happy how this is turning out. Hannah, I was so afraid all those years of telling you about your father. I was wrong, and I'm sorry. I'm so happy Jenny's here and that we all met. It's like a weight has been lifted from me."

"It's okay, Mom. You had your reasons. As you always told me, everything happens for a reason. I'm whipped and need sleep. I think Jenny's probably ready to get some sleep too."

Jenny nodded. "Yeah, my eyes are starting to go shut. Thanks so much for tonight and for having me. I'm happy too. It's like I found a whole new family."

Hannah and Jenny left and got ready for bed. Jenny crawled under the covers and closed her eyes, but as soon as she did, she thought of Frank. She couldn't understand her attraction to him. Then she thought of Jean Luc. She'd never seen him other than in his race gear and in a shirt and trousers. But she still knew he had the same broad shoulders and narrow hips as did Frank. Maybe she was transferring the attraction she really had for Jean Luc to Frank. Her mind raced with fantasies about both men. The only man she'd ever known was Chris, and though his body wasn't fat, it was fleshy and soft. Not like Frank. And not like Jean Luc. She remembered the hug and the kiss they shared at Le Castellet and how hard his body had felt. Sleep eventually came, and Jean Luc and Frank filled her dreams.

After breakfast the next morning, Jenny went with Meg to see her studio. Meg turned on the light.

"Here, let me show you these so you get an idea of my art." She showed Jenny several finished paintings.

Meg noticed the confusion clouding Jenny's face. "Yes, they are a bit much, aren't they? I was working on changing my brushstrokes, and maybe discipline won out over my better artistic sense as these don't work anything like I wanted. Here are two older paintings. You can see the difference."

Still confused, Jenny said, "No offense, but I don't know what I'm looking at. I never paid much attention to art."

Meg laughed. "No offense taken. My work is abstract art. The easiest way to explain abstract art is that it isn't meant to depict some recognizable scene but is intended to evoke emotion."

"Okay, now I can understand, because I get a sense of exhilaration in looking at the one on the left. The one on the right gives me a sense of foreboding. Plus, they both seem pleasing to my eye."

"You got pretty much what I was trying to do with these. And thanks for the compliment. But you're a writer, right?

That's an art unto itself. Hannah mentioned your book, and I'll look for it the next time I'm in town. I'd love to read it."

"I'll warn you, it's not a real happy book. It's a third-person account loosely based on my life, mostly fiction, but many of the circumstances actually happened, sort of an enhanced memoir. So you'll get sort of a glimpse into my childhood. There are only a few who actually know this, so I trust you to keep what I just told you confidential. My editor and publisher don't even know."

Meg gave a warm smile. "Never heard it."

The next week, Jenny accompanied Hannah and Meg to yoga, and she and Hannah went with Frank one day into San Francisco to see one of his jobs. Jenny was awed by his skill in restoring doors and making moldings for the old Victorian style houses that were so prevalent in the city.

Hannah took Jenny to the city twice to sightsee. During one trip, Hannah took her to City Lights Bookstore. Jenny was overwhelmed as she had been at Shakespeare and Company and spent hours browsing, limiting herself to only six books. She thought about all she brought home from Paris sitting unread at home on her bookshelf.

Meg, Hannah, and Jenny were sitting on the patio waiting for Frank to come home when Hannah's phone buzzed. It was Russell, and she went into the house to talk.

When she returned fifteen minutes later, Meg asked, "So is he on his way back? He's been there now for over two weeks."

Hannah didn't reply for a few moments as she was still digesting the conversation. "Well, no. He's decided to stay and do a six month retreat. He said he realized how much stuff from his childhood he hasn't dealt with, and in the last two weeks, it's all been surfacing. He's had some good meetings with Rinpoche and between them, they feel it will be most beneficial for Russell to spend the time in contemplation and finally come to grips with his past and the control issues he's been dealing with lately."

Meg nodded. "I think it's a good idea. I've noticed how he's been lately, how he's been treating you. He's been getting a little too uptight."

Jenny frowned in confusion. "What's a rinpoche?"

Hannah answered, "The word rinpoche in Tibetan translates to 'precious one.' It also means that he has achieved enlightenment in a past life and wouldn't have to have any more rebirths. A rinpoche is regarded as one who has great compassion and has elected to come back in human form for another life, or lives, in order to teach us how to attain enlightenment. His name is Tenzin Lhundup Karma, and he's the head of the center. He has the equivalent of probably two or three PhDs and is really smart and a beautiful human being. I was up there two different times. I'm sort of jealous of Russell."

She shrugged. "Now we'll have to cancel our next tour. And that's okay. There's new material I want to develop. I think Mick'll be okay with it. I know he has several consulting jobs lined up and will be happy not to have the pressure of trying to do consulting work along with prepping for six weeks on the road. Mick holds a PhD in economics, focusing on the Pacific Rim and international trade. He's always in demand.

"Mick and I'll be doing our weekly gig downtown tomorrow night. I'll miss Russell's backup, but Mick and I work well together for harmonies. You're all coming down, of course."

Meg nodded. "Of course we will."

On Friday morning Jenny awoke to a text from Jean Luc inviting her to come to the Belgian Grand Prix at Spa-

Francorchamps the next week. He mentioned he was in a tight race for the championship and she brought him luck. The last comment made her smile.

She went to meet Hannah for the morning meditation session that Hannah insisted upon every day.

"Sleep well?"

"I did. I had a text from Jean Luc inviting me to Belgium for the Formula 1 race there. He never gives up, like he'll send his private jet for me and everything."

"A private jet? Really? He would do that? Private jet and all? Really? Is this guy rich or what?"

"Oh yeah. He makes a boatload of money driving a car fast. A really big boatload." Jenny laughed.

"You should go, Jenny. It'd be more exciting than hanging around here."

"You know I just got out of that relationship with Chris, and I already had trust issues. I just don't think I can trust a man right now, and I'm afraid of getting into another relationship."

"But you like this Jean Luc?"

Jenny stared out the window. "Yeah. I really do. I really do like him. He makes me feel respected and wanted in, I don't know, in a really sincere way I guess."

Hannah cocked her head and regarded Jenny thoughtfully. "You know, you've brought up Chris every time we talk about relationships. How long are you going to let him hold your power? How long do you want to live under his shadow? There're good guys out there, Jenny. Russell, who I love completely. Then there's Mick, who's a great guy. And Frank, who has been my father. I love and trust those three guys more than I can say. Excuse me for saying, sis, but I think you need to redirect your thinking. Let's go and meditate. We'll talk later."

An hour later, the two women emerged from the quiet solitude of the meditation room and went to the kitchen to brew some tea. As the water was heating, Jenny said, "You're right. I am still living under the Chris cloud. Maybe I should go and see what happens. Maybe something will work out … or not. But I want to hang around with you. Maybe we should both go. It'd be great to have you with me. Want to?"

"Really? He wouldn't care?"

"As long as I was there, he wouldn't care one bit. In fact he'd probably be excited to meet you. He is a truly nice guy."

"Text him back and tell him your sister is coming with you."

Jenny checked time differences in her head. "Yeah. I'll call him now."

It only took a moment until he answered. "Jennifer?"

"Hi, Jean. Yeah, it's me. Got your text this morning, and I think I might come. But on the one condition that I can bring my sister, Hannah, with me."

"Of course you can bring your sister. I didn't know you had a sister."

"Half sister actually, and I didn't either until a few weeks ago. It's a long story. I'll explain when I get there. If there's any chance you might see my grandparents, please don't say anything. They don't know, and we need to be the ones to tell them."

"But of course. I will send my plane for you and make all the arrangements for you and your sister, Hannah. You make me so happy. It is so beautiful there in the Ardenne Forest. It will be a great weekend. Thank you. I will be anticipating seeing you. I am so happy. Do not worry about anything. I'll send you all information on when the plane will arrive in Durango for you."

"Oh, wait. I'm not in Durango. I'm in California, by San Francisco. We'll have to leave from here."

"That will be no problem. I will send you flight information. Oh, *ma cherie*. I'm so happy I could fly."

"Just be careful when you're driving that red car and don't think about flying."

"But of course. I am always careful. I will send information soon. I will be happy when you are here. Goodbye, *ma cherie*."

"Quit calling me that, and I look forward to seeing you too. Bye." She could almost see him doing a fist pump, but her heart was pounding, and she was short of breath. *Darn you, Hannah.*

Jenny called for Hannah. "Hey, there you are. Get your passport ready, and we need to go shopping for some new clothes."

That night at the historic bar on the waterfront with historic black and white pictures hanging on the walls, people sat on stools at a bar once frequented only by hard men who stood, drinking warm beer or whiskey, smoking cigars or chewing tobacco. The old, worn planked wooden floor was now filled with tables of people enjoying pizza, craft drinks, and Sonoma wines. At one of those tables Meg, Frank, Karen, and Jenny sat enjoying Hannah and Mick's music, eating good pizza along with beer and wine.

Chapter 33

A few days later, Jenny and Hannah sat comfortably in Jean Luc's private jet somewhere over the Atlantic Ocean, drinking champagne, heading toward Liege-Bierset, Belgium.

Hannah grinned. "This is amazing. I'm not used to this sort of luxury."

"Yeah, knowing Jean Luc, I'm wondering what our hotel will be like. I'm sure we'll be treated like royalty, so get ready. He said he had reserved us a suite with two bedrooms."

They exited the craft and a stylishly dressed woman Jenny thought she recognized met them. "Welcome. I'm Gabriella. We met briefly at Le Castellet when I strapped you into the car before your ride with Jean Luc."

"Gabriella. I thought you looked familiar. How are you? I was so scared that day I hardly remember anything."

"I am well, thank you, but you had fun that day, no?"

"I did have fun. As scared as I was, it was fun. This is my sister, Hannah."

"Hello, Hannah. I am happy to meet you."

Jenny asked how the season was going, and Gabriela replied, "The season is crazy as always. But Jean Luc is a nice man to work for. He is generous and considerate. I worked for one other driver before, and he was a terrible man. I could never do enough for him, and when he wanted me to go to bed with him, that's when I decided to quit. Jean Luc heard of it and asked me to be his assistant. I was very lucky."

"That's good. Your job sounds exciting, traveling all over the world," Jenny said.

"It is exciting, but it can be very difficult sometimes. Always different time zones and jet lag. It's a male world. I get many unwanted remarks. Some of the male crew treat me like I'm helpless and might break. Others want to get me in bed. I miss my family and friends at my home village. I plan on this to be my last year with the team. I'm hoping Ferrari might give me steady work at Maranello. I can be closer to home in Italy then. I have maybe some other opportunities also."

Jenny nodded. "I understand how tiring all the travel can be from my own brief experience. I hope you can stay with Ferrari."

"Thank you. Now we must go. Traffic will be getting bad."

Hannah pressed her nose against her window, not missing a thing, and Jenny stared out her own window as they drove by well-kept farms and through a beautiful forest.

Jenny thought about her upside-down life. Though her friends and family were deserting her, she'd found a sister in California. She loved her house in Durango but liked being in Paris with its creative vibe, and she discovered she liked California.

It seemed the Durango she first knew had lost some of its earlier charm, maybe because she'd been there for a while, and the newness had worn off. And an increasing number of tourists flocked there now, overwhelming the downtown and the mountain trails. Many of her favorite musicians had relocated elsewhere. Everything seemed to be in a state of flux. Her world had broadened from the confines of Durango. She could live anywhere. She wasn't sure where she should be.

She thought of her finances. Even though her book sales were tapering off, she had a goodly sum invested. Her trust-fund account would offer her minimal support if nothing else, and she owned her house free and clear.

But her new book was at a standstill. She decided she had to quit running around, get serious, and focus on her writing.

Gabriella snapped Jenny away from her thoughts. "We are at the Radisson Blu Palace where you will be staying. It is about twenty minutes to the track, but it's late now, and Jean Luc will be back soon. Everything is arranged for your suite. You do not need to provide any gratuities as that has also been taken care of. Charge anything you need in your room. You will have time to settle in and freshen up. I've been assigned to be your driver, and I'll give you my cell number to call anytime you need a ride."

Jenny and Hannah thanked her as they pulled up to the front entrance. A doorman promptly greeted them and escorted the two women and their luggage into the European-modern lobby, bright, minimalist, with tasteful splashes of color.

Jenny spied the swimming pool and hot tub on the way to the elevators. "Hey, let's unpack and head down to the hot tub for a soak."

"Awesome. I'm ready," Hannah replied.

Their spacious fourth-floor suite reflected the lobby, ultra modern, but nicely appointed and comfortable. They selected their bedrooms and unpacked. Jenny put on her swimsuit and the soft fleece robe she found in the bathroom, which was almost as big as her bedroom at home, and slipped into the slippers that matched the robe.

"Hey, Hannah, you ready?"

"Yeah, let's go. I'm ready for a soak and a cool drink."

"Me too."

As they prepared to enter the hot tub, a waiter approached. "May I bring you a refreshment, Mesdemoiselles?"

They checked out the drink menu he offered, and feeling a bit extravagant, Jenny decided on a Cranberry Pear Champagne cocktail. Hannah ordered the same. They slipped into the hot water.

Hannah grinned. "I could get used to this sort of lifestyle way too easily."

Their drinks arrived, and they sipped the delicious cocktail, savoring the combination of fruit and champagne as the hot water soaked away the miles.

After fifteen minutes they were ready to move to the pool to cool down, then to a lounge chair. The waiter came by, and they each ordered another drink.

Hannah said, "God, Jenny. Thank you. This is amazing. I'm in Europe. I always dreamed of coming here but never believed I could ever afford it. This is so great." She giggled with delight, helped along by her cocktail.

Jenny felt a presence and looked up into Jean Luc's wide grin. "I am so happy to see you here and enjoying the hotel. That is good. You must do a full spa treatment while you're here." He leaned over and gave her the customary *bisous*. "May I sit?"

She felt her heart flutter. "Of course you can sit. You're the reason I'm here. Jean Luc, this is my sister, Hannah."

"He took Hannah's hand and kissed it then also gave a

bisous. "I am honored to meet you, Hannah, sister of Jennifer. You are both so beautiful. I shall be the envy of every man here with two beautiful women. Your trip was okay? And you are being treated well by the hotel?"

"Stop it, Jean Luc," Jenny said. "You embarrass us. Yes, our trip was fine, and the hotel is amazing. Thank you."

"I apologize; I wish not to embarrass you, but the truth is the truth no matter. I'm sorry I'm so late. I thought I would be here sooner, but there are problems with the car and getting the proper downforce."

"No problem. It's nice to see you again. Are you doing okay? And what's a downforce?"

"It is adjusting the front and rear wings to maximize grip on corners but allow the car to have quickness on the straights. It is a delicate balance. This is especially so on this track with tricky corners and long straights like the Kemmel Straight. And I am doing fine, thank you."

Jenny sensed Jean Luc's discomfort. "You seem preoccupied. Would you rather we weren't here? Are you worried about the race? We can be on our own if you have things you need to do. I understand."

"No, no, I'm happy you are here. But, yes, my mind is on the race. The car is not working properly. We are doing everything we can. I will be required at the track all day tomorrow for practice and then Saturday for more practice and qualifying. So, we won't be able to spend much time together. Then there is the race Sunday. You will be alone more than I planned. But we will have time after Sunday. No?"

Jenny smiled. "If that's what you're worried about, don't be. We'll be fine. Hannah and I will find things to do. Please don't worry. Focus on the race. We'll have time afterward. Okay?"

"Okay. Thank you, Jennifer. I shall now go and prepare for

dinner. Can you meet me in the restaurant at seven?"

Jenny checked the time. "I think we can. Hannah? Seven okay?"

"Sounds great. We should go too and get cleaned up. I think I'm happy you made me get that sexy little dress."

On Friday Jenny booked herself and Hannah for a full spa treatment. "This is way too extravagant, Jenny," Hannah protested. "We shouldn't. It's too expensive."

"It's okay. Jean Luc told me last night that we should enjoy any and all amenities available. He's happy we're here and wants us to enjoy our time."

"But I've never been this extravagant."

"So this is your chance; now be quiet and enjoy it."

After their morning and early afternoon of luxuriating with massages, wraps, facials, manicures, pedicures, and several other treatments, they spent the rest of the day languishing by the pool.

On Saturday Jenny and Hannah went to watch qualifying for the race. Gabriella delivered them to the Ferrari pit garage where they were both given the royal treatment. They were supplied with the sound-canceling earmuffs and given the option of staying down in the pits or going above where they could see some of the track. There were several large flat screen TVs for more track coverage. Of course there was champagne and food. They elected to go above where there were a number of other specially invited guests.

Hannah was giddy with the excitement of it all, especially when a handsome Italian man began flirting with her. She smiled politely, dissed him, and whispered in Jenny's ear, "I heard someone saying there's a famous movie star here. Do you see anyone?"

"I haven't seen a movie in forever and pay no attention to

who's famous these days, so no, I have no idea. Qualifying's starting. Let's go outside to watch. Put on your earmuffs. It's gonna be loud."

The two of them watched as Jean Luc struggled with his car and barely made it into the final ten to get time for the coveted pole position. As the dust cleared, Jean Luc was sixth, relegated to the third row.

That night the three of them met for dinner, and the mood was dark. A usually upbeat Jean Luc was unusually quiet, being unhappy with the car, his performance, and where he placed on the starting grid. The dinner was short, and he retired early for a good night's rest. Jenny and Hannah went to the bar where a quartet played some old jazz standards. They drank champagne and enjoyed the quietude of the music, but a growing apprehension settled in Jenny's gut.

On race day Gabriella took Jenny and Hannah to the track early. They went up to the same room as yesterday where a crowd of spectators and hangers on gathered. Jenny inadvertently scanned the crowd for any sign of the Russian women, worried that they might somehow appear, but then she remembered they'd been arrested.

The starting grid was in place and the warm up lap completed. The lights went on one by one, then went off and the race began. Jean Luc got off to a bad start and lost one position. *Shit, like I was supposed to bring him luck?* she thought. Jenny's apprehension increased with every passing lap, seeing how Jean Luc was struggling.

The race went on at the usual frantic pace. Drivers began their pit stops for new tires. Hannah was astounded that the pit crews could change four tires in less than three seconds. She was totally into the action.

It was lap forty-seven when the yellow flags came out.

Word spread quickly that there was a crash at the famous Raidillon/Eau Rouge corner, a tricky sweeping uphill with a quick sweeping right-hand corner at the top. With the cars being almost airborne, the corner had to be executed expertly and precisely.

The red lights went on, signaling the halting of the race, and all drivers had to go into the pits until such time as the track was cleared of the debris from the crash. Jenny's breath caught and her apprehension went into full-scale dread as she watched the cars come into the pits. There was only one Ferrari, and it wasn't Jean Luc's.

Jenny's heart seemed to lodge in her throat. She felt weak and grabbed Hannah for support.

"Jenny? Are you okay?"

"He's not coming into the pits. He was in that crash. I know it."

Hannah touched her arm. "I'm sure he's okay."

"How can you fucking know? Oh shit! Oh shit! Please let him be okay."

Jenny elbowed her way to one of the flat screens to see what happened. A camera on the site showed the carnage of wheels, axles, other car parts and the cockpits of four cars. She saw drivers exiting or being helped to exit the remains of their cars. Then the camera flashed on the red car where several track marshals gathered around. An ambulance arrived, and the EMTs extracted a red-suited man, laid him on a stretcher, put him in the ambulance, and sped off with lights flashing and klaxon sounding. Jenny's heart pounded in fear. She turned, pushed through the crowd, and ran down to the pits to find Gabriella, who was gathered with concerned members of the crew.

"Gabriella! Do you know anything? Is he okay?"

"We do not have any reports yet other than Jean Luc is being rushed to the hospital. We have been told that another car went airborne and hit him full force with its rear end and it hit so hard, it crushed the cocoon. The team principal and I are going now to the hospital. Marco here will take you to your hotel when you're ready." She introduced Jenny to Marco. "I'll call or text as soon as I know anything."

"I'm ready to go back now. I just have to find my sister."

She went back up to the hospitality room and spied Hannah watching one of the flat screens. "I need to get out of here," Jenny said. "You can stay if you want, but I have to leave. I have to leave now."

"I'll come. Jenny, he'll be okay."

"How the fuck do you know he'll be okay? How the fuck can you say that?" she screamed.

Hannah reached for her hand and pulled her into a hug. "I'm sorry. I don't know what to say."

Jenny lost it and began sobbing. Hannah led her through the staring crowd and down to where Marco was waiting. He escorted them to the car and took a sobbing Jenny and a distraught Hannah back to the hotel.

Chapter 34

Gabriella sent a text at 4:00 p.m. saying that Jean Luc had extensive injuries to his right side and was headed for surgery. At 7:00 p.m. Gabriella called Jenny and said, "We have an update on Jean Luc. His surgery went well, and he will be flown to Paris tomorrow. He will be admitted into the Hôtel Dieu Hospital where he'll have more surgery. The surgical team here has done all they feel comfortable doing with the resources of a small hospital. But he is in stable condition. We haven't been permitted to see him and won't until tomorrow in Paris if Hôtel Dieu Hospital will allow it. His family has been notified. We'll fly out tomorrow, and you're welcome to join us."

"Thanks, Gabriella. How extensive are his injuries?"

"The surgeon wouldn't say. All we were told is he has broken bones, and his femur was shattered. It will be a long recovery, I think."

"But these cars are supposed to be so safe. How could this happen?"

"With that car going airborne and crashing into the side of his cockpit with the rear of the car which is the gearbox and motor, both solid and unforgiving, it crushed the cockpit. It was a situation not planned for. I was told the FIA governing body will be assessing it and maybe make new safety recommendations."

"But he will live?"

"Yes. He will live."

"What time do you leave tomorrow?"

"Ten o'clock. Shall I pick you up at nine?"

"Yes. Please. We'll be ready. Thanks for everything."

Jenny clicked off and sat staring at nothing. "Hannah, we're going to Paris."

"Your grandparents are there, aren't they?"

"Yes they are, and they're your grandparents too."

"Oh, God, I never thought of that. They are. Oh, God. What'll they think? What'll they do? Just showing up. Maybe I can just be your friend."

"No way. They're great. They'll be happy. It'll be interesting though."

"What do you mean, interesting?"

"It'll be a shock for sure. Just like it was for me. Remember, I passed out."

"Oh crap. Now I'm nervous."

"Don't be. Just be you. It'll be fine."

On the short hop to Paris, Jenny felt tense and fearful. She then noticed how tense Hannah was, not having said a word since they left the hotel. Jenny reached over and squeezed her hand. "Don't worry. It'll be fine."

As they began their descent to land, Gabriella said, "A van will be meeting us. Where can we take you?"

"Thanks, Gabriella. I should have told you, I notified my

grandparents, and they'll be meeting us, so we won't need to go with you."

"There is no problem. Maybe we will meet at the hospital?"

"I hope we do. I so appreciate all you've done. Thank you."

"It was my pleasure. Transporting you was one part of my job I like very much."

A few minutes later, they'd landed, disembarked, and found Dean and Susan waiting for them. Jenny introduced Hannah to her grandparents as a close friend, putting off the inevitable of telling them Hannah was their granddaughter. Hannah smiled while wringing her hands. Jenny noticed Susan glancing at both of them quizzically, but she said nothing.

They arrived at the apartment, and as soon as they were inside, Jenny called Gabriella to see whether there was any news.

"He has been admitted to the hospital and will be in surgery this afternoon. We will not be allowed to see him until maybe tomorrow depending on how he is. His parents are there and were able to see him briefly before the surgery. We'll be staying at a nearby hotel. I will send you the address as soon as we're located. Maybe we will meet for coffee tomorrow?"

"Thanks, Gabriella. Let me know where you are, and we'll meet. See you tomorrow."

After clicking off, Jenny filled everyone in on what she'd heard about Jean Luc.

Susan said, "You know where the guest bedroom is, Jennifer. I should check the fold-out bed in there to make sure it's okay. If you don't mind sharing the bedroom and bath."

"Susan, Dean," Jenny said, "let's sit for a minute. We have something to tell you."

They both looked at her with a puzzled look, but sat as ordered. Hannah looked even more apprehensive than Susan.

Susan asked, "Is something wrong?"

"No. Nothing's wrong. It's just that we won't mind sharing the bedroom and bath since we slept together in my camper for two weeks."

Susan's eyes widened and she blurted out, "Is Hannah your girlfriend?"

"No. She's more than that, she's my half sister and … and … and your granddaughter."

A long silence ensued as Susan and Dean digested the information. "I don't understand," Susan said, "your half sister? Our granddaughter? I don't understand."

"It's true, Susan. Let me explain." Jenny told the story of her trip to California, camping on a beach next to Hannah and her friends and what had happened after that. When she finished, there was another long silence.

The first thing Dean asked was, "Does Julian know?"

"No. We were planning on going to Durango to see him when we decided on going to Spa for the race."

Jenny glanced at Hannah, who was white as a ghost and looked like she might pass out.

Dean's face had lit up into a broad smile. "Well, this is certainly quite a surprise. And I will add, a nice surprise. Hannah, welcome to the family."

Susan got up and said, "Hannah, come here." They met in the middle of the room, and Susan embraced her like she might never let go. "This is wonderful. So wonderful. We have two beautiful granddaughters. I just can't believe it. I thought there was something, some sort of resemblance when I saw you two, but I couldn't place it. Now I know."

Tears ran down both women's faces, and Jenny felt her own eyes begin to tear up.

Susan let go. "Oh my. I need a tissue."

"I think we all do," Dean said. "This calls for a celebration. Let's go down to the plaza and have dinner with champagne. And we'll drink a glass for Jean Luc. Let's celebrate our new granddaughter and the fact that Jean Luc, while badly injured, is alive and will heal."

When Jenny called Gabriella the next morning, her call went straight to voicemail, so she decided to go to the hospital to see if she might find out how Jean Luc was doing. Dean and Susan wanted to spend time with Hannah get to know her and show her some of Paris, so she stayed behind.

Jenny went into the reception area and heard someone call her name and turned to see Danielle. "Jennifer. Jennifer. You are here. We didn't know if you would come." She greeted Jenny with *bisous* and a long warm hug.

"How is he?" Jenny asked. "Will he recover? Can I see him?"

The receptionist overheard and said, "Only immediate family are permitted to see him and only for a short time. You have American accent, so not family."

Daniella answered sharply, "She is family as far as we are concerned and will be permitted to see him when he's ready!"

The woman's eyes grew large. She said something terse in French, huffed, and walked away.

"He had surgery yesterday to do some more repair on broken bones and was given pain drugs so he couldn't talk much. He may be able to talk more this morning. Robert is up in the waiting room on his floor. I'd just stepped out for a little walk and some fresh air. Come. We'll talk when we get upstairs. Robert will be overjoyed to see you."

They found Robert in the waiting room, and after another warm greeting, they sat.

"How is he?" Jennifer asked again.

Robert answered, "The doctors say he will recover. But it will be long and hard. He may never drive races again. His right femur and hip were fractured. His right scapula was damaged. There are no internal injuries. He will be very happy you are here. Lisette is coming, and her flight will be landing soon, so we must leave shortly."

They made small talk about Jenny's trip. Other than that, they remained lost in their thoughts.

Later in the morning, with Jean Luc still not coherent from the pain meds, Jenny went to the hospital cafeteria for a coffee and snack. Danielle and Robert left to pick up Lisette,

Around 2:30 in the afternoon, a doctor came out of Jean Luc's room, writing on his clipboard. Seeing Jenny he stopped to report. "I have just examined Mr. Bonnet, and his vitals are excellent. He is awake, and he may have visitors, but please, be brief."

With some trepidation, Jenny went to his door. "Jean Luc?"

"Who is it?" he responded dully.

She wasn't prepared for the bandaged body she saw. The once-beautiful physical specimen looked like it had been deflated to a fragment of its former self.

"It's Jenny, Jean."

"Who? Jennifer. You are here." He closed his eyes and tried to focus. "I am a mess, no?"

Jenny had to smile. "Yes you are, but you'll be okay. I think they've you all put back together."

He smiled weakly. "I messed up badly. I remember going into that corner thinking I could overtake those three cars. I knew better. I should have waited. I was frustrated, and now I lie here, broken."

"Hush. It happened, and you're alive and will heal. It'll take time, but you will heal. You have lots of people who love you and are cheering you on. Now healing will be your job."

"The doctor will not tell me if I will ever be able to drive again."

"That's because he can't predict the future. Give it time. Focus on healing."

"Yes. I know. I'm very tired. Are my mother and father here?"

"They were here but left to get Lisette from the airport and will be back later. I can hang around until they get back."

"Jennifer, I am tired and want to sleep, but I must tell you that I am in love with you, and I shall never give up loving you."

Jenny felt tears welling up. "I know. I love you too, Jean Luc." She went to his bedside, placed a hand on his face and gave him a gentle lingering kiss. "Close your eyes and rest. I'll see you later." His only response was a smile, and he closed his eyes.

As she was leaving the hospital, she met the Bonnet family. Lisette did the usual *bisous* and gave Jenny a long hug. "I'm so happy to see you, Jennifer. I'm sorry we meet under such circumstances, but I can't wait to tell you all about New York and everything. Are you leaving?"

"Yes. I have to go. He woke up for a few minutes, and we talked briefly. He's cognizant of what happened and his injuries. But he just went back to sleep. I'm sorry you missed him."

"We will wait. He'll wake again soon."

"Why must you leave?" Danielle asked.

"I need fresh air and want to spend some time with my grandparents. I've hardly seen them since I got here. I'll be by again tomorrow. You all need to be here for him now. I'll be back." With that, she left.

She got a cab to Saint-Michel and, as she walked toward the apartment on rue Danton, realizing her hunger, she stopped at the Brasserie Le Saint André where she'd always had breakfast when she visited a few months ago. She went in, but her friend Camille wasn't there. Disappointed, Jenny ordered her usual.

Chapter 35

For the next week, Jenny spent most of every day at the hospital with Danielle, Lisette, or Robert when they were there. Jean Luc had two more minor surgeries and, now well screwed back together, was on his way to recovery. Having been in great physical shape before the accident helped him improve every day. The doctor already had him doing some bedridden physical therapy.

Hannah went with Jenny to the hospital a few times whenever Dean and Susan weren't occupying her time. Overall, they had hardly seen each other since they got to Paris. One night they managed to escape their grandparents and went for dinner to have some uninterrupted time together.

They chose a restaurant right by Saint-Michel Plaza and sat outside in an alcove of plants, which offered privacy even though there were other diners all around. As dusk gathered, delicate lights turned the dining area into a magical place. They each ordered a glass of champagne and took a big sigh.

Jenny said, "At last. Dean and Susan can be a bit much,

can't they?"

"Yeah, but it's great to know them and spend time. I always knew my other grandparents, that is until they died in that car crash. That was devastating. But now I get to have new ones. And, get this, they never closed out your brother Michael's trust fund and are in the process of transferring it over to me. I can't believe it. That's so generous. I've never had any money or resources until I met Russell. He's generous, but it's still all his. I feel a new independence."

"Speaking of Russell, you haven't said anything about him. He should be done with his retreat soon."

"Well, that's another thing; he texted me last week that he's planning on staying longer now, maybe for the rest of the year."

"Really? Wow. What do you think?"

"It certainly impacts our music. We were really starting to shine and had more tour dates lined up, which we have to cancel. Our agent wasn't the least bit happy when I told her. But we'll be fine. If that's what he needs, I fully support it. When I had those bad times a few years ago, I was able to get myself back together with Rinpoche's help."

The waiter arrived to take their food order, and after ordering their food and more champagne, they continued their conversation.

"So, Jenny, what's up with Jean Luc? I see you two together and see how you look at each other."

"I know … I know. I think I'll stay here for a while and see what happens. I admit, as much as I've tried not to, I've fallen for him. I think I fell in love with him before I ever left Paris. I just didn't want to admit it to myself."

"From what little I've seen of him, I think he's a really nice guy. Genuine. Even with all his money and rock-star status."

"Yeah. He is. I don't how or if it'll ever work out with us with his life being here and mine back in Colorado. We'll see. Are you planning on heading home soon?"

"Not sure. I'm liking Paris and may hang out here for a while. I've thought about finding a decent guitar and maybe doing some busking and some writing. There are some open mics I'd like to go to. It'd be a different vibe here than in the US. I think Susan would love it if I stayed forever."

Jenny laughed. "I know. They're great, and I like being with them, but sometimes I need my own space. Right now, I need to get working on my book. My publisher's getting impatient, and I can't afford to lose them since they did a brilliant job publishing and promoting my first book. Sales are beginning to dwindle, as are my royalties, which is okay. I've put away a lot of that money so I'm good."

"So what's your solution? Where can you go to have peace and quiet to work?"

"I don't know. I'd like to go home. There I could have my own space. But I don't want to leave while Jean's, well, you know. Maybe I just need to find a good coffee shop that doesn't mind me hanging around all afternoon."

The waiter again interrupted them, wanting to know if there would be anything else. When they said no, he handed them the bill and left.

They were a bit drunk, and when they got back to the apartment, they bid good night to Dean and Susan and went to their bedroom. Jenny giggled as they got ready for bed and said, "Maybe you'll find a nice Frenchman for your entertainment while Russell's busy finding himself."

Hannah threw one of the pillows from her bed, hitting Jenny squarely in the face.

"Okay. Game on, sister." Jenny grabbed a pillow and

walloped Hannah to which Hannah reciprocated, and it erupted into a full-fledged pillow fight with laughing and squealing. Finally, they collapsed into fits of laughter.

A knock sounded on the door. "What's going on in here?" Susan opened the door, seeing the chaos of the two sisters, both rolling in laughter, their beds a mess, pillows lying on the floor.

Both tried to stop laughing, but kept breaking into giggles. Hannah said, "Nothing, Susan. Sorry."

Both sisters looked guiltily at Susan, doing their best to control their giggles.

Susan smiled. "It makes me so happy to hear you two. After Michael and everything, to hear you two having fun and laughing makes me so happy I could cry. I love you both so much. I'm so grateful for you, Hanna, and for you, Jenny. I—" and there were no more words.

Both young women went and embraced her. "We love you too, Susan. And, we're grateful for you and Grandpa."

The next morning Hannah went with Jenny to the hospital. Jean Luc went for physical therapy at eleven, so they left and walked back to Saint-Michel and went to the Brasserie Le Saint André for a croissant and coffee. As they approached the brasserie, Jenny realized how much she enjoyed being back in Paris. She'd spent so much time here before she so abruptly left. Camille was working and lit up when she saw Jenny.

"Jennifer. You are back. I knew you were leaving. I have missed you. Are you okay?"

"Hi, Camille. It's great to see you again. I left in a hurry for the States. I'm sorry I never said goodbye and apologize for never communicating with you." She saw Camille looking at Hannah and introduced them. She told her of the attack and attempted kidnapping. And then went on to tell of Jean

Luc and his crash.

Camille looked at her for a few moments and then began to giggle. "I heard about that incident. It was you who stabbed him in the ass? You really did?" Her giggles were contagious and all three of them were soon trying suppress their giggles.

Jenny took a breath and answered, "Yes, I did, as hard as I could and my knife went in deep." At that they all laughed full on, and tears ran down their cheeks.

They over their laughter and Jenny asked, "How are you, Camille? How have you been?"

"I have been enjoying my summer, but I may not return to university."

"What? Why?" Jenny asked.

"My roommate and friend has moved back to our village to help with the family vineyard. I cannot afford rent by myself and also afford university. I have interviewed possible roommates, but I cannot find anyone I want to live with. Everyone seems to be too wild or not of good character. I am sad, but I must work full time here now for my uncle so I can pay my rent."

Jenny was about to speak, but Hannah interrupted her. "Are you thinking what I'm thinking?"

"Maybe. That we should rent it as a place to work?"

"Exactly."

Camille seemed about to say something, but then eyed the other two with a quizzical expression. "I do not understand. You both want to rent it? There is only one bedroom."

Jenny smiled. "Hannah is a musician and songwriter. We're both looking for a place to write away from our grandparents, who never leave us alone when we're there with them. We would pay you full rent but only be there during the day. Could we look at it to see if it would work for us, and for you, of course?"

"I will be happy to show it to you. I'm off at three o'clock. I will give you the address and will meet you there."

"Perfect," Jenny said. "We'll see you then." They finished their coffee and paid their bill. "See you at three," Jenny said in parting.

The two of them wandered around some of the narrow cobblestone streets that wound about the arrondissement, discovering little shops with antiques—some with rare books—boulangeries, boucheries, and shops selling fresh veggies. Then they came across a shop with an old sign that read "Instruments de Musique".

Hannah peeked through the dirty window. "Oh, let's go in. Maybe they have a guitar. Let's go see."

Jenny smiled at Hannah's excitement, like a little girl in a candy shop. The inside was dark and smelled of dust and tobacco smoke. An old man sat in a chair in the corner, smoking a pipe and reading a book. Hannah eagerly scoped out the shop, seeing only violins.

The man looked up. "*Bonjour, Mesdemoiselles. Vous cherchez á acheter un instrument?*"

"*Bonjour. Parlez-vous anglais?*" Jenny asked.

"It is poor, but I can a little. Will you look for a violin, maybe?"

Hannah responded, "No, I'm not looking for a violin. But do you have any guitars?"

"Ah. A *guitare*. Yes. I have only two old ones. They are in the back. I will find them."

The man slowly got up and ambled through a curtained doorway. They heard him rummaging around, and a few minutes later, he brought out two, setting the cases on the counter. With little room on the small counter, he opened the first somewhat worn and ratty case which revealed what appeared to be an old Martin guitar with a small body and a shorter twelve-fret neck rather than the more usual fourteen-fret neck.

Hannah looked at the guitar as if it were a newborn baby. Then she gently rubbed her finger across the silky top. "May I look at it more closely and play it?"

"Of course, Mademoiselle. I apologize; it has been a long time. The strings are old, and it will not be in tune."

"No problem."

Hannah carefully took the guitar from the case and inspected it. The top finish had a worn aged look, but the rest looked good with no marks or cracks.

"Here is a stool, Mademoiselle. You may sit and play. *Non?*"
"*Merci, Monsieur.*"

She sat and tuned the guitar to a pitch that she could hear in her head after so many years of playing and began to gently play some chords. After she noodled around getting the feel of the instrument, she launched into playing and singing one of her own slower ballads.

She finished and the old man wiped away a tear. "*Magnifique, Mademoiselle. Magnifique.* Even with old strings, you make it sound so wonderful. This guitar was made for you. You must have it. It has been in my shop for many years. Now it must be yours." He thought for a long moment and said, "I will sell it to you for €300." He paused. "I traded it for a violin with some American many years ago. Maybe €300 is too many to ask?"

Hannah looked inside the guitar. "Excuse me for a few minutes. I need to look this up." She spent a few minutes on her cell phone, closed it and smiled. "I will give you €6,500 for it."

He gave her a puzzled look. "I say €300 and you say €6,500? Most want to bargain for cheaper. I don't understand."

"This guitar was made in the 1940s and is worth at least that much in America, Monsieur. The Brazilian Rosewood that the back and sides are made from is now endangered and hasn't been available for many years. This is a rare guitar, and I cannot cheat you. I will happily pay that much for it."

The man looked at her and looked down, shaking his head, mumbling something about crazy Americans, then he looked up at her and smiled. "If you are certain, Mademoiselle. It is so much."

"I have to be honest. It would be wrong of me if I bought it for less. Can you do credit cards?"

He grinned from ear to ear. "Of course. Of course. I wish I had some better strings for you, but I am only much equipped for violins."

Jenny, who'd remained in the background during the transaction, said, "Monsieur, would you make the bill of sale out for what you wanted to sell it for originally to save import-duty tax? No one will ever know but the three of us."

"Ah, you are a smart woman to think of that. I will make out two, one for €300 and one for €6,500. Use which one you choose."

Everything was completed; they exchanged thank yous and goodbyes, and they left the shop.

"I can't believe I found this guitar in Paris of all places. I've wanted one of these forever, but never had the funds for any that I came across. With Dean and Susan's generosity, I can afford this. I love it. Now we have to find a music store where I can get some strings and the other accessories I'll need."

Hannah searched on her phone for music stores that might have what she wanted. The store was beyond walking distance, especially carrying her new guitar, so they found a taxi. They arrived and Hannah told the driver to wait. Jenny waited in the taxi, and Hannah went in with her guitar and reappeared within fifteen minutes holding a small bag and her guitar in a new sturdy case.

"Now we have to go and meet Camille," Jenny said.

Camille's apartment was in an old four-story building a few blocks from the Sorbonne on rue de l'Odéon, not far from the Luxembourg Gardens and on the same street where Sylvia Beach opened the original Shakespeare and Company at 2 rue de l'Odéon, in 1919, which served American expats, such as Ernest Hemingway and F. Scott Fitzgerald, until she closed the store in 1941 when the Nazis occupied Paris. She never reopened the store.

They rang the buzzer to her apartment; the door lock clicked, and they entered the vestibule where the concierge, an older man, eyed them.

"We are here to see Mademoiselle Gauthier. She is expecting us."

"Ah, yes. She is number 410. The lift is there," he said, directing them to the left.

"Merci, Monsieur," Jenny said. They turned to the lift, but it was so small that it would not accommodate the two of them and a guitar.

"I can use the stairs," Hannah said. "You take the lift."

Jenny rode the ancient lift as it slowly ascended to the fourth floor. When she arrived, she found Hannah, already there, waiting. They found number 410 and knocked. Camille answered and invited them into a small but adequate sitting room furnished with a small couch, two uncomfortable-looking chairs, and a small coffee table. A kitchenette with a small dining table and two chairs occupied the left side of the room. Tall French doors opened onto a small balcony overlooking rue de l'Odéon. The walls were painted a calm off-white, and a few pictures hung here and there.

"Let me show you the bedroom with the desks where you'll want to work," Camille said.

She showed them into a small bedroom with two single beds, side tables, a lamp, an armoire, and two small desks with shelves above the writing surfaces. The room also had tall French doors which opened out onto a small balcony overlooking a narrow side street.

Jenny sighed and said, "I love it. Do you have Wi-Fi?"

"Yes, we have good Wi-Fi. It is very fast here."

"I'll rent it for six months. After that I'm not sure. Actually I'm not even sure about six months."

"And you will not stay here?" Camille asked.

"No. I'll stay with my grandparents. They like having me there and would be hurt if I left and stayed elsewhere."

"I understand," Camille said with disappointment in her voice.

"I can have the funds wired to your account. I'll check with my bank tomorrow. I'll need your bank, account, and routing numbers." Jenny looked over, saw that Hannah was getting antsy, and realized she wanted to get back, restring and play her new guitar. "We have to leave. Our grandparents are expecting us. I'll call you as soon as I find out about the money. Thanks."

"Wait. I will get you the keys." Camille went to a drawer in the kitchen, then quickly wrote something on a slip of paper and returned. She handed Jenny two sets of two keys each. "This one is for the front door, and this one for the apartment." Then she handed a slip of paper to Jenny. "This is the Wi-Fi password and account codes."

"Thanks, Camille. We must go."

"Yes. We will talk soon."

The two women left, using the stairs, and decided to walk back to rue Danton. "This is perfect. Now we have a place where we can write in peace without Susan interrupting to chat all the time."

Hannah laughed. "This will be great. Our own space with peace and quiet."

Chapter 36

Every morning over the next few weeks, Jenny left early to go to the hospital to spend time with Jean Luc and left when he went for physical therapy, which was normally at eleven thirty. They talked about everything. He taught her to play chess, and Jenny took him in his wheelchair out to a close by brasserie for coffee and croissants.

Afterward, Jenny headed to Camille's to write. Hannah was generally already there working. Late in the afternoon, they headed back to Dean and Susan's for wine and to talk about their day. And the two sisters managed one date night together every week.

Hannah played some open mics at various venues, having a great time, and was well received. She had offers from two places to play one or two nights a week. She used her California material interspersed with some new songs inspired by being in Paris.

One evening while Hannah was playing a gig and Dean worked in his office, Jenny and Susan were having an after-dinner glass of port when Susan asked, "So what's going on with you and Jean Luc?"

Jenny considered the question for a few long moments. "He makes me feel good. I like being with him. It seems we never run out of things to talk about. Sometimes we just play chess and don't talk. I just like being with him. It seems, I don't know, it just seems natural being with him."

"Are you in love with him?"

"I guess I might be. After Chris, my trust issues became front and center again. I think I can trust Jean Luc. I want to trust him. I know I'm afraid of commitment again. I'm trying to let this thing with Chris go and be done with it once and for all and move on."

Susan nodded, and Jenny continued, "You know, there are only four men I loved or thought I loved. There's Dean of course. Then Will, who I genuinely love as a father. And Julian, of course. Then there was Chris who was the first boy I thought I was in love with and maybe I was. But, with Jean, I feel different; it's a different feeling from Dean, Will, Chris, or Julian. I don't know how to explain it other than I feel a deep connection to him, something more than mental or the funny feeling I had in my gut with Chris. It feels different, on a deeper level. Does any of this make sense?"

"It makes a great deal of sense. Have you talked to him about how you feel?"

"No."

"Maybe you should. Tell him how you feel. See how he feels."

"Oh, Susan, I already know how he feels. That's what scares me. He has claimed to be in love with me after the third time he saw me."

"You may not know, Jennifer, but Dean and I met at a

party while he was still in law school. We dated three months, and he proposed, and I said yes. We were married two months later, and I've never regretted it for a moment. I knew by our second date that he was the one."

"Really? How could you know? In such a short time?"

"When you know, you know. And you know about Jean Luc."

Jenny didn't respond for a minute, considering everything she'd just heard. "I don't know; I'm scared, Susan."

"It's always scary, but listen to your heart, to your gut. Listen to your intuition. Trust your feelings, not your brain."

Jenny laughed. "I trusted my feelings with Chris, and that turned out well."

"You just told me how you felt with Chris and the difference with Jean. Plus you were still recovering from your childhood and all the trauma. You were inexperienced with men. We never said anything and probably should have, but Dean and I had concerns. We were thankful and happy when he left."

"You never said anything? Why?"

"Would you have listened?"

Jenny chuckled. "Probably not."

With that, Susan finished her port. "I'm ready to turn in. Thanks for talking."

Jenny finished her port as well. "Thank you for listening and for your advice. I love you, Grandma. I'm so grateful to have you."

"Thank you, dear. I'm grateful to have you."

With that they got up and exchanged cheek kisses and a hug. Susan headed to her bedroom, and Jenny took the glasses to the kitchen.

The following day when she arrived at the hospital, Jean

Luc was dressed, and everything he'd had with him during his stay was packed up. He boasted a big smile. "I'm being released this morning and can go home. I'm very happy."

"That's great news."

"Yes. My doctor says I am healing well but will need home care. I'm excited to be away from here and back in my apartment. We have found an organization that will provide me with care for twenty-four hours every day. I will still need assistance because my arm and shoulder are not ready for any weight. Will you still come and visit me in the mornings? My apartment is a distance away from where you stay."

She leaned closer and gently touched his cheek. "Of course I will."

Chapter 37

Jean Luc's apartment was in the eighth arrondissement off Boulevard Haussmann, which would be a long walk. Jenny checked on using the metro underground which seemed easy enough. On the morning after his parents took Jean Luc back to his place, Jenny walked out the door of her grandparents' apartment and was met by a middle-aged, well-dressed man standing by a black Mercedes with darkly tinted windows. "Mademoiselle Morse?" he asked.

Startled, she asked, "Who are you? What do you want?"

"Monsieur Bonnet has sent me to take you to his apartment."

Flashbacks of the attempted kidnapping made her shudder with fear, her heart rate accelerated, and she reached for her knife as she slowly began to back away. "Get away from me. Now!"

The man's eyes widened, and he moved toward the car. "But Mademoiselle, I was ordered to bring you to his apartment. He is expecting you."

"Just get away from me. Tell whoever sent you to leave me fucking alone."

The man got into the Mercedes. "Yes, Mademoiselle. I will relay your message." He sped away.

Jenny leaned against the building and took some deep breaths, trying to calm herself. After a few minutes, her heart slowed down; she shook her hair and walked confidently to the underground.

She found the apartment in a Haussmann style building. The concierge greeted her, and she told him who she was.

"Ah, yes. Monsieur Bonnet is expecting you, apartment 236. The lift is over by the staircase." He pointed her in the direction.

"Thank you," she replied as she headed for the stairs.

She rang the door buzzer and was greeted by a severe-looking woman of some indeterminate age who spoke with a heavy French accent and carefully chosen words. "Welcome, Mademoiselle Morse, I am Solange, Monsieur Bonnet's nurse. He is in the library. Follow me."

Jenny entered the modestly furnished apartment, which did not fit with the elegance of the building or the large living-dining room. Pictures of his family and several of Jean Luc standing in his racing uniform holding trophies or posed with other men and women sat on a sideboard, and several abstract paintings graced the wall. Sunlight streamed in through two sets of French doors onto polished parquet flooring partially covered with a large rug. A comfortable light-tan leather couch faced two matching chairs over a glass-topped coffee table. A modern dining table with six matching chairs took up the rest of the area, which was close to a doorway she assumed was the kitchen.

She entered the library and saw Jean Luc in his wheelchair

talking with the man she'd just chased away after he offered her the ride in the black Mercedes.

"Jennifer, come meet Antoine. He said you refused to ride with him."

"Yes I did. I had no idea who he was. You could have at least texted me to let me know. Do you remember I was almost kidnapped not too long ago?" she said testily.

"I'm sorry. I should have texted you. I thought you would appreciate the ride. How did you get here? Taxi?"

"No. I rode the underground, which was just fine," she answered sarcastically, not sparing the annoyance she felt.

An uncomfortable Antoine said, "I should leave now." He slipped out the door, closing it softly behind him."

"I apologize. I should have informed you. I am sorry. Will you have coffee?"

"Don't try to be nice. I'm mad at you. I was scared, Jean. I was ready to pull my knife and attack him. That would have been great, wouldn't it? Crazy American woman attacks chauffeur. God, that would've been all I need."

"I am so sorry. I was getting settled in and was not thinking clearly. I am sorry."

"Okay. Okay. I know I overreacted, but he scared me, being there, waiting. I should apologize to Antoine. He was just doing his job."

"He will understand. He is a chauffeur for hire, and I use his services when I am here and need such service. He is very nice."

"I still should apologize. Excuse me." She left, and a few minutes later, Jean Luc heard them laughing.

Back in the library, Jenny scanned the bookshelves which were almost devoid of books but filled with trophies and more pictures of his racing career. He noticed and said, "I've had

good times and much success with racing cars. And now—"
His voice faltered and he turned away from her.

"And now? Are you okay? What's wrong?"

He took a deep breath and wiped his good arm across his eyes. "And now, I must retire. I must leave racing."

"But why? You're an amazing driver."

"Not anymore. This crash has made me realize how vulnerable I am. I made an error in my judgment and risked others and wrecked their cars. I was responsible."

"Jean Luc, I've read several articles about the race, and no one blamed you for what happened. It was actually one of the other drivers that caused it all. It was an accident."

"I know what others say. But Eau Rouge is a tricky corner, and I was trying to overtake. My aggressiveness pushed the other driver into an error. But I know I am responsible. I knew better. I have driven that corner many times and know it is tricky.

"My contract is up this year, and Ferrari is indicating they may not renew it. I would be able to pick up a ride in a lesser team maybe. But they all know I made a bad error. I must retire."

"But, retire from what you love? You're not that old. There are other drivers who are older."

"I know. But they have not made such a bad error as I have. And, I'm not sure I will ever trust my judgment on the race track again. I don't know if I will even be physically able to drive again. I may not be able to move my legs to get into a Formula 1 car. I have lost much physical strength. My doctor has told me it will take maybe a year before I am able to walk well and use my right arm again. Then I would need another year maybe to get my strength and stamina back to be able to withstand the rigorous racing. I may never have the confidence again.

"I must add that not having to be traveling and racing in different parts of the world has given me a new perspective on my life. It has been good to be with my family and you all the time. With my racing schedule, I see very little of them. I once had friends and companions. I see them no more. It is not such a glamorous life as others think. It can be very lonely. I have only one real friend, Wolfgang Werner, who is my team head mechanic. We spend much time together when we are traveling here or there. It is the right thing I must do."

His words reminded Jenny of what Gabriella had said about the stress working in Formula 1 had on one's personal life, and in thinking about it, her own life when she was on the book-tour circuit. "What will you do? Racing has been your life."

"I don't know. Ferrari or some other team may want me for a consultant. Maybe I can do race commentary or interviews. I can devote more time to my foundation and raise money. Right now, I am being very sad and do not want to talk of this anymore."

"I understand. It will be your decision. But I'm sad also. It's so hard to say goodbye to someone or something that's such a great part of your life."

Jenny got up and gave him a tender kiss and a long hug, longer than necessary. "I love you, Jean Luc Bonnet." She didn't want to let go; she wanted to stay in his arms forever.

He smiled sadly at her. "I love you also, Jennifer Morse."

Chapter 38

The weeks went by and October arrived. Autumn was everywhere with leaves turning colors and a definite chill in the air. Jenny's routine was the same every morning: going to Jean Luc's, and writing every afternoon.

Hannah was busy with writing new music and performing at a number of clubs in the city. Jenny, and sometimes Dean and Susan, went to listen. Jenny and Hannah had become inseparable except for the mornings.

The second week in October, the two sisters were having a night out together when Hannah announced she would be returning home. "Russell is leaving the retreat center next week. Truth is, Rinpoche is kicking him out. Apparently he told Russell it was time to go home and back to the world and me. Rinpoche always liked me better," she said with a champagne-induced giggle.

"Are you ready to go home?" Jenny asked. "Things are going well for you here."

"I know. I hate to leave, but it's time. I'll miss you and

Dean and Susan. I love all of you, and they have been so gracious to me. But it's time. I have new material, and we need some band time for rehearsal. We have to get ready for an upcoming tour, and now that we'll have new material, we might get that next CD recorded. What about you? How long will you be here? What are your plans? What about Jean?"

Jenny pondered the questions for a few moments. "I don't know. I've made good progress on my novel. Paris is inspiring for me. I have a great writing space and a good routine going. I know you and Russell will be busy when you get home. Jean Luc? I don't know. But I do know I'm in love with him."

"Have you told him?"

"Yeah. Once. Right after his crash and he was in bad shape. It just came out without me thinking. Then again when he told me he was retiring and was very sad."

"But do you love him or only want to love him?"

"Yeah, I'm sure. It's so different from Chris who always seemed to be there, almost hovering until he wasn't. Jean Luc is easy to be with. We talk, play chess, read books, listen to music. My time with him always goes by much too quickly."

"But you realize you are there like only three-to-four hours, then you leave for another life with your writing and me and our grandparents. You've never really spent all day, everyday night, weeks, months on end. You're a free spirit. Can you be tied down? And he lives here. Are you willing to stay permanently in Paris?"

Jenny again pondered the questions posed to her, things she'd thought about but usually pushed aside, hoping answers would come in time.

"I know and I don't know. I don't know what'll happen once I get this book finished. I miss home. I'll miss you. And I can't go on staying with Dean and Susan forever. Lately I'm getting the impression they'd like some privacy and to be by themselves. They never say anything of course."

"Maybe it's both of us being there. Once I'm gone they might feel better?"

"Maybe. There's so much to think about. I liked it when my life was simpler all those years ago when I lived out of a backpack in the mountains. So much has changed."

Hannah said, "Only one thing is for certain, change is inevitable."

That night Jenny lay awake thinking of all the questions hidden away in a place in her mind where they lay dormant until Hannah's questions brought them to the surface. She realized just how much she missed her home.

She thought of Will and Helen and realized that she hadn't talked with them in so long. She considered the time difference, two fifteen here; that was six fifteen there. She snuck quietly into the kitchen to be as far away from the bedrooms as possible and called.

Helen answered. "Jenny? Jenny. Will, it's Jenny. Come here. I'm putting it on speaker. Jenny, how are you? We think of you all the time. It's so good to hear your voice. What time is it there?"

"Two fifteen. I couldn't sleep, and I knew I needed to talk to you. I have so much on my mind right now. I realized you'll be leaving for Mexico soon. Then I realized I want to get back home, but everything is so complicated."

Jenny unloaded everything about Jean Luc, her writing, her wanting to stay by him, her wanting to be home again. Then she stopped to take a breath, and Helen jumped in. "We're planning on leaving in two weeks. We'd love to see you before we leave. You'll be welcome to visit us in our winter paradise anytime."

Will jumped in, "When will I see a manuscript for your book? I'm looking forward to reading it."

"I'm very close to finishing it. Maybe by the time you leave? I don't know, but I'm close."

Helen said, "Maybe you should bring this young man with you? It sounds as though he's a big reason for you staying."

Jenny said, "He is. But he lives here. I don't think he'll leave."

"Have you asked him?"

"No."

"You should. We'd love to talk longer but we're on our way out for dinner. Please call us again soon."

"I promise. Thank you both for always being there for me. I love you both."

"We love you too. Talk again soon."

Jenny went back to bed, having made up her mind about what she was going to do. She closed her eyes and was asleep in an instant.

The next day she saw Camille at the brasserie and told her she and Hanna would be leaving sooner than she'd planned. Camille was crestfallen and wanted to refund the rent Jenny had paid upfront. Jenny refused, saying a deal was a deal and it was she who was stepping away. She hoped Camille would find a suitable roommate before spring semester began. They promised to meet again soon, either in Paris or in the US since Camille wanted to visit Jenny in Colorado.

When she saw Jean Luc that morning, the first thing she said was, "Jean, I'm going home in a week, and you're coming with me. I see how slowly you're progressing, and I think you need some real physical therapy. These doctors and PT people here mean well, but you're gonna be ages getting back on your feet unless we up your game."

"Up your game? What does that mean?"

"It means you are going to quit being pampered and get off your butt and get to work. You should have been out of that wheelchair weeks ago."

He looked at her incredulously. "You say my physical therapy is not good? I need my wheelchair. I need a nurse."

Jenny said, "You say all that, but it came to me last night how you've just been cruising along when you need to get yourself back into shape. I have a good friend who is a physical therapist and have seen how she works with athletes. She is demanding and makes them work, but they're up and going way faster than you'll ever be at this rate. You'll stay with me. I know where she worked and there are excellent physical therapists there. I'll be your nurse or whatever. You don't need a nurse, you need to get going. I have to go home, and I want you there. I want you there because I love you and want to be with you. Period."

He looked at her, stunned by her outburst. "Jennifer, I have never heard you being so forceful. It is a good quality that makes me love you more. Please let me give it some thought."

"You have a week."

On their last night in Paris, as she and Hannah stood on the little balcony off their bedroom to watch the sun setting behind the Eiffel Tower, Jenny knew that a chapter of her life was coming to a close, and a new one was waiting, yet to be written.

Chapter 39

Jean Luc's plane made a soft touchdown at SFO, San Francisco International Airport. The attendant opened the cabin door, and Hannah ran down the stairs and into the arms of a waiting Russell. They embraced and kissed until Jenny thought their lips would be chapped. When they had, at last, broken apart, Hannah led Russell into the plane to meet Jean Luc.

After introducing the two men and some small talk, Jenny said, "We'll be out to see you soon and retrieve my van. I'd love to see Meg and Frank again as well as Mick and Karen."

"We could also drive it to Durango. It'd be a fun road trip."

"Yeah, but you're gonna be busy. We'll talk and figure it out either way. I'd love to have you come to visit. I'm gonna miss you so much, Sister. I cherish the time we had together, and I want to have more." Her voice quavered and tears formed.

Hannah wasn't able to reply, she could only give a long hug. She quickly turned and went down to the tarmac wiping her eyes on her sleeve, and she and Russell walked away.

After a short flight to Durango, Jenny found the wheelchair van which she'd rented waiting for them. She and the attendants got him loaded and secured, and then they headed for her house, stopping for a quick run through at the grocery store for food and supplies.

Once the attendants got Jean Luc into the house, she called Helen.

"You're home. We can't wait to see you. We'll be out, and we'll pick up some take out, Mexican or barbeque on the way?"

"I got food. You don't have to."

"No argument. Mexican it is. We'll be there within the hour."

Jenny got Jean Luc situated in the larger guest room. She was grateful that when Will remodeled the house he made everything handicapped accessible. She was just finishing when Will and Helen arrived with food and what was needed for margaritas.

They charged in with hugs and greetings. After giving all their attention to Jenny, Helen turned to Jean Luc. "And you must be the man we've heard so much about. Welcome." She leaned down and gave him a long, warm hug.

Will followed with a handshake. "Great to finally meet you, Jean Luc. And you drive for Ferrari. I'm jealous. It must be amazing."

Jean Luc took a breath. "Thank you, but please call me Jean. It is a pleasure to meet you, Helen and Will. And I used to drive for Ferrari. I have recently retired from racing. With my accident and my age, it is time. I must move on with my life." He looked at Jenny with a loving smile which Helen didn't miss. She glanced at Jenny to see her returning the look.

Will reached into their bag and pulled out everything for margaritas. "Since we're having Mexican, we should have a margarita before dinner." He got four glasses from the cupboard and made the drinks while Helen sliced lime and Jenny got the ice.

Jean Luc asked, "What is a margarita? I have not had this drink before."

"Jean Luc, you mean to tell me you have been in Austin, Texas, and Mexico City and have never had a margarita? Surely you must have had Mexican food," Jenny said, feeling giddy with having people she loved around her in her house.

"No, Jennifer. I never drank any alcohol when I was racing, and I always made sure to eat only what I knew. I could not afford any problems in my stomach in the middle of a race. What is a margarita?"

"It is tequila, triple sec, lime or lime juice," Jenny replied. "We use a squirt of Orange Stevia for sweetener, ice and top it off with water. Some places line the top of the glass with salt, but I skip that. You're in for a real treat. This is from the best Mexican food restaurant in Durango. What did you bring?"

Will answered, "Chicken and beef enchiladas, some chili relleños, red and green salsas, pico de gallo, tomato/avocado salad, and of course, rice and refried beans."

"Wow," Jenny said, "we can eat for a month. Let's get ready. I'm hungry. How's your margarita, Jean?"

"It is very good, very refreshing."

"Then let's eat. I'm starved."

They sat and passed around the food while answering Jean Luc's questions about it. He was warned to taste the salsas before slathering them on as the red one was very hot.

"This is amazing," Jean Luc said. "I have been missing out on this delicious food all my life. Now I shall eat more of this Mexican cuisine."

They finished with sopapillas and honey along with

Mezcal for a digestif.

Will helped Jenny and Helen clear the table, and he went back to talk with Jean Luc as the two women put away the leftover food and put the dishes in the dishwasher.

Helen said, "You know, Jenny, I haven't seen you so happy, relaxed and at ease in a very long time. You and Jean seem so good together, something I never felt with you and Chris. It was like there was always tension underlying everything you said or did, like you were afraid you might ruffle his feathers."

"Really? Hmmm, I think you might be right. Guess I never thought of that. Yeah, Chris was always so sensitive about everything, like he never felt adequate. I know he considered himself a failure at writing after his book bombed. But that was his own fault for not wanting any advice. Well, that's all history now. Jean is different. He's very self assured. Of course he was a highly successful race-car driver. That might be a big part of it. But he's vulnerable also.

"His retirement was really hard for him, and I know it bothers him as to whether he made the right decision or not. The main thing is I want him to get back up and going. The doctors and PT people in Paris were too easy on him. He should be walking by now. I have him scheduled with the Orthopedic Consortium in the morning. I made sure all his records were sent to them and that they'd received them before we left."

"So what are the long-term plans? You were adamant that it would never work since he lives in Paris."

"Well, since he's retired, he won't be constantly traveling all over the world. He's thinking of selling his airplane since it's expensive, and he can charter a plane if he needs … or fly commercial. And he's not needing to be in Paris all the time. He was both reluctant and excited to come here. We'll see how he settles into our lifestyle."

"Well, I hope it works for you two. You seem good together, and I can tell he adores you just by the way he looks at you. Are you in love with him?"

"Yes, very much in love. It's so easy. We've never had sex, and though I want to, it's okay that it hasn't happened yet. His injuries have prevented that anyway, but truthfully, I can't wait. I really want him."

Helen smiled. "I'm happy for you, Jenny, unbelievably happy. I hope it all works out for you two."

"I think it will. We have a lot of things to work out that we've been avoiding. I don't know. Just have to see."

"Now … I need to know about your newfound sister. What's that about?"

"It's quite a story. The guys are talking, so let's crack a bottle of wine and head for the porch. I'll turn on the heater."

Two hours later, Will interrupted them. "Okay, enough girl talk. Jean is tired and so am I."

"Okay," Helen said, "we do need to go. You must be exhausted too, Jenny."

"Now that you mention it," she said with a yawn.

They said their goodbyes and good nights. Jenny got Jean Luc situated, and she collapsed into bed and fell instantly asleep into a dreamless night.

The next morning she helped him get into the shower, got him breakfast, and then the wheelchair van and attendants arrived to take him to the meet with the orthopedic doctor. He'd already reviewed Jean Luc's records and did some follow up x-rays. From the new x-rays the doctor felt he should be able to begin putting weight on his leg, and his shoulder and arm were also mended enough to begin using crutches as needed.

Then there was PT. They wanted him for two hours for an evaluation and to create a plan. Jenny left and went first to the bookstore she hadn't been to in forever and browsed and bought two new books, even though she had half a dozen from Shakespeare and Company at home and that many from City Lights still in California. Then she went to Raven's Coffee shop for a coffee and to kill time. Everything was still the same there, and the owner happened to be working, so they spent some time catching up. Then Jenny went out to the patio to people watch and reminisce about years past when she met with Kelly or Helen there for coffee and gossip. She missed Kelly and, of course, Helen would leaving for Mexico in a few days. She felt very alone with her closest friends gone.

Jenny returned to the PT rooms, and the wheelchair van took them back home. Jenny wished she had a handicapped ramp so she could dispense with the van and the two attendants but figured the need for the wheelchair would be short lived.

Jean Luc was both exhausted and excited. "Jennifer, they showed me no mercy. They said I have been 'sandbagging.' I don't know what that means. They said I was more than ready to move along from what I was doing in Paris and needed to 'up my game' like you said. What does 'sandbagging' mean? I don't understand all these English terms."

Jenny couldn't help but laugh. "'Sandbagging' means slacking when you need to be working up to your potential rather than laying back. What else?"

"They worked out a regimen of exercises I can do at home and some I will need to go a gym to do. Are there any gyms here?"

"Oh yeah. We have any number to choose from, but I have one in mind that I think you'll like."

"And they had me getting up and into my wheelchair by

myself. It is hard, but I can do it. They think only another week maybe before I can be out of it and walking with crutches for balance. I'm so happy. And I'm so tired. I go back in three days."

"We have a number of world class athletes that live and train here," Jenny said. "Plus there are many amateurs, so our PT people are geared up to get people back on their feet quickly."

"I had a personal trainer before my crash," Jean Luc said, "but I let him go since I have now retired. He kept me in shape but never made me work as hard as I did today. I am grateful that you made me come here. I am already enjoying the peacefulness and the beauty of where you live. It is so quiet. I am now anxious to see your mountains you talked about."

"You'll see them soon enough. Let's get you home and let you rest."

Chapter 40

Within two weeks, Jean Luc was able to put away the crutches and walked with a cane assist, mainly for balance. He progressed quickly, spending two hours a day at the gym. By the second week in November, he was able to drive and had bought a new Jeep Grand Cherokee with all the bells and whistles, and even paddle shifters, which reminded him of his Ferraris.

Thanksgiving was in two weeks, and Jenny was resigned to spending it alone with Jean Luc who didn't know anything about Thanksgiving. When the day came, Jenny explained the what and why about the holiday. Rather than a turkey and all the traditional food, she made a pot of chili with cornbread.

Jenny and Hannah texted or talked several times a week. Neither wanted to be the one to tell Julian about his other daughter. On December 1st they were talking about their Thanksgivings, and Jenny said, "Why don't you and Russell come for Christmas? I'll coerce Julian and Cheryl to come out for the night. It might be the most appropriate time we'll ever have."

Hannah hesitated, then said, "I think it's a great idea, we can tell him together. Russell likes to go to Iowa to see his parents at Christmas, but he's being pretty malleable these days, so I don't see a problem getting him to agree. We can always go there before or after. I really miss you."

"I miss you too. It'll be great just to have you here. Now I'm excited and can't wait."

After they finished talking, Jenny called Julian for the invite to which he agreed would be a great idea. Jenny hadn't seen him and Cheryl since she'd been home and Julian was anxious to see her and meet Jean Luc.

Jenny never did any Christmas decorations, so the next weeks were filled with Jenny and Jean Luc shopping for lights and other decorations and getting everything in a celebratory mood.

Jean Luc was now walking cane free and building back his strength in his arm and leg. Along with PT, he was seeing a good sports chiropractor and getting acupuncture treatments. He was far from 100 percent but had good stamina and was a big help in the preparations.

One day while they were putting up outdoor lights, Jenny said, "You know, there are only two guest rooms. We need to put Hannah and Russell in yours and Julian and Cheryl in the other."

He looked at her with a frown. "But where will I go?"

"In with me, of course."

"But Jennifer, we aren't married."

"So? Why will that make a difference? We're living together. I'm totally in love with you and have no problem with you sleeping with me. Actually, I would like you sleeping with me. I want you next to me. We don't have to have sex if you're not okay with it."

"Maybe I should sleep on the sofa."

"No way. God, Hannah and Russell aren't married. They've been together for years. It'll be okay. You're moving in tonight because tomorrow is December 20th, and they're arriving on the three o'clock flight from Phoenix. So when we're done here, get your stuff into our bedroom. I've cleared some drawers for you."

He looked at her. "But—"

She cut him off. "No 'buts,' Frenchy. I thought Frenchmen were good at seducing girls."

"We like to seduce but not sleep necessarily. To us it is like a game, maybe?"

"Well, you just lost this game, mister."

That night at ten o'clock, teeth brushed and pajamas on, a modest, reluctant Jean Luc slipped beneath the covers with his body hugging the edge of the bed. She slid over next to him, got up on her elbow and gave him a lingering good-night kiss. The kiss lasted, then another, then another; one thing led to another, and thirty minutes later, they lay naked snuggled against each other, both spent, their breathing starting to calm down.

"I love you, Jennifer."

"I love you too, Jean Luc Bonnet."

Within minutes, both were asleep.

After Hannah and Russell's flight arrived thirty minutes late, there were hugs, kisses, and handshakes, they picked up their luggage from the carousel, piled into Jean Luc's Cherokee and headed home.

Jenny, who was still glowing after last night's adventure, showed her guests to their room. Hannah noticed the silly grin and lack of focus, and when Russell left, said, "You're being weird, sister. What's up? Is it having us here?"

Jenny grinned. "No. Not at all. It's just that we spent the night together last night … for the first time. Does it show that bad?"

"Oh yeah. Jean too. You're both being weird. First time, eh? Must have been good."

"Yes, amazingly good. How's Russell since he returned?"

"He's great. He's settled back into life as we knew it. We're back having fun with the music rather than being all anal about it. However, news is Karen is pregnant."

"Oh my God! Really? So what does that mean with Mick and your group?"

"Sadly, he'll be bowing out except for local gigs, and that's even a maybe. He always has more consulting offers than he wants and obviously makes a lot more doing them than playing with us. And with a baby coming and everything, he's had to make some decisions. We hate to lose him, but understand and support him and Karen. It'll be different with just the two of us when we're on the road. Which leads me to ask, might you be interested in selling us your camper van? We can downsize now since it'll be only the two of us. And your camper is way more comfortable."

"I can't answer that right now. I'll have to think about it."

"No rush. We thought you might want to get rid of it."

"I'll talk to Jean about it and let you know."

Russell called out, "Hey, what're you two doing in there?"

"Just some girl talk."

They spent the rest of the day and evening catching up and getting to know Russell and him getting to know Jenny and Jean Luc. The two couples easily connected and had all sorts of stories to share.

The four of them finished decorating, and they spent the

next few days with Jenny and Jean Luc showing them the town and the area. But there was always the underlying tension of anticipation of how Julien would react.

And then it was Christmas Eve late morning, and Julian and Cheryl would be arriving any minute. Jenny and Hannah were ready to start drinking tequila shots to quell their nervousness.

A knock came on the door. Jenny said, "Shit, they're here. Showtime. Let the fun begin." She opened the door.

"Hi, Dad. Hey, Cheryl. Welcome and Merry Christmas

Julien said, "Merry Christmas to you. Your house looks great."

"Come in and give me your coats. I'll show you to your room. Oh, first, let me introduce you; this is Jean, visiting from France. And this is Hannah and Russell, friends from California."

Cheryl smiled and Julien said, "Pleased to meet you all."

"We'll be back in a minute," Jenny said, ushering them to their room.

Jenny and Hannah were in the kitchen preparing lunch with Jean Luc and Russell sitting at the counter talking about racing. Julien and Cheryl joined them. The conversation turned to everyone saying who they were and what they did. Lunch was served and they all sat at the counter, informally eating sandwiches and drinking iced tea.

After lunch Jenny said, "Dad, Hannah and I have something to tell you … alone. Come with us into the living room."

He gave them a curious look, got up and followed them. "Sit down, Dad."

"What's going on?" he asked.

Jenny told him about her trip to California and meeting

Hannah and Russell at the beachside campground. "Well, we were talking about things, and it came up that … Well, it came up that Hannah is Meg's daughter from the commune. And … and she's your daughter. Meg was pregnant with Hannah when she left."

Everyting became dead quiet. Cheryl, Jean Luc, and Russell were listening from the kitchen and made not a sound.

Julien cocked his head, like he was trying to let this information sink in. He looked at Hannah, then Jenny, seeing for the first time both carried his features. He looked away and said, "I need some air. Excuse me." He got up and walked out onto the south deck into the warm sun and sat staring out into nowhere. Jenny and Hannah left him for a few minutes before joining him. He had tears running down his cheeks.

Jenny and Hannah pulled up chairs and sat with him. Jenny said, "I'm sorry. We didn't mean to upset you, but you had to be told."

"How's Meg?" he asked with a shaking voice.

"She's great," Hannah said. "She said to say hi and sends her warmest regards."

"It's all so crazy. She saw what was happening, everything I was too blind to see. She begged me to go with her or at least let you and Michael go with her. But I was too stubborn and wrapped up in my grief and stupid shit. I was trying to drown my grief in alcohol and drugs. We know how that turned out. I … I don't know what to say other than I'm so happy that you found me, Hannah. I don't deserve either of you two beautiful women for my daughters." He put an arm around each of them and pulled them into a tight embrace.

Both the women snuggled in and returned the embrace. He loosened his grip and took a deep breath. "I'm sorry. But all my shit suddenly was staring me in the face again. I know

I've told Jenny a million times how sorry I am, and now I'll tell you, Hannah. I'm sorry. Meg was an amazingly wonderful woman, and I was in love with her. If only I'd have listened to her. She's okay with this?"

"She encouraged it and was happy that it was finally happening. She protected me for a long time, or thought she was anyway, but I'm happy to finally meet my father. We have a lot to catch up on."

"Then let's begin catching up," Jenny said. "Plus the sun is going down, and it's freezing out here. Let's get inside."

And they all did just that, catching up, laughing, crying and having the best Christmas Eve ever. Jenny and Hannah had made a big pot of chili in the slow cooker that morning; it smelled delicious, and everyone was hungry. After dinner was finished and cleaned up, everyone gathered by the tree to open presents. After a few hours of presents and joviality, Jenny hadn't yet found anything from Jean Luc. She didn't say anything but started to gather up the wrapping paper.

Jean Luc said, "Oh wait. There is one more." He reached into his pocket and pulled out a small box. "Jennifer, I think this is for you."

She looked at what he handed her and sucked in her breath as she started opening it. There it was, a nicely cut diamond set between two small gray moonstones, the color of her eyes. She stared at it, her heart racing.

Jean Luc took it from her, removed the ring, knelt before her, took her left hand and slipped it on her finger. "Jennifer Morse, there is no other and never will be any other but you that I shall love. Will you do me the honor of marrying me?"

Tears ran down her face. With a trembling voice, barely a whisper, she said, "Yes."

Chapter 41

Jenny and Jean Luc were married the next June at the chalet at the top of the Grizzly Ski Lift at Purgatory Mountain Resort. They took their vows looking out east toward the San Juan Mountains. So many memories ran through Jenny's head of the two years she'd spent as a homeless refugee and all that had ensued since.

And now here she was, surrounded by people she loved: her father, her grandparents, and even her family from Iowa including her grumpy old grandfather, Harlan, who couldn't pass up flying on a charter jet that Jean Luc sent to fly them all to Durango. Then there were Helen and Will, along with Camille who came with Robert, Danielle, and Lisette. Kelly, Peter, and Amanda and her husband were also there. Hannah was her maid of honor with Kelly, Lisette, and Camille as bridesmaids. Wolfgang Werner and Juan Sanchez, both friends from his Formula 1 days, were Jean's best man and groomsman.

A year and a half later, Jenny gave birth to twins, a boy and girl. They were named after Jenny's mother, Melissa, and after her brother, Michael.

Jenny's new book was published a year later and was equally as successful as her first, even without the extensive book tours that her agent had required for her first book. She was a mother now and paced herself accordingly. She was also working on her third novel.

Epilogue

Jenny and Jean Luc had decided that Durango would be their primary location. He enjoyed the quiet life of Durango, especially now that he wasn't traveling around the world to a different place every few weeks. He kept his Paris apartment and sold his Monte Carlo residence, and they bought another house in Sausalito to be close to Hannah and Russell when they often times visited there..

Dean and Susan eventually moved back from Paris and, having decided that their house was more than they needed, moved into a retirement community at the north end of town. So Jenny and Jean Luc bought their house and rented the north valley house as an Airbnb. With the twins and Jean Luc's business south of town, it was more convenient.

Jenny's phone buzzed, and she answered the call from Jean Luc.

"Hi, sweetheart. We've had a last minute cancelation and have time at one thirty if you'd like to try out our new Porsche 911 for a few laps. It's pretty sweet. Wolf and I each got a turn with it this morning."

"That sounds great. I was just heading out for a run and was dropping the kids off at Will and Helen's, but a few laps sound like a lot more fun. I'll be there in about a half hour."

"Good. Oh, I need to tell you, I've had an update and the plane will be here late this afternoon, so we can leave for Paris for sure tomorrow afternoon as we first planned. Will that be that okay?"

"Yes. I have everything packed for the kids and me. It'll be great to see your folks and Lisette."

"Wolf is set to take over. Things at the driving school are slow right now. We have only a few reservations for day drives, so it's a good time for me to be away."

"Hey, we can talk later. I'll see you in a bit. But I'd rather you warm up the Ferrari for me … not in a Porsche mood today." She headed out south of town in her BMW to meet Jean Luc and do some laps around the three-mile road circuit that Jean Luc and his good friend from his Ferrari days and their wedding's best man, Wolfgang Werner, had built.

He and Wolf came up with the idea of a driving school where people could come to learn the fine points of driving fast on a track, or who just wanted the thrill of driving a Ferrari, Porsche, BMW, Mercedes, or McLaren on an unrestricted track with professional guidance. Jean Luc's research indicated there were a lot of wannabe racers out there, and a lot of the wannabes had a lot of money. And, now in its second year, between the drivers' school, day drivers, and the go-cart track with a stable of electric go-carts, they employed ten people including an office manager and scheduler, several mechanics, groundskeepers, and general maintenance personnel.

Jenny got to the track and kissed Jean Luc on the cheek. "I'm gonna get suited up. Will you strap me in?"

"Of course. Can I come with you?"

"Naaah. I can handle it on my own."

A Note from the Author

Acknowledgments

I wish to thank my wife, Julianne Ward, for her patience and encouragement. Also, I wish to thank my publisher, Tahlia Newland, for all her amazing help, encouragement, and patience to get me through this project and to Rose Newland for her beautiful cover design and formatting.

Other books by this author

San Juan Sunrise,
Book One of the Jennifer Morse Series

The Awakening of Russell Henderson,
The story of Russell and Hanna

Grandpa's Horse and Other Tales,
An Anthology of Short Stories